How could he?

For *years* Isobel had lived for some sign of attention from this man. Any sign would have done—a letter sent to the convent in Conques, perhaps…even a simple message. He had done nothing.

And now he had the impudence to wait until they were in a smoky inn to kiss her. In a whorehouse, to be precise. He was kissing her as a pretence, the devil. He didn't want her. Her pulse thudded. She *liked* his kiss.

When a large hand crept to her cheek, cradling it in its palm, making tiny caressing circles with its fingertips, pleasure shot along every nerve. She bit back a moan. It was fortunate that his hand hid her face from onlookers. She felt hot and confused. *He doesn't want to do this. He doesn't know me.* In the years she had lived in the south he had not shown the slightest interest in her welfare. *I am just another trophy to him. I am a prize. Lucien is marrying me for my inheritance.*

And then his mouth was on hers again and her thoughts were scattered.

Duty, Honour, Truth, Valour

The tenets of the Knights of Champagne
will be sorely tested in this exciting new
Medieval series by Carol Townend.

The pounding of hooves,
the cold snap of air, a knight's colours
flying high across the roaring crowd—nothing
rivals a tourney. The chance to prove his worth
is at the beating heart of any knight.

And tournaments bring other dangers too.
Scoundrels, thieves, murderers and worse are
all drawn towards a town bursting with deep
pockets, flowing wine and wanton women.

Only these three knights stand in their way.
But what of the women who stand beside them?

Find out in
Carol Townend's
Knights of Champagne
Three Swordsmen for Three Ladies

LADY ISOBEL'S CHAMPION

Carol Townend

First published in Great Britain 2013
by Mills & Boon, an imprint of Harlequin (UK) Limited,
Large Print edition 2013
Harlequin (UK) Limited, Eton House, 18-24 Paradise Road,
Richmond, Surrey TW9 1SR

© Carol Townend 2013

ISBN: 978 0 263 23290 5

Harlequin (UK) policy is to use papers that are natural,
renewable and recyclable products and made from wood grown in
sustainable forests. The logging and manufacturing process conform
to the legal environmental regulations of the country of origin.

Printed and bound in Great Britain
by CPI Antony Rowe, Chippenham, Wiltshire

Carol Townend has been making up stories since she was a child. Whenever she comes across a tumbledown building, be it castle or cottage, she can't help conjuring up the lives of the people who once lived there. Her Yorkshire forebears were friendly with the Brontë sisters. Perhaps their influence lingers…

Carol's love of ancient and medieval history took her to London University, where she read History, and her first novel (published by Mills & Boon®) won the Romantic Novelists' Association's New Writers' Award. Currently she lives near Kew Gardens, with her husband and daughter. Visit her website at www.caroltownend.co.uk

Previous novels by the same author:

THE NOVICE BRIDE
AN HONOURABLE ROGUE
HIS CAPTIVE LADY
RUNAWAY LADY, CONQUERING LORD
HER BANISHED LORD
BOUND TO THE BARBARIAN*
CHAINED TO THE BARBARIAN*
BETROTHED TO THE BARBARIAN*

**Palace Brides* trilogy

**Did you know that some of these novels
are also available as eBooks?
Visit www.millsandboon.co.uk**

AUTHOR NOTE

Arthurian myths and legends have been popular for hundreds of years. Dashing knights worship beautiful ladies, fight for honour—and sometimes lose honour! Some of the earliest versions of these stories were written in the twelfth century by an influential poet called Chrétien de Troyes. Troyes was the walled city in the county of Champagne where Chrétien lived and worked. His patron, Countess Marie of Champagne, was a princess—daughter of King Louis of France, and the legendary Eleanor of Aquitaine. Countess Marie's splendid artistic court in Troyes rivalled Queen Eleanor's in Poitiers.

The books in my *Knights of Champagne* mini-series are not an attempt to rework the Arthurian myths and legends. They are original romances set around the Troyes court. I wanted to tell the stories of some of the lords and ladies who might have inspired Chrétien—and I was keen to give the women a more active role, since Chrétien's ladies tend to be too passive for today's reader.

Apart from a brief glimpse of Count Henry and Countess Marie, my characters are all fictional. I have used the layout of the medieval city to create my Troyes, but these books are first and foremost fictional.

DEDICATION

To Karen, with love

Chapter One

October 1173—in the east tower of
Ravenshold, in the County of Champagne

With the tip of his dagger, Lucien Vernon, Comte d'Aveyron, prodded what looked suspiciously like a dead sparrow. 'Is that what I think it is?' He grimaced as he surveyed a table littered with leavings. There was a handful of tiny bones; any number of butterflies' wings in a clay pot; and a mortar holding a gnarled fragment of bark that Lucien was pretty certain would never be seen in either kitchen or infirmary. The pestle was chipped, and the surface of the table was lost beneath a dusting of dead flies, leaf mast, beech nuts and acorns.

'Dried bat?' his friend Sir Raoul de Courtney suggested. 'Or perhaps a toad?' Raoul was examining a stoppered glass jar filled with cloudy liquid, his expression finely balanced between intense curiosity and disgust. Daylight was squeezing past a frill of cobwebs hanging in the lancet window. Holding the jar to the light, Raoul eyed the contents. *'Mon Dieu!'* He dropped the jar on to the table with a thump that sent up a haze of dust. His lip curled, disgust had won out over curiosity. 'Holy hell, Luc, haven't you seen enough? Let's get out of here.'

Lucien scrubbed at his face, fingers lingering for a moment on the ragged scar on his left temple. The scar was throbbing, as it had been since he had learned of Morwenna's untimely death, as it always did when he thought of her. 'My apologies, Raoul, I thought I might find something here, some explanation as to why Morwenna died. Did I tell you I had to bribe Father Thomas before he would permit her to be buried in the graveyard?'

Raoul shook his head, his eyes were sympathetic. 'I heard that rumours of witchcraft were doing the rounds. Who started them this time, any idea?'

'No. I had hoped to find answers here but...' Lucien shook his head. A wave of regret swept through him—if only things could have turned out differently. He hadn't seen Morwenna in what—two years?—and now she was gone. Guilt clawed his insides; regret was bitter in his mouth. He jerked his head at the table. 'Despite all you see here, she was no witch.'

'I know that.'

'She was just…she was obsessed.' Lucien dragged in air. The place smelt musty. It smelt of death. It was as though time had stopped at the top of the east tower—everything was frozen at the point of dissolution. 'Morwenna wasn't obsessed in the early days…'

'She was beautiful then?'

'A goddess. Raoul, if you could have seen her before we married…'

'I know you don't hold with witchcraft, Luc, but it strikes me she bewitched you.'

Lucien's laugh was curt. 'I was fifteen.' He stared at the glass jar on the table and grimaced. 'Many young men are bewitched at that age. You, I seem to recall—'

Raoul held up his hand. 'Point taken. There's no need to drag my past into this.' He eyed a mouldering heap of chestnuts and shuddered. 'For God's sake, you'll learn nothing here. My advice to you is to burn everything in this room. It wouldn't do for Lady Isobel to see it.'

'There's no rush,' Lucien said. 'Lady Isobel's not due for another month.'

'Ah, Luc…about that…' Raoul's nostrils flared. 'Never mind, I'll tell you outside.'

'My priorities are the hall and bedchambers,' Lucien said, reviewing all that needed to be done before his betrothed arrived. 'Then there are the stables...'

'Don't forget the kitchens,' Raoul put in. 'Let's go, the air in here is fetid. Burn all this, that's what I say.'

Lucien shook his head. 'Not until I have reassured myself that Morwenna's death was no accident.'

'It was an accident, Arthur was clear on that. Luc, it might be better if you accept that sometimes there are no answers. Search through this tower all you like, but you'll find nothing more substantial than Morwenna's dreams.' Raoul reached for the door latch. 'As you say, there's plenty to get your teeth into elsewhere.'

Lucien nodded, Raoul was in the right. His betrothed, Lady Isobel of Turenne, would be here within the month, and Ravenshold wasn't fit for a beggar, never mind its future mistress. The armoury and tack room needed restocking; the Great Hall needed scouring from rafters to floor; the stables were infested with rats; the kitchen garden had run to seed; the orchard needed pruning... Lucien hadn't got as far as the cellars. He shuddered to think what else he would find. Chaos and neglect were everywhere. Domestic duties had not ranked highly among Morwenna's priorities.

Lucien took a last look round the tower room. His

dead wife had called it her workroom. Plaster was peeling from the walls; there was a pile of debris under the table; a broken stool; a curl of yellowing parchment…

'This is not a happy place.' Lucien pulled the door shut with a decisive click. 'Morwenna certainly held on to her dreams. It's a pity they didn't extend beyond this chamber.' *It's a pity they weren't based on reality.*

Raoul was in full retreat, hurrying down the twisting stairs that led to the bailey. After a moment, his voice floated up. 'Let's take a turn along the curtain wall, Luc. I need fresh air.'

'Amen to that, but I've yet to inspect the kitchen and cellar.'

'Check your wine stocks later.'

In the bailey, Lucien was met with a dazzle of autumn sun, and he took a deep, cleansing breath. A momentary diversion would be a relief after the atmosphere of sadness in the tower. Unfortunately the autumn sun revealed more neglect outside. There were cracks in the water troughs. Drifts of leaves in every corner. In the forecourt there were ruts in an area he would swear had been paved on his last visit.

Raoul was talking to Sergeant Gregor up on the walkway, and Lucien climbed the steps to join them. From the top, most of Lucien's Champagne holdings were visible. He let his eyes slide past the church and village, moving over the tidy vineyards and neat fields beyond. What a blessing that he had given Morwenna no influence beyond the castle. The contrast between the air of desolation within the walls and the orderliness without was marked. In the fields, the crops had recently been harvested and sheep were grazing on the stubble. The grapes had been gathered from the vines.

Rooks were flying round a nearby stand of trees. In the distance, he caught the tell-tale gleam of the sun bouncing off a helmet. A small party of horse-men was approaching on the road from Troyes. It was probably a merchant come in the hope of selling his wares. Resting a shoulder against the cold stone of a merlon, Lucien nodded at Sergeant Gregor as he saluted and returned to his post. Raoul looked very serious. Too serious. Lucien folded his arms and lifted a brow. 'You've something to say?'

Raoul hesitated.

'Don't tell me, the smith couldn't mend your hel-met and you want to borrow one of mine for the tournament?'

'No, that's not it.'

His stance was guarded enough to give Lucien a prickling of concern. 'Raoul?'

'Sergeant Gregor has just confirmed some news from Troyes.'

'Oh?'

'She's here, Luc.'

Lucien felt himself go still. 'She? Who?'

'Lady Isobel of Turenne. Your betrothed.'

In a heartbeat, Lucien was back in the shadowy cool of the Abbey at Conques. He was a lad of fifteen, and he was shaking in his boots at the enormity of the lie his father was forcing him to tell. Lady Isobel de Turenne had been eleven, as he recalled. Lucien had been so ashamed, so guilty, that he had barely looked at her. She had been slim. A child. And he had been forced to swear a sacred oath to marry her, an oath he had never been sure he would be able to keep.

'Isobel? In Troyes?' He shoved his hand through hair that was as black as night. 'What the devil do you mean? She's not expected until next month.'

'She rode into town last eve,' Raoul murmured. 'It's my guess she'll want to see you as soon as she may.'

Lucien swore under his breath. *No!* This was the last thing he wanted. He wasn't ready to greet his betrothed—Ravenshold simply wasn't fit to be seen. He gestured at the leaf-strewn bailey; at the hall and towers that were all but lost behind great swags of ivy. The jingling of bits and the clopping of hoofs told him that the merchant and his party had almost reached the gatehouse. 'She can't come here, look at the place.'

'That's up to you, of course. But I thought you should know that Lady Isobel and her party have taken lodgings in the Abbey de Notre-Dame-aux-Nonnains.'

Lucien stared at his friend, knots pulling at his guts. 'Blast the woman, she's far too early.'

Raoul gave him a puzzled look. 'You sent for her after Morwenna's death. What difference can a month make?'

'I made it plain when I wrote to Viscount Gautier that Ravenshold would not be ready to accommodate his daughter until Advent at the earliest.'

'I suspect it's more than Ravenshold that's not ready,' Raoul said softly.

Lucien narrowed his eyes. 'And what might that mean?'

'Luc, you did your duty by Morwenna and that is in the past. You deserve better, you deserve a marriage that will give you sons and daughters. You are my friend, I want to see you happy.'

'You—an unmarried man—equate marriage with happiness? On what basis?'

Raoul gripped his shoulder. 'You did what you

could for Morwenna. *Mon Dieu*, you did more than anyone else would have done. Go to Troyes, and go today. Meet Lady Isobel and you will see she is not another Morwenna. Far from it, Lady Isobel has grown into a lovely young woman.'

Lucien frowned. 'How would you know?'

'I met her last year at the Abbey in Conques. It was before her mother died. They were there to honour St Foye.'

'You've never mentioned this before.'

'What was the point? I knew you'd never abandon Morwenna.'

Lucien's thoughts were churning. He did need heirs and despite Raoul's doubts, he knew himself to be ready for his second marriage. Although he would be the first to admit that he had hoped for more time. Isobel would likely expect an explanation for the length of their betrothal. Nine years! He hadn't yet thought of a tactful way to explain it. If he told her the truth he would feel as though he were betraying Morwenna. 'Love is out of the question, of course,' he said, thinking aloud. Love had betrayed Lucien before, he wasn't about to let that happen again. 'I will marry the girl, since my father wished it. I will honour our betrothal agreement, and she will give me heirs. That is as far as it will go.'

'My guess is she'll want to see you today,' Raoul said, watching him.

'Today? Lord, Morwenna is scarcely in her grave.'

'It is not too soon.'

'I have neglected Lady Isobel. I have lied to her.'

'Make it up to her. You have charm, or, at any rate—' Raoul grinned '—you used to have charm.'

The hoofbeats were close, the merchant's party was approaching the gate. The merchant had his wife with him, Lucien realised, as he heard a woman laugh. It sounded light. Carefree.

'Thank you, Pierre,' the woman said. 'I enjoyed the ride, very much. It was most invigorating, particularly after Captain Simund refused to let us travel at more than a snail's pace yesterday.'

There was a brief pause. Then a man, Pierre presumably, murmured a response. 'You are welcome, my lady.'

My lady? This might not be a merchant and his party then. *My lady?*

The woman spoke again. 'This is it? Ravenshold?'

'Yes, my lady, this is Ravenshold.'

A horse snorted, a bit jangled.

Raoul looked at Lucien. 'It sounds as though your hospitality is about to be tested.'

'Not if I can help it, the castle isn't fit for swine.'

Raoul leaned out through a crenel and flinched. 'Oh, Lord.'

'What?' Squeezing into the next crenel, Lucien craned his neck to follow Raoul's gaze. There was no sign of any merchant, just a young girl with an escort of four. *Four men-at-arms?* For one young girl? She must be of some importance. She was examining the curtain wall with such attention, one might think she had never seen one before.

The girl was blonde. A beauty in a burgundy-coloured gown and cloak. She had twisted her veil and wound it round her neck for the ride, but a few strands of yellow hair framed her face. She had rosy cheeks and a delicate profile. Her lips were the colour of ripe cherries. Lucien caught only a glimpse of her eyes. They were green as emeralds and framed with luxuriant eyelashes that were unusually dark for someone so fair. They made him long for more than a glimpse. Her horse—a black mare—had the dust of the road upon her, but she looked as though she had Arab blood-lines.

Raoul caught him by the belt and dragged him back from the crenel. His mouth quivered.

'Raoul, what the devil…?'

'If you are not ready for visitors, you had best stay out of sight.'

A line of machicolations was built into the battlements. The one at Lucien's feet funnelled that bright girl's voice up to the walkway.

'Pierre, please ask that guard by the gatehouse if Lord d'Aveyron is here.'

'Yes, my lady.'

The horses moved off.

Fighting free of Raoul's grip, Lucien leaned out. The girl was riding astride—she rode easily and naturally, as though born to the saddle. 'I ordered the guard not to admit visitors,' he said.

'Very wise in the circumstances,' Raoul said. He was struggling, not entirely successfully, to hold back a grin.

'What's up?'

Raoul opened his eyes, failing utterly to keep his grin in check. 'Nothing.'

'Raoul?'

Raoul's eyes danced, and when he would not respond, Lucien turned back to the crenel. The girl and her party had finished their exchange with the guard and were back on the road to Troyes. 'That girl is uncommonly attractive.' As he spoke, it occurred to him that the most attractive thing about her was that air of innocent enjoyment.

Raoul gave a crack of laughter that sent a pigeon flapping from its roost.

Lucien frowned. 'You don't agree?'

'You don't recognise her, do you, Luc? You have no idea.'

'What are you talking about?'

'That attractive girl is not just any girl. Or, rather, lady.'

'You know her, Raoul?'

'Of course. And so should you.'

A sinking feeling told Lucien that he was not going to like what was coming next.

'Luc, she's yours. That is Lady Isobel of Turenne. Your betrothed. I suspected when I met her that she might turn out to be very…direct.'

Luc shoved his head back through the crenel. A small cloud of dust marked the end of the road where it disappeared into the woodland beyond the vineyards. He thought he saw the swirl of a burgundy cloak. 'Isobel,' he murmured, under his breath. 'Hell. Where did you say she was lodging?'

'The Abbey de Notre-Dame-aux-Nonnains.' Raoul's mouth lifted. 'Your betrothed is eager to meet you.' Elbowing Lucien aside, Raoul peered down the road, but the little cavalcade had been swallowed up by the forest. His expression sobered. 'Forget the guilt, you can claim her with all honour. She has waited a long time.'

Lucien rubbed his hand round the back of his neck. 'I must say, I'm surprised to see her so early.'

'Once you had written to her father, I suspect he packed her off in no time. He will be anxious to be rid of her.'

Cold fingers feathered across the back of his neck. 'What's wrong with her?' *Lord, don't say I'm to be stuck with another disaster for a wife...another Morwenna.*

'If you had kept in touch with Turenne you would know why Lady Isobel is *de trop*. Viscount Gautier has remarried. I gather his new lady is keen to have Turenne to herself.'

'I see.'

'Poor girl, turfed out by her stepmother.' Raoul made a clucking sound. 'And here you are, turning her away at the gate because Ravenshold is a little run-down.'

'A *little* run-down?' Lucien said, exasperated. He had a strong dislike of being cornered, and by arriving early that was exactly what his betrothed had done, she had cornered him.

'I take it you will be riding into Troyes this afternoon?'

'Yes, damn you, I shall.'

Count Lucien d'Aveyron turned on his heel and made his way along the battlements and down into the bailey. He did not have to look back to know that Raoul was grinning.

Chapter Two

'It is not right that you must share my punishment,' Lady Isobel de Turenne muttered to her companion, Elise. 'You did not ride out of Troyes without permission.'

Isobel and Elise were sitting in a square of sunlight in the cloisters of the Abbey de Notre-Dame-aux-Nonnains, repairing a blue altar cloth for Advent. The sewing was intricate, with hundreds of complicated knots and swirls. The Abbess had given it to Isobel because she had wanted her to do penance for wayward behaviour. Isobel couldn't help but notice that the blue of the cloth was an exact match to the blue field on Count Lucien's colours. Was that deliberate?

'You should have sought my permission, Lady Isobel,' Abbess Ursula had said, on Isobel's return to the Abbey. 'And as for you leaving the town itself... well! You must take better care of yourself. Anything might have happened, anything. The Winter Fair is almost upon us—Champagne is bristling with beggars and thieves.'

No matter that Isobel had reassured the Abbess that she had been quite safe with her escort. No matter that she had reassured the Abbess there had been no sighting of any beggar or thief. Privately, Isobel found it hard to see that riding out to Ravenshold had been so great a sin—she had come to Troyes as a result of Count Lucien's summons.

She'd wanted to meet him. She'd wanted to see Ravenshold. But Abbess Ursula thought she should wait until the Count came to claim her. The Abbess ran the Abbey's school for young ladies and disciplining her charges came to her as easily as breathing. Isobel's behaviour had been unladylike, and penance must be made.

Isobel and Elise had been sewing for hours. However, it was a mystery as to why poor Elise, who had the misfortune to seek shelter at the Abbey shortly after Isobel's arrival, must join Isobel in her penance. Isobel couldn't deny that she was glad of her company since her maid Girande was languishing in the infirmary with a malady picked up *en route* to Troyes.

'I am sorry, Elise,' she said. 'I wish you didn't have to pick up a needle to expiate my sins.'

'I like sewing, my lady. I find it restful.'

Isobel had no response to that. Elise might find sewing restful, but Isobel's fingers were cramped from hours of needlework. She hated sitting still.

Abbess Ursula had instructed Isobel to use the time to reflect on the duties Count Lucien would expect her to undertake when she became his wife. Instead, Isobel found herself reflecting on the character of her fiancé, and on why he had taken so many years to summon her. *Nine years. I have waited nine years for this man. Why? Did he loathe me on sight?* However many times Isobel told herself that, since she and her betrothed had hardly spoken to each other nine years ago, it was extremely unlikely that he disliked her on sight but doubts remained.

The guard at the gatehouse denied Count Lucien was there, but I saw movement up on the battlements. Of course, it might well have been another guard, but Count Lucien is here in Champagne. When will he come for me, when...?

Doubts swirled through her mind, twisting and turning like the swirls on the altar cloth. *Has he no feeling for what it is like to be betrothed to a man who ignores one so completely? Did word reach him of Mother's difficulty in bearing a son? Was it in his mind to reject me because I may not be able to give him an heir?*

'Did you see Lord d'Aveyron, my lady?' Elise murmured.

The sunlight flashed briefly on Isobel's needle as she formed a silver knot and drew the thread clear of the silk. 'No, I haven't seen him in years.'

'You and the Count were betrothed as children?'

'I was eleven when we were betrothed.'

Elise's head bent over the altar cloth. 'Were you pleased to have been chosen by so great a tourney champion?'

'The match was made by our fathers. Count Lucien wasn't a great champion then—that came later.' Isobel sighed and wriggled her fingers to ease the cramp. 'But, yes, I was pleased. At the time.'

Elise made another of those encouraging noises as Isobel remembered. She was reluctant to give voice to all she felt for Lucien Vernon, Count d'Aveyron. Shortly after their betrothal, she had been sent to St Foye's Convent to be schooled to be his wife. Over the course of the years her feelings towards him had evolved. Isobel lived in an age when girls were married young. And though there were aspects of married life she was uncertain about, she wanted her marriage to take place.

'My friend Lady Jeanne de Maurs married when she was twelve,' Isobel murmured.

'Madame?'

'She left St Foye's shortly after. Another friend, Lady Nicola, was wed at thirteen. The marriages were not consummated until later, but they were married. They had status. Helena and Constance left at fifteen, Anna at sixteen...'

'Count Lucien kept you waiting.'

Isobel focused on the sunlight sliding over the stones between the fluted pillars. 'I am twenty, Elise. It was a great shame to be the oldest girl at St Foye's who was not destined for the Church.' Isobel fell silent. She felt far more than shame, she felt forgotten. Unwanted. Unloved. *What is wrong with me? Why did he not call for me sooner?*

Someone coughed. 'My pardon. Lady Isobel?'

Sister Christine had entered the cloisters and was standing by a pillar.

'Sister?'

'You have a visitor. He is waiting to greet you in the Portress's Lodge.'

A visitor? He? Isobel felt Elise's gaze on her. 'Who? Who is it?' she asked, though the sharp jolt in her belly told her the answer.

'Count Lucien d'Aveyron, my lady. Your betrothed.'

Mouth suddenly dry, Isobel handed her end of the altar cloth to Elise. *At last!* She was surprised to note her hands were steady. In her mind's eye she could see a pair of vivid blue eyes. She had always remembered his eyes.

She cleared her throat. 'Elise, would you care to accompany me?'

Elise hesitated. 'Sister Christine will be with you. Do you need me to come too?'

'I would welcome your support.'

'Then of course I shall accompany you.' Elise folded the Advent cloth, and placed it carefully in the workbox.

In the corridor outside the Portress's Lodge, a quatrefoil was cut into the wall. 'One moment, Sister,' Isobel said, pausing briefly to glance through it as she straightened her veil.

Lucien Vernon, Comte d'Aveyron, was stalking the length of the lodge, boots sounding loud on the stone-flagged floor. Light from a narrow lancet fell directly on him, giving Isobel an impression of long limbs and hair that gleamed as black as jet. One look and she sensed impatience in him. Here was a man who was not used to waiting for anyone.

Isobel recognised the square jaw and regular features, but not the ragged scar on his left temple. *Count Lucien must have received that at a tournament, for there was no scar on the day of our betrothal.* Oddly, the scar did not detract from his looks, if anything it enhanced them. This was no callow youth, but a man of experience. A powerful and handsome man.

'Lady Isobel.' Sister Christine urged her into the lodge, and before Isobel knew it she was facing him. Lucien Vernon, Comte d'Aveyron, champion of tournaments beyond counting. Her betrothed.

She dropped into a curtsy. 'Lord d'Aveyron.'

Taking two swift strides, the Count lifted her hand in a firm grasp. As he bowed over it and kissed it, a tremor shot through her. *At last.* Count Lucien might not be used to being kept waiting, but he hadn't hesitated to make her wait. *I have waited nine years for this moment.*

'My guard mentioned that you rode to Ravenshold this morning,' he said. 'I apologise that you were turned away, but I didn't look to see you until Advent.'

Hearing censure in his tone, Isobel felt herself flush. 'Once my father received your letter, he was anxious that I should come without delay.'

Blue eyes studied her. 'I trust your journey was not too taxing? You are recovered?'

'Yes, thank you, my lord. I enjoy riding.' Had Count Lucien always been so tall? For a moment he was a complete stranger rather than the man Isobel had been betrothed to so long ago. His eyes met hers and then she knew it was he. She had never forgotten that he had the bluest eyes, they were warm as a summer sky. The colour was unexpected in someone whose features were otherwise so dark. Unforgettable. As for the warmth—that had faded from her mind with the slow turn of the years. Seeing it again, she was emboldened to add, 'It has been a long time.'

'It has been too long. I know it, and am sorry for it. However, I am delighted to see you again.' He led her towards the light, holding her at arm's length while he continued his appraisal of her. 'I would have come for you sooner, but…'

'You were occupied with your lands, with tournaments.' Isobel kept her head high, appalled to feel herself flushing as he ran his gaze up and down— hair, mouth, breasts… This was her betrothed of many years, yet he was making her feel nervous— edgy in a way she didn't understand. Why did his gaze make her feel so self-conscious? She wished she could read him. What was he thinking?

And why was Elise hovering out in the corridor when she had made a point of stressing that she would welcome some support?

'You have grown into a strikingly beautiful woman,' Count Lucien said, softly. 'I find myself regretting the duties that have kept us apart for so long.'

Isobel sent him a direct look. It had been a relief when she had heard that *finally* Lord d'Aveyron's summons had arrived at Turenne, and she wanted him to know that she had not enjoyed the wait. He ought to know. 'Duties, my lord?' Conscious of Sister Christine hovering by the door, she lowered her voice. 'It has been *nine* years. My lord, I know you have become a great tourney champion, but must you attend every tournament in Christendom?'

She caught a slight grimace, quickly concealed.

'A thousand apologies, my lady. King Henry and King Louis disapprove of tournaments, which means that sometimes one must travel long distances to find the best of them.' He lifted his shoulder. 'The prize money can be good.'

Isobel stared at him. Lucien Vernon held so much land it was hard to believe that he struggled to raise revenues. He had estates in Champagne, Normandy and the Auvergne—plenty of resources, surely? Something felt wrong. Was he so ambitious—so avaricious—that he must win every prize in Christendom? And if so, why had he not married her sooner? She was an heiress.

Later, I will go into this with him later. I cannot

ask revealing questions with Sister Christine hanging on our every word.

Count Lucien smiled and she felt it in her toes. His eyes were not pure blue, they had black and grey flecks in them and they were very penetrating. Disturbing. Isobel did not remember them being quite so disturbing nine years ago.

She steeled herself against him. It stung to look into those thick-lashed eyes and recall that he had not cared to visit her in nine years. Their match might have been arranged by their fathers, but from the moment Isobel had met him she had been drawn to him. Once the delays had started and she had realised that he did not feel the same way about her, she knew that when she next faced him, she must conceal the attraction she felt. An attraction that was still there, despite the years of silence.

Even then, there had been a hint of the devil about Count Lucien d'Aveyron. Today, it was strong. She could feel it in his touch—in the way a smile or a glance weakened her self-containment. The nuns had never mentioned that men possessed such power. It was…unsettling in an exciting, shivery way.

Such power was dangerous. Such power was to be resisted. Particularly when she found it in the man who had shamed her. *He ignored me for years! I will not grant him power over me.*

Count Lucien was her betrothed, that much was set in stone. Isobel had never wished to escape their marriage, but if she wanted to keep her self-respect, she must guard her heart. This man would soon be claiming her body. It was a husband's right and she was realistic enough to know that even if she wanted to she would not be able to hold him at bay. But he would never touch her soul.

Nine years, he ignored me for nine years...

'My lady, as you are doubtless aware, I sent for you because it is time for our marriage. It will be soon.' His fingers squeezed hers, warming her inside all over again.

There was movement behind her. Abbess Ursula had entered the lodge—the ruby at the centre of her silver cross was glowing like an ember. Elise trailed in behind the Abbess, moving unobtrusively in the shadows behind her.

'Count Lucien.' Abbess Ursula inclined her head. 'I assume you have come to arrange your wedding. Did you have a particular day in mind? I take it some time after the turn of the year will be convenient?'

'The turn of the year? Lord, no. Since Lady Isobel is here I see no reason to delay.'

The Abbess drew her head back. 'Count Lucien, Advent is almost upon us. You are doubtless aware there can be no weddings in Advent, and it will be hard to arrange it before then. I realise Lady Isobel is already chafing at her confinement here, but her early arrival has thrown us into disarray and—'

'I am aware of all that,' the Count said, voice dry. 'And I intend to take responsibility for Lady Isobel's care as soon as possible. Our marriage will take place before Advent begins.' He looked at Isobel. 'Do you care to choose the day, my lady?'

Isobel thought quickly. 'I should like to marry on Winter's Eve,' she said, picking a day at random.

'Winter's Eve?' His blue eyes were thoughtful. 'I'm taking part in a local tournament the following day, but I imagine that might be arranged.'

The Abbess frowned. 'But my lord, Winter's Eve…that doesn't give us long to prepare.'

'I am sure the bishop will accommodate us. And should he prove difficult, I expect you, Abbess Ursula, as cousin to King Louis, to use your influence.'

Isobel's mind was awhirl. In truth, she was in a state of shock. Not once in all that time had he shown the slightest interest in her. She had grown used to his neglect. But thankfully it seemed he really did intend to marry her. Of course, she would feel happier if he hadn't made it plain he would be squeezing the ceremony in before one of his all-important tournaments…

The Abbess sighed. 'Winter's Eve is not the best

of days for a wedding, my lord. You may not recall, but in some quarters it is known as Witches' Eve.'

'Is it?' the Count said, stiffening.

It might be wishful thinking on Isobel's part, but it was as though he disliked the way the Abbess was so dismissive of her suggestion. *Is he to take my part against the Abbess? Is he to be my champion?* It was a novel feeling. Isobel felt herself begin to soften towards him.

You fool, have the long years taught you nothing? You mean nothing to him.

'Reverend Mother, are weddings actually forbidden on Winter's Eve?' he asked.

Abbess Ursula shook her head. 'No, my lord, but—'

'Then Winter's Eve it is.'

The Abbess gave a curt nod. 'As you wish, my lord.'

Blue eyes held Isobel's. 'My lady, you realise our marriage will take place before word reaches your father? Viscount Gautier will not be witnessing our wedding.'

'I am reconciled to that,' Isobel said. 'I realised some while ago that my father would not be attending the ceremony.'

'Oh?'

'He no longer enjoys full health.'

Count Lucien's expression was sympathetic. 'I was saddened to hear of your mother's death in the summer, I didn't know Viscount Gautier was also in poor health.'

Isobel nodded, and jerked her gaze away. Grief welled up and the narrow window behind Count Lucien was lost in a mist of tears. Her wounds were too raw for her to speak about her poor mother. 'Father has remarried. I am sure he will have mentioned this in your exchange of letters.'

'Yes, so I recall.'

In her heart, Isobel felt her father had betrayed her mother by remarrying so soon. The words caught in her throat.

It irked her that after prevaricating for so long, Count Lucien had merely to snap his fingers and she must come running. Her new stepmother, Lady Angelina, must have been thrilled when his summons had arrived, for she had wasted no time in packing Isobel off. Isobel could have remained at St Foye's, but the convent was clearly too close to Turenne for Lady Angelina's comfort. Notwithstanding this, Isobel would have felt she was betraying her father if she complained at being so easily dismissed.

If only her father had ridden to St Foye's to bid her farewell. Conques was not far from Turenne. Isobel understood that his illness had probably prevented it, but she would have liked a private message of Godspeed. Instead, her father had simply forwarded Lucien's summons to Mother Edina. And Mother Edina had duly relayed it to Isobel along with the news that her escort awaited outside the convent gates, and would she please pack up her belongings without delay.

She cleared her throat. 'My lord, despite his marriage, Father is not in good health. He will remain in Turenne.'

'I hope he recovers swiftly,' the Count said.

He looked so sombre, Isobel had a depressing thought. If her father and Angelina had a son, and despite her father's ill health that was possible, then Isobel would no longer be an heiress. Was Count Lucien regretting arranging a marriage with a woman who might never come into an inheritance?

I want Count Lucien to want me! I don't want him to reject me because he considers me a poor prospect.

How lowering to feel this way.

'Count Lucien, a word if you please?' The Abbess gestured him to one side. They went to stand under the window and although Abbess Ursula's tone became confidential, she had a carrying voice. 'I cannot help but notice that Lady Isobel is in need of…discipline. I fear her father gave her too much licence at Turenne.'

The Count drew his head back. 'Lady Isobel has spent much of her time in St Foye's Convent—I would venture that the good nuns there, rather than Viscount Gautier, are responsible for her upbringing. She will not prevail on your hospitality for long. I am making arrangements for her to lodge at Count Henry's palace.'

'Lady Isobel's maid is sick, my lord. Lady Isobel will have to remain here until the girl has recovered.'

Before she knew it, Isobel had stepped forwards. 'I am perfectly capable of packing my belongings myself, Reverend Mother.'

'And I should be pleased to help,' Elise said, from her place in the shadows.

The Abbess lifted an eyebrow. 'Very well. I suppose I should expect nothing less.'

'What can you mean?'

'Lady Isobel, from the moment you have arrived, you have shown little sense of propriety.' She huffed out a breath and frowned at the Count. 'Your betrothed needs a firm bridle, my lord. This morning she left the convent without permission. It grieves me to confess that she has been wandering about the county like a pedlar's daughter.'

Lucien watched a flush run into Isobel's cheeks.

She was staring stolidly at a cross on the wall. *She came to find me.* She might have arrived in Troyes a month before she was expected, but Abbess Ursula was not going to be permitted to bully her. 'Lady Isobel rode to Ravenshold,' he said. 'Unfortunately, I had given my men orders to admit no one and she was turned away.'

'Be that as it may, Lady Isobel should not have left the Abbey without my leave.'

Isobel stepped forwards. 'I took an escort.' Large green eyes turned towards him. 'My father's men-at-arms escorted me from Turenne. They did not leave my side for a moment.'

Abbess Ursula made a clucking sound with her tongue. 'Lady Isobel should not have gone without my permission. Such disobedience. Such wilfulness. I am sorry to have to tell you, Lord d'Aveyron, but you will find Lady Isobel needs a *very* firm bridle.'

'I am certain you exaggerate.' Thus far, Lucien was surprisingly pleased with the way his betrothed had turned out. So much so, that he was beginning to think that his luck might have turned. It seemed that way.

Isobel was pretty, nay, pretty was too pallid a word for Isobel's golden beauty. She was beautiful. And she had a demure look to her—that neat figure, that simple gown—that gave the lie to the warnings the Abbess was giving about her character. Isobel looked to be precisely the sort of good, biddable wife he wanted. A lady. Someone who—unlike Morwenna—had been bred to duty and obedience. Isobel of Turenne would give him children and she would look after them. And Lucien would be free to manage his life and his estates as he always did. Just look at her. The golden hair concealed by that veil was, he suspected, more soft and fair than that of Queen Guinevere. Were those cherry-coloured lips as sweet as they looked?

'I do not exaggerate, my lord, I assure you,' the Abbess said. 'At any rate, you will be pleased to hear I have put a stop to such behaviour. I have dismissed her escort.'

Lucien felt himself go still. Isobel was no longer a child, and she would shortly be his bride. It was one thing for the Abbess to chastise Lady Isobel whilst she was in her charge, but that she should take it upon herself to dismiss Viscount Gautier's escort was unthinkable. 'You did what?'

'I sent them to Troyes Castle.'

'You did not have that right, Reverend Mother,' Lucien said, softly. 'Viscount Gautier sent that escort for Lady Isobel's protection.'

'My Abbey is a house of God, not a barracks!'

'None the less, you should not have dismissed

Lady Isobel's escort. I am confident that if Viscount Gautier trusts his men to accompany his daughter from Turenne, they are more than competent to protect her whilst she explores Champagne.'

Abbess Ursula looked sourly at his betrothed. 'Have it as you will, my lord. Since Lady Isobel promises to be rather too lively a guest for my Abbey, I am happy to wash my hands of her. It would not do for her to disrupt my other ladies.' Her breast heaved and she swept to the door. 'Count Lucien, never say I did not warn you how wilful she is. I wish you joy. Come along, Sister, I want to discuss your idea for the sisters' stall at the Winter Fair.'

Lucien watched her go. 'What a dragon,' he murmured.

Isobel could not be sure she had heard him correctly. 'My lord?'

'We shall be married in little over a week. I would be honoured if you would call me Lucien. And I should like to call you Isobel, if that is acceptable?'

'I...yes, of course,' Isobel said, bemused to be granted this privilege after years of being forgotten. Many wives were never given permission to dispense with the formalities. *He ignores me for years, and suddenly I am free to call him Lucien?* It made no sense.

He turned to Elise who seemed struck with shyness and would not look at him. 'Who is this?'

'A friend. My lo—Lucien, this is Elise…Elise, this is my betrothed, Count Lucien d'Aveyron.'

Head rigidly down, Elise made her curtsy. 'Good day, *mon seigneur*.'

'Good day, Elise.' The Count—*Lucien*—glanced through the door and back at Isobel. 'Is your maid very sick?'

'I don't think it is serious, but she's been put in the infirmary.'

'What's wrong with her?'

'I am not sure. I suspect she ate something that disagreed with her. She has been most violently ill.'

'Can she be moved? If not, I will send someone back to fetch her when she is recovered.'

Isobel's heart lifted. 'I'm leaving *before* our wedding?'

'If you are in agreement, I see no reason why you should not leave today. But Ravenshold is…unprepared for your arrival. I have asked Count Henry if you may stay at his palace here in town. I am waiting to hear if there is space for you.'

Isobel felt a flutter of excitement and found herself smiling. She had not wanted to show pleasure that Lucien had at last come to greet her. She had meant to be cool, but he had caught her unawares with his offer to remove her from the Abbey that day.

Today! All my life I have been shifted from convent to convent and now...

Freedom!

I must be calm. I must not let him see how I have longed for this day. Yet I must not alienate him either. I shall have to do my best to please him.

Abruptly, her mood darkened. She could not forget that her mother had died in childbirth. *Unless I want Mother's fate to be mine, how can I welcome him into my bed?*

Crowding into her mind came another memory, that of her friend Lady Anna. Scarcely a month after a smiling and happy Anna had left St Foye's Convent for her wedding, she had come racing back. Anna had been pale. She had lost weight. She had taken Isobel aside and started muttering darkly about the horrors—yes, horrors had been the word she had used—of the wedding bed. Anna had only just started when there had been a fearful clamour at the convent gates. Anna's irate bridegroom had come to claim her.

A blink of an eye later, Anna had left St Foye's a second time. Isobel never heard from her again. A year later, she learned that Anna had died in childbed. Exactly as her mother had done.

I may never be able to give him an heir. Mother tried again and again to give Father a boy. She died trying. Am I to die in like manner?

'I shall send word to Count Henry's steward, and see how swiftly arrangements may be made for you.' Lucien sent Elise a charming smile. 'If your friend agrees to accompany you, the proprieties may still be observed. Even the Abbess could not cavil at the arrangements. Well, my lady, what do you say?'

Isobel had opened her mouth to reply, when a novice hurtled into the lodge.

'Where's the Abbess?' the novice gasped. Her face was the image of distress.

'Talking to one of the sisters,' Lucien said. 'Why?'

'The relic!' The novice was shaking from head to toe. 'My lady, the relic's been stolen!'

Isobel froze. 'I beg your pardon?' When she had come from the convent in Conques, she had brought a relic with her—a scrap of cloth reputed to have come from St Foye's gown. The relic was highly treasured by the nuns in the south, and it was a great honour to have been entrusted with transporting it.

'The altar's been smashed in the Lady Chapel and...' the novice bobbed a curtsy '...excuse me, my lady, I must find the Abbess.' She vanished as quickly as she had appeared.

Lucien looked questioningly at Isobel. 'Relic?'

'A fragment of cloth that belonged to St Foye.'

'You brought it with you?'

Isobel nodded. 'The relic is lent to this Abbey until the end of the Winter Fair. Since Father gave me an escort and I wanted to return the nuns' hospitality, I offered to bring it. It brings pilgrims—'

'And revenues,' Lucien put in, drily.

'I suppose it does bring money, but...' Isobel looked earnestly at him. 'Excuse me, my lord, I feel some responsibility for that relic.' Without another word, she picked up her skirts and hurried out of the lodge.

Lucien followed, somewhat bemused at the interest his betrothed was showing in the theft of a fragment of material that might or might not have belonged to some long-dead saint. She had largely been brought up by nuns, that must explain it. He followed her into a paved yard and past a series of columns—the cloisters that adjoined the Abbey Church. She moved with grace, giving him a chance to see that her figure was most pleasing. As the sunlight lifted the edge of her veil, he glimpsed a thick plait, burnished to gold by the afternoon sun.

The little novice had run off into the cloisters, in search of the Abbess. Lucien followed Isobel into the cool shade of the church where a wooden screen separated a series of side-chapels from the main nave. Eyes round with shock, she had paused at the entrance to one of the chapels, and was absently resting her hand on a carved angel. Her hand was delicate, fine-boned and ladylike. Lucien had never before thought of a hand as being pretty, but Isobel's was.

Several people must have been at their devotions in the Abbey Church when the thief had struck. A number of townsfolk and a handful of sisters were standing with their noses pressed against the carved screen, watching what was going on in the chapel.

Reaching Isobel as she stood in the chapel entrance, Lucien was startled by an impulse to cover that pretty hand with his. He was in God's house, and the nuns would definitely disapprove. Experimentally, he placed his fingers on the back of her hand.

Instantly, Isobel was tense, taut as a bow. Her green eyes flickered, and slowly—it was the subtlest of movements—she shifted her hand so that it lay alongside his on the wooden screen. Almost touching, but not quite. As a rebuttal it was subtle, but it gave him a jolt. It made him realise that Isobel of Turenne might not find it easy to forgive him for their much-delayed marriage. Wooing this woman might not be easy. *She is hiding much anger.*

Dark-robed nuns stood like statues around the

edge of the side chapel, stunned by the sacrilege. Peering past them, Lucien saw a brightly painted slice of sandstone with several trefoils cut into it. The altar frontal. Someone had hacked away the border between two trefoils, leaving a ragged black hole. On the tiled floor lay a rope, a crowbar, and a number of sandstone shards.

Skirts sweeping though the shards, Isobel crossed to the altar and the nuns parted to let her through. She bent and took a closer look. The relic must have been housed in the darkness behind the altar.

Isobel straightened, turning to look at him. 'The reliquary is gone,' she said. Her gaze went past him, focusing on one of the bystanders. She stiffened. *'My lord, look!'*

A hooded man in a shabby brown tunic was struggling to lace up a pouch. Incredibly, Lucien caught the rich gleam of gold and the sharp shine of blue enamel. A Limoges reliquary box. A box that in itself would almost be as priceless as the relic within it. The man sidled to the church door and nipped through it.

'Did you see?' Isobel breathed, brushing past him. Lucien nodded. 'Limoges reliquary.'

'The nerve of the man, pretending to be a pilgrim.' Isobel was already halfway across the nave. 'I have to catch him.'

Striding after her, Lucien frowned. He caught her hand. '*You?* It is not your place to catch thieves.' When her green eyes flashed, he tightened his grip. 'Isobel—'

Wrenching her hand free, Isobel dived into the sunlight.

Chapter Three

Lucien stared after her. *She disobeyed me!* It was rare that Lucien's orders were disobeyed, but it did happen. He sometimes had trouble with young squires when they first joined him, but they soon learned that if they were to succeed they had best obey him. He marched into the sunlit courtyard. It would be the same with Isobel, she would soon learn.

He felt a momentary pang for the bride he had envisioned—pretty, demure, obedient. Lucien had hoped his second wife would put his wishes first; he had hoped she would quietly take charge of the domestic side of his life, leaving him free to focus on military matters.

Lucien was honouring the betrothal contract with Isobel of Turenne because it had been his father's wish. He had long regretted his inability to grant his father that wish, just as he regretted the bitter quarrel that had followed. A quarrel that had never been mended. Finally he was in a position to honour that betrothal contract, and it was a blow to discover that Isobel of Turenne was not the demure lady of his imaginings. She needed schooling.

He gritted his teeth. She seemed intelligent; she would, he hoped, be a quick learner. She had reached the convent gate. He watched her slight figure whip through it, veil and gown flying, and increased his pace. It was a pity the nuns had not instilled in her the importance of obedience. Clearly, it was up to him to teach her that particular virtue...

Isobel picked up her skirts, raced through the courtyard, and burst into the street. She had no idea why the urge to catch the hooded man had spurred her into such unladylike action, but the thought had been accompanied by an irresistible rush of excitement. *He must be caught!*

Her heart was pounding. She had brought the relic with her from the south, and she felt responsible for it. It was only being lent to the Abbey here for the duration of the Winter Fair and if it was lost, the good sisters at St Foye's in Conques would be seriously impoverished. Pilgrims flocked to pray over it, and their offerings brought in much-needed revenues. Those nuns had looked after her for years.

She could not stand by and watch while their precious relic was stolen.

Brisk footsteps were coming up behind her. Count Lucien. She heard him murmur something to the startled nun at the Abbey gate.

The relic!

Ahead, the thief—Isobel had marked his shabby brown cloak and hood—slipped round a corner. She hurtled after him. The street was narrow and the way was all but blocked by wooden stalls. Townsfolk and merchants were haggling over prices. The Winter Fair had not officially begun, so this must be a market area. On either side, tall houses loured overhead, and a line of shop-fronts opened directly on to the road. Isobel skirted a pottery stall and a couple of wine-merchants.

'Excuse me.'

'Watch it! Don't shove.'

Ahead, the brown hood bobbed up and down in the press.

'Stop that man!' Isobel cried, pointing. 'Stop, thief!'

The townsfolk turned. Stared. Pulse thudding, Isobel forged on. The brown hood…she could no longer see it. Her chest was tight, and by the time she reached the end of the street, her lungs were aching. The brown hood had gone.

She was drawing breath at a small crossroads as Lucien ran up. 'Which way, my lord? You're taller than me, did you see where he went?'

A lock of dark hair fell across the jagged scar on Count Lucien's temple. Strong fingers wrapped round hers. 'My lady—Isobel—what in blazes are you about?'

She gestured at the crossroads. 'Where did he go? Did you see him?'

Count Lucien's grip shifted, strong fingers banded like iron about her wrist. 'It is not wise to run about Troyes unaccompanied at this time of year.'

'But, my lord, the thief...' Pulling against Lucien's hold, Isobel peered down a shadowy alley. A pair of lovers were locked in a passionate embrace. The man had lifted the woman's skirt; Isobel caught a shocking glimpse of white thigh. Flushing, she drew back, and frowned through her embarrassment. 'My lord, please release me.'

The look on that woman's face...she looked as though she were in ecstasy. *Ecstasy?* That did not tally with anything the nuns or her mother had told her. Or Anna for that matter...

'I shall release you when you understand that it is not safe to be running about the town like this. Lord, have the nuns taught you nothing? You ought to take more care of yourself. As you have already seen, the town fills with thieves at this time of year.'

Isobel twisted her wrist, but her betrothed had not finished.

'My lady, the Winter Fair attracts men of all stamps. I would have your promise that you will take care. Further, I would have your assurance that in future when I say you nay, that you heed me.'

Her heart lurched. 'Luc—my lord?'

'Did you not hear me back in the church? You are to be my countess. It is *not* your place to catch thieves.'

'My apologies, my lord.' Isobel bit her lip. Those blue eyes were boring into her, hard as sapphires. She had heard him, but in the rush of excitement her one thought had been to keep sight of the thief. *Holy Mother, don't tell me Lucien is going to turn out to be an arrogant boor like poor Anna's husband.* In her mind, Lucien was a tourney champion, not an arrogant boor.

Avoiding that hard, accusing gaze, Isobel risked a glance down another alley. There was no sign of the brown hood. 'He got away.'

'Isobel, leave it. Count Henry's knights will deal with him.'

'But, my lord, there must be something we can

do. St Foye's is not as rich as the Abbey, they cannot afford to lose their relic.'

Lucien felt a pang such as he had not felt in years. His anger began to dissipate and he could not account for it, save to conclude that Isobel's green eyes were altogether too appealing. Her chest was still heaving from her race through the streets. Her cheeks were flushed and several blonde wisps had escaped her plait and were curling about her face. She looked more human than she had done in the convent lodge. And doubly attractive. He became conscious of a strong feeling of possessiveness, akin to pride. *She is mine.* When slightly dishevelled, Isobel de Turenne was extraordinarily desirable. He could imagine just how she might look after an encounter with a lover…

The shiver that ran through him was easy to place. Desire. It had been surprisingly invigorating chasing after her. It was as though she had awoken something primitive in him, something that had been sleeping for far too long. *She is very beautiful.* How many years had it been since Lucien had allowed himself the luxury of feeling this sort of desire? Without wanting to analyse it, it had been far too long. Lucien was somewhat put out to find that the desire he felt for Isobel was not entirely comfortable.

It was mixed with regret. With uncertainty. *How will she react when she learns about Morwenna?*

'My lady, there are officers in Troyes responsible for maintaining order. It is their duty to catch the thief, not yours. You...' Lucien paused for emphasis '...are a lady, not one of Count Henry's Guardian Knights.'

'Guardian Knights?'

'The Count of Champagne has established a *conroi* of knights to maintain law and order at the time of the Fairs. He would be most offended to hear that you were taking on their duties. As would his knights.'

Those great green eyes lowered, she appeared to be studying the wall of the house behind him. 'Yes, my lord.'

Slowly Lucien released her, and when she did not dart off again down a side street he let out a breath he had not realised he had been holding. *What a sight she had made though, tearing through the town!* Lucien had had no idea that a girl, hampered by trailing skirts, could run so fast. *She is as fleet as a doe.*

'You really want to catch that man.'

'As I said, St Foye's is not a wealthy convent, my lord. There is no treasury filled with silver and gold as there is at the monastery. The nuns need that relic, it's almost all they have.'

Lucien leaned his shoulder against the oak frame of one of the houses. She really seemed to care. It was possible she was using the theft as an excuse to escape the Abbey. Likely, she had spent too much of her life penned up in a convent. Lucien pushed back the guilt, although he couldn't blame her if she felt that way, it would drive him mad to be so cooped up. 'I am told you have only just arrived in Troyes,' he said.

'That is so, we arrived at the Abbey yesterday.'

'And before that? How much time did you spend at St Foye's Convent and how much in Turenne?'

'Mostly I was with the nuns, my lord. Although, I did come home occasionally…' her face clouded '…when my mother needed me.'

Yes, there is no doubt of it. Isobel is using the theft as a means to escape the confines of the Abbey. I would do the same in her place. And she mourns her mother, deeply.

Lucien could not help her over her grief for her mother, but he could offer her assistance elsewhere. He crooked his arm at her. 'Since we seem to have lost our quarry, perhaps you would permit me to show you the town?'

Her answering smile was bright and innocent. It

should not have set off a disturbing ache in Lucien's belly. *Desire.*

'Thank you, my lord. I should enjoy that very much.'

Lucien tucked her arm into his. He had surprised himself with his offer to show her around Troyes. *I like her. I like Isobel de Turenne.* Of course, she must learn the value of obedience, but after nine years of hell, maybe his luck was turning. *I will teach her to behave with decorum. Outside the bedchamber. Inside, however...*

He shot her a look. She was walking demurely at his side, every inch the lady again, which was promising. If the memory of their frantic hunt through the streets had not been so vivid, he would think he had dreamed it. A tell-tale curl, freed at some point during the chase, curled down her breast. There was a wildness about her. Lady Isobel de Turenne had learned to look demure, but not so far beneath the surface there was a hint of the wild, a lack of artifice. He rather liked it.

They walked slowly to the end of the alley and arrived in a square near one of the canals.

'These canals power the water mills, there are several in Troyes,' he told her. 'And, of course you must see Count Henry's palace.'

'I'd love to. I've seen so little.'

That twist of hair rippled and gleamed like spun gold. And her lips—they truly were the colour of ripe cherries.

'Abbess Ursula was going to confine me to the Abbey precincts after I...' she flushed '...rode out to Ravenshold.'

'Oh?'

'I didn't have leave to go.' The flush deepened. 'Truth to tell, I knew she would withhold permission, so I didn't ask. I only saw Ravenshold from the road. I should have liked to see inside.'

Lucien murmured something non-committal about how he would have been there to greet her if he had known she was planning to arrive so soon. He led her on to the bridge over the canal. 'I take it that was when the Abbess dismissed your escort?'

'When we returned to the Abbey, she packed them off to the barracks at Troyes Castle. Two of them have never left Turenne before, I hope they are all right. Pierre is sure to be missing Turenne.'

'And you? Will you miss Turenne?'

Her look was impenetrable. 'Me? No, my lord.' She paused, adding softly. 'I have been trained to be your wife, my home is with you.'

However softly she uttered it, it remained a rebuke. Lucien felt his face stiffen, he was not used to criticism. Particularly since she had every right to be aggrieved. He had kept her waiting.

Searching for a less contentious topic, Lucien leaned on the guardrail at the centre of the bridge, and directed her attention to Count Henry's palace. This was a long, three-storied residence lying alongside the canal. The lower windows had old-fashioned Roman arches, but the stonework above the upper windows flowed in curves that were distinctly arabesque, mirroring a design Lucien had seen in the Aquitaine. The higher windows were glazed.

'There's Count Henry's palace, where you will lodge until our wedding.'

Intelligent green eyes fixed on the palace. 'There's a landing stage.'

'I don't expect it's much used, except for delivering supplies to the kitchens and so forth.' He watched her study the palace…the landing stage… the canal, and was taken with an impulse to run his finger down the line of her nose. He wanted to turn her face to his, to taste those tantalising cherry-coloured lips…

'Thank you for showing me, my lord. I look forward to moving in.'

Lucien cleared his throat. 'As I mentioned, I have asked if there is space for you today, but with the Winter Fair about to begin, the town is bursting at the seams. We may have to wait a few days for an apartment to fall vacant.'

'There's no need to bespeak an entire apartment, my lord, I know I arrived earlier than expected. I am happy to share a chamber with other ladies. I am used to it.'

'I shall bear that in mind. Come, let me take you to the garrison, it's not far from here.'

'I can see my men? You are thoughtful, my lord. Although I should be returning to the Abbey soon. The Abbess will—'

'The Abbess can hardly object to my squiring you about town. I am your betrothed.'

'I wish we had found the relic,' she said. 'Did you know it works miracles?'

Lucien went cold. Isobel's remark, innocent though it seemed, had him instantly on his guard. He couldn't stomach a second wife who believed in miracles. Morwenna had given him a lifelong aversion to such nonsense...

'Yesterday a young woman was brought into the church,' she was saying. 'Her legs were paralysed. When she lowered her scarf through the aperture in the altar, it touched the reliquary and her paralysis left her.'

Lucien felt a prickling of unease. 'You believe that?'

She glanced at him, observed the way he was

watching her, and a small line appeared on her brow. His betrothed was clearly more sensitive to subtle shifts of mood than Morwenna had been.

'I believe the young woman believed it, my lord. And I know she walked from the church, because I saw her myself. As to whether it was a genuine miracle…' she lifted her shoulders '…who can say? I do know the relic brings revenues to the nuns, revenues they use to do many good works. Why, the sisters at St Foye's…'

Lucien hid his unease and they strolled towards Troyes Castle with Isobel earnestly listing the many good works the nuns undertook in Conques. Lucien found himself torn. Isobel de Turenne was, on the surface, everything a man could want. She had poise, beauty, breeding. And that tantalising hint of the wild. He would not have been surprised to learn that Lady Isobel de Turenne was the subject of many a *chanson*. Knights would be happy to wear her favour and fulfil quests for her.

However, this mention of miracles worried him.

'I do not hold with miracles,' he said, carefully. 'It seems to me that belief in miracles is a poisonous combination of delusion and wishful thinking.'

'Poisonous?' Green eyes fixed on his. 'Sometimes delusion can be a good thing, my lord.'

'Can it?'

'You are too cynical, my lord. You forget, I saw that young woman walk with my own eyes. Before yesterday, she hadn't walked for years.'

Lucien shook his head. Isobel's convent innocence was refreshing, but such naivety could be dangerous. 'I cannot help but wonder how you knew the young woman had not walked for so long.'

'I asked her.'

'And you believe everything you are told?'

Isobel's brow wrinkled. 'Not everything, but I believe the young woman was telling the truth. You will doubtless say her paralysis was caused by a paralysis of spirit. I saw someone find her feet again. Delusion?'

'Probably.'

She gripped his sleeve. 'My lord, does it matter what caused that young woman's paralysis? Does it matter what cured her? If a scrap of cloth helped in any way, I cannot see the wrong in it. One way or another, faith cured her.'

The moat and drawbridge of Troyes Castle were at the end of the street. Covering her hand with his, Lucien led her towards it. 'My lady, do you not think there are those in the Church who might take advantage of the credulous with all this talk of faith and miracles?'

Her veil shifted as she tipped her head on one side

and considered his question. And then she was smiling up at him, and the world seemed to shift beneath his feet. *She is so lovely. So innocent.* He almost missed a step. At one time, Morwenna had been his pattern of perfection, which was doubtless why Isobel's golden hair and striking green eyes brought an unwelcome question to the forefront of his mind.

Do Isobel's heart and spirit mirror her external beauty?

'Yes, my lord, that has occurred to me, but I truly do not think it matters.'

'No?'

'No.' She spoke with calm certainty. 'If someone uses a relic as a means of thinking themselves into health, in my view that is all to the good.'

'We are back to faith again, I see.'

She smiled. 'So we are.'

'My lady, will you not agree that if someone can think herself into health, then the opposite may also be true? She could think herself ill.'

'Possibly, I am not sure. These matters are too deep for me. All I know is that I saw that woman walk again.' Her mouth turned down. 'I can't help feeling responsible for the relic since it was I who brought it from Conques. I owe a debt of gratitude to those nuns. Is it so wrong to want it returned to them?'

He stiffened. 'I advise you to leave it to the Guardians.'

The castle portcullis and barbican stood a few yards away on the other side of the drawbridge, they had almost reached the barracks. Lucien guided her on to the drawbridge, noticing that his rebuke had hit home, she was avoiding his eyes. 'I am wise to you, my lady,' he said, lightening his tone. 'If you are completely honest, you will admit that catching the thief was not all you wished to do when you ran into the streets.'

White teeth bit into a full lower lip. 'Oh?'

Lucien leaned in and a delicate cloud of scent enfolded him. It was like a breath of summer air. Honeysuckle and roses. 'You wanted to explore.'

Her sudden, deep flush told him that he had struck a nerve. 'My lord, I...'

'There's no need to dissemble. You are not a woman to be kept in a cage, not even a gilded one. Your loyalty to the sisters in the south is admirable, and I do not blame you for seizing the chance to snatch a breath of freedom.' He gestured at the barbican. 'This is where we shall find your men. Come, allow me the pleasure of continuing to escort you.'

As they crossed the drawbridge and entered the bailey, Lucien realised that he was not simply giving lip-service to the usual courtesies. It was indeed a pleasure to escort her.

After years of being cloistered, Isobel found it something of a novelty to be on the arm of a man with Lucien Vernon's influence. At the garrison, a quick word from her betrothed had them swiftly ushered across whispering rushes into a hall larger than any Isobel had seen in the south. In size it rivalled the Cathedral in Conques.

Wide-eyed, she looked about her. Without question, this was a hall for soldiers, but she had never seen such splendour. Rank on rank of knights' pennants hung from the beams, their colours—red, green, gold, blue, silver—were brightened by light filtering through traceried windows. Flames flared in a cavernous fireplace. Antique arms gleamed on the walls. The table on the raised dais at the end was covered in a damask cloth so dazzlingly white it almost blinded. Stacks of wooden serving dishes were piled on side-tables; there were rows of wine-jugs; trays of clay goblets...

'The Countess of Champagne is the daughter of King Louis, is she not?' she asked.

'She's his daughter by his first wife, Queen Eleanor.'

Lucien answered absently, his attention had been

snared by a man drinking ale at a side-table. The man's clothes and spurs proclaimed him to be a knight. As Lucien went to join him, Isobel heard her name.

'Lady Isobel!' Her father's man, Captain Simund, was bowing at her side. 'It is a pleasure to see you, my lady.'

'Thank you, Captain, I am glad to see you. I wanted to apologise for your dismissal from the Abbey.'

'Do not fret, my lady, I understand.' Captain Simund's gaze fastened on Lucien. 'Is that Count Lucien, my lady?'

Isobel nodded. 'When he has finished talking to his acquaintance, I shall introduce you. Tell me, Captain, are your billets acceptable?'

'Thank you, yes.'

'And the others—are they well? I was particularly concerned for Pierre.'

'We are in good spirits, my lady. If I may be so bold…' Captain Simund hesitated '…the men are happier here than they would be at the Abbey. We don't have to tiptoe around. We don't—begging your pardon, my lady—have to watch our tongues every moment of every day.'

'Captain, I am glad to hear it,' Isobel said, warmly. 'I feared Pierre might miss Turenne.'

'Not a bit of it, my lady.'

After Isobel had introduced Captain Simund to her betrothed, she and Lucien left the garrison.

'I shall show you more of Troyes, you will feel at ease if you know your way about,' Lucien said.

'Thank you, my lord, so I will.'

Thus it was that a word from her betrothed to a guard on the city walls gained admittance to the boardwalk ringing the town. On one hand, out across the dry moat, the County of Champagne stretched away to the horizon. On the other lay the town—it was like looking down at a vast parchment map of Troyes. Inky smoke trails wafted heavenwards through a dozen tiled roofs. If the streets had once followed a plan, they no longer did so. Wooden houses were crammed in higgledy-piggledy, no two were the same.

'The roof tiles are a safeguard against fire,' Lucien told her.

'What about that one?' Isobel asked, seeing thatch among the tiles.

Lucien shrugged. 'Not everyone keeps to the rules. I expect Count Henry will fine whoever lives there.'

There were straight roofs and sagging roofs— some green with moss, others black with mildew. Every now and then a tree poked up from a garden or square. Alleys and side streets ran every which way. The place was a maze.

'From here you can see that the barracks are inside the old Roman walls,' Lucien said, pointing. 'As is St Peter's Cathedral, we shall be married in the porch. Look, there's the Bishop's palace....'

As Lucien talked, they promenaded slowly around the walls. He had covered her hand with his own. Isobel did not think he was aware of what he was doing, though she was very much aware of him. He ran his thumb softly over her knuckles and she felt him quietly taking measure of her wrist.

Something inside her trembled and her cheeks were hot. Lucien flustered her. Why had no one warned her she might react in this way? In truth, he had done little, merely stroke her wrist with those long fingers...was her response normal? She had no way of knowing. Nuns—sworn to a life of celibacy—never spoke of such things.

Isobel stared across the city roofs, hoping Lucien would think she was attending to his every word rather than wondering at sensations such as she had never felt before. Such *disturbing* sensations...

'And this quarter here...' Lucien's voice changed, and when she steeled herself to meet his gaze, she caught the tail end of a smile and her gut clenched. *He should smile more often, it takes years from him.*

His nose wrinkled. 'I wouldn't recommend you venture into those particular streets.'

Isobel couldn't help notice that Lucien's eyes were lingering on her mouth. 'Those streets are dangerous?' she asked, thoughts beginning to whirl as she came to a realisation. *Lucien is attracted to me. Perhaps he is as attracted to me as I am to him...*

How am I to keep him at bay if there is an attraction on both sides? With Mama's history, I can't risk a pregnancy. Her mother's pain-filled cries echoed through her mind, she had fought so valiantly to give birth to an heir. *That will not be my fate.*

'They are dangerous if you have a sensitive nose.' Lucien grimaced. 'That's where you'll find the tanneries.'

A pungent smell proved the truth of his words. They hurried past holding their breath, and came down from the walls by a grain market. After crossing a square containing a handful of market stalls, they entered a shadowy street where the upper storeys of the houses leaned to within inches of their neighbours opposite.

Isobel's gaze fell on a man weaving his way through the townsfolk. It was only a glimpse—an unshaven face peering out from beneath a brown hood—but it was enough. She gripped Lucien's arm. 'My lord!'

Lucien narrowed his gaze as he scoured the street. Children and dogs were racing in and out of the crowded alleyways, blocking his view.

'There, my lord, by that tavern.'

Vivid blue eyes met hers. 'Isobel, I warn you—'

'He's going inside!'

The door shut. Isobel released Lucien's sleeve and picked up her skirts.

'A moment, my lady.' A firm hand held her in place. 'That's the Black Boar, you weren't thinking of challenging him in there?'

'He shall not have that relic.'

She took a step, but Lucien blocked her, shaking his head.

'My lady, I should not have to remind you—it is *not* your place to chase him.'

Isobel opened her mouth to object, but disapproval was large in his eyes and the words froze on her lips.

He swept on. 'Firstly, the man would have to be insane to have kept the relic on him, he will have passed it to someone else. Secondly, it will be dangerous for you to approach him. You must take more care. It's likely he saw you run out of the Abbey—you weren't particularly discreet.'

'But—'

'And thirdly, it's entirely possible the women inside will tear you to pieces.' Lucien ran his hand round the back of his neck. 'My lady, the Black Boar is not a place for ladies of gentle birth.'

Isobel did not know how it was, but in an instant she understood what he was saying. 'It's a brothel?'

'My lady!'

She put up her chin. 'You are shocked. I may have lived much of my life in a convent, but I have heard of such places. And you have no need to worry that I shall ask how you know it's a brothel. I have been well schooled.'

'Well schooled?' He looked at her. 'That I would seriously question.'

Her chin inched higher; she knew her cheeks must be aflame. 'I have learned enough to know that ladies must never question their menfolk on such matters.'

Dark colour ran into Lucien's cheeks.

'My lady, I assure you I have never set foot in the Black Boar.'

Isobel gave him a considering look. His tone—and the earnest expression in those blue eyes—told her he was speaking the truth. 'I admit, that is a relief.'

She tucked her arm into his, and smiled up at him. Once again, he was looking at her mouth, his expression unreadable. Her stomach tightened. It could be her imagination, but she rather thought his mouth was edging into a reluctant smile. 'My lord,

I am no faintheart. If *you* are with me, I am certain all will be well...'

He shook his head, even as Isobel saw—yes, it was a definite smile. *The man really should smile more often.*

'I will be your champion, of course.'

I amuse him. 'Thank you, my lord.'

Lucien pushed at the inn door and they stepped over the threshold. It was a relief to know that Lucien had never patronised it, but Isobel could not help but wonder whether there were other, similar, establishments that he *had* patronised.

Chapter Four

Inside, smoke gusted from a central fire. The shutters were closed and the air was stale. The stench was overpowering. Candle grease, mutton stew, and human sweat. Customers hunched round the fire, leather mugs in hand. Rushlights guttered, sooty streamers trailed upwards.

'Hell of a draught,' someone bellowed.

A boy leaped at the door, and the gloom deepened.

Isobel gripped Lucien's arm, he had been right to warn her about this place. For all her bravado, she had never been in an inn like this. A full-bosomed woman was leaning through a serving hatch. The cut of her gown would doubtless give the Abbess an apoplexy. Faces turned towards them—unearthly in the fire-glow.

Isobel had lost sight of the thief. Several girls were moving among the customers—bright hair ribbons shone through the murk: yellow, violet, blue. The girls' clothes were cleverly laced to show off swelling breasts and slender waists. Isobel found herself staring.

A potboy materialised. 'Drink?' He looked Isobel up and down. 'Or is it a bedchamber you are wanting, sir?'

Isobel's cheeks scorched. When Lucien's stern expression lightened—*he is amused*—she avoided his eyes.

'We would like a cup of your best red, thank you,' he said. 'We shall take it over there, in the corner.'

The thief was at a table lit by a cloudy horn lantern, deep in conversation with a woman in a moth-eaten shawl. Lucien handed Isobel to a bench a few feet away.

'Can't we get any closer?' Isobel murmured.

Lucien's lips curved as he settled next to her. Taking her hand, he lifted it to his lips, and her stomach turned over. His blue eyes were as intent as a lover's. 'We can get as close as you wish, my dove.'

Isobel huffed out a breath. Lucien was almost on top of her, the long length of his thigh was warm against hers. She wrenched her hand free and glared at him. 'My lord, that was not what I meant, and you know it.'

Lucien's hand—as warm as his thigh—slid round her waist. 'Try to look more encouraging,' he murmured, his voice as caressing as his hand. 'They take us for sweethearts. Scowl like that and they will become suspicious. We will learn nothing. At the moment your presence is tolerated because they hope I will pay for a private chamber.'

Isobel swallowed. Lucien's smile, though charming, was altogether too practised. She recalled how his skin had darkened before they had entered. *Lucien might not have been in this particular inn before, but he is not inexperienced. He...* Her heart seemed to stutter, and when she noticed his gaze drop to her mouth, she realised with a jolt what was coming.

'Oh...no.'

'Oh, yes. Come here, little dove.' Pulling her against him, Lucien lowered his lips to hers.

Isobel froze. Her fingers clenched into fists, fists she pressed up against his chest, pushing against him. But not too hard. She was curious. And furious.

How could he!

For *years* Isobel had lived for some sign of attention from this man. Any sign would have done—a letter sent to the convent in Conques perhaps...even a simple message. He had done nothing. He had ignored her—year, after year, after year.

And then he had the gall to wait until they were in a smoky inn to kiss her. In a whorehouse, to be precise. She heard a strangled sound and, realising it was coming from her, silenced it. He was kissing her as a pretence, the devil. He didn't want her. Her pulse thudded. She wished he would stop, she couldn't breathe. She was going to faint. Lord, no, she wasn't, she *liked* his kiss.

His mouth softened and he eased back. 'Relax, Isobel, you will convince no one like that.'

She pushed against his chest with little effect, her strength had deserted her.

When a large hand crept to her cheek, cradling it in his palm, making tiny caressing circles with his fingertips, pleasure shot along every nerve. She bit back a moan. It was fortunate that his hand hid her face from onlookers. She felt hot, and confused, and…her womb seemed to ache. *He doesn't want to do this. He doesn't know me.* In the years she had lived in the south he had not shown the slightest interest in her welfare. *I am just another trophy to him. I am a prize. Lucien is marrying me for my inheritance.*

And then his mouth was on hers again and her thoughts scattered. Isobel forgot they were in the Black Boar; she forgot why they were here; she forgot everything. The nuns, the relic, the thief—they no longer existed. The world had narrowed down to Lucien, to the arm wound round her waist, to the lips on hers. There was simply nothing else.

Lucien's scent, musky and mysterious, surrounded her. His touch warmed her blood, her breasts felt heavy. The need to unclench her fists and wind her arms about his neck was irresistible. He was making her want to kiss his cheekbones and that scar on his temple. He was making…

She felt his tongue on hers and gasped. His tongue? She tore her lips from his.

'Wh…what are you doing?'

His eyes—it must be something to do with the mean light—were almost black. 'Kissing my betrothed,' he murmured.

Something thumped on to the table.

'Your wine,' the potboy said. He had a distinct snigger in his voice. 'Are you certain you won't be wanting that bedchamber, sir?'

Isobel moaned with the shame of it and, even more shaming, found herself wrestling with the impulse to hide her face against Lucien's chest.

The dark head shook. 'No, thank you. We are… negotiating terms. Later perhaps.'

'Negotiating terms?' Isobel glared at him. 'I hate you, I really hate you.'

'No,' came the soft answer. 'Thankfully, I don't think you do.'

He had done kissing her, it seemed. Strong hands were smoothing back hair that had escaped from her veil. He kept her tight against him—the arm encircling her waist felt proprietorial. And so it was, she supposed. *I am his betrothed. His heiress. I am his latest trophy.*

Lucien leaned against the wall of the inn, taking her with him, making her drape her arm about him. 'There, isn't it a relief to have got it out of the way?'

'Got what out of the way?' Isobel spoke sharply, hoping to conceal the most unsettling discovery. She liked being tucked against Lucien almost as much as she liked kissing him. It felt as though they belonged together. She was not feeling unalloyed pleasure though. She also felt anger—but whether she was more angry with herself or with him she could not say.

This man ignored me for years. I am nothing to him but a means to an end.

'Our first kiss.' Lightly, he touched her nose. 'On the whole, it was quite enjoyable. Far better than I had hoped.'

She ground her teeth together. *On the whole...* 'Lucien, I swear—'

'Yes, yes, you hate me.' Leaning towards her, he kissed her ear. Except that he wasn't really kissing it, he was using the kiss to conceal the jerking of his head towards the next table. 'Listen…can you hear?'

Isobel fought to ignore the rush of tingling evoked by his kiss and concentrated on the nearby table. Two heads, the shawled and the hooded, were close together.

'Your man said to tell you that he will be at the next tournament,' the woman said.

The thief wiped his nose with a ragged sleeve. 'I take it you don't mean the Twelfth Night joust in Troyes Castle?'

The woman laughed. It was a dry sound, like the rustling of leaves. 'Don't be a fool, that one will be bristling with Count Henry's Guardians. I am speaking about the All Hallows Tourney at the Field of the Birds. I am told…' the woman lowered her voice and Isobel barely caught the words '…your man has a buyer in mind. He will pay well for a relic that belonged to St Foye.'

'Better than last time?'

'*Much* better. He will meet you at the beginning of the tourney, at the vespers when the young knights run through their paces.'

'*Before* the vespers?'

'Yes.'

Firelight glinted in a shard of broken glass by the thief's elbow. 'Where? Where shall I meet him?'

'He will find you.' The woman gave a snort of laughter. 'He ought to know you by now.' Keeping her shawl firmly about her, she rose and scurried out.

Careful to keep her voice low, Isobel looked at Lucien. 'Did you see her face?' *Where is the Field of the Birds?* Isobel was bursting with other questions, but she bit her tongue on the rest, the hooded man was too close.

Lucien's hand tightened its hold. 'No. You?'

'Not so much as a hair on her head.' Isobel sighed and tried to put space between them. As she did so, she realised with horror that whilst she had been listening to the conversation on the next table, Lucien had taken possession of her other hand. Their fingers were entwined. How had she not noticed? Under the pretext of picking up her wine, she hastily disentangled herself.

She took a wary sip. The wine was earthy and faintly sour; it had an unpleasant undertone that defied identification. Ordinarily, Isobel wouldn't dream of drinking it, but she was glad to have the excuse to edge out of Lucien's arms. He discomposed her. He made her forget herself. Shooting him a glance, she caught his eyes on her, distant, watchful.

'Must you look at me like that?' she asked.

'You are not as I expected.'

'If you had troubled yourself to visit me at Conques, you would have come to know me.'

His face went hard. 'It is not necessary to know a woman in order to marry her.'

Isobel stared. 'You are blunt, my lord.' Her fingers curled into her palms. 'You want my lands.'

Lucien leaned in. His eyes were no longer dark as they had been when they had kissed, they gleamed with intent. *Ruthless, he is utterly ruthless.* Those eyes were the eyes of a man who never took his eyes from his target. 'I admit your lands will be useful,' he said quietly. 'My lady, only a fool would turn down the chance of enlarging his estates. But I am not marrying you solely for your lands. I am marrying you to honour the oath I swore at our betrothal. My father was sorely disappointed at the delay. I did him wrong in the matter of our marriage and that wrong has sat heavy in my mind for years. The time has come to put it right.'

Isobel frowned. 'Your father died some years ago. Why wait till now to honour your oath to wed me?'

It was as though Lucien had not heard her. That hard gaze shifted to the jug of wine, although she doubted that he saw it.

'I need an heir.'

Isobel's hand jerked. Wine slopped on to the table.

An heir. He means a male heir, the one thing my mother could not give my father. The one thing Isobel was afraid she would not be able to give him. Lucien's mouth, the mouth that had stirred such feelings in her, was set in a hard, uncompromising line. When Lucien put his mind to it, he would be relentless. What would happen to her if she failed him as her mother had failed her father? Two great fears twisted together in her mind: *I may not be capable of giving him an heir. I may die in the attempt.*

He reached for his wine, drank, and gave an eloquent shudder. '*Mon Dieu*, Isobel.' He prised her cup out of her grasp and dragged her to her feet. 'Don't touch that pi—er, swill, else you'll be joining your maid in the infirmary. We're leaving.'

As they squeezed past the tables, the thief looked up. His lip curled and he reached for his dagger.

Isobel made a small sound of distress.

Shielding her with his body, Lucien urged her past the fire. 'As I feared, he noticed you giving chase.' He pushed a coin into the potboy's waiting hands. 'I shall escort you back to the Abbey.'

'Thank you, my lord.'

Outside, Isobel heaved in a lungful of fresh air. Lucien took possession of her hand. He didn't tuck it into his arm in the more formal manner; instead, he held it at his side, as though they were sweethearts.

As he wove his fingers with hers, something knotted up inside her. It was very painful. Rather like longing for something one could never have. She was not this man's sweetheart—he was marrying her to honour the arrangement his father had made. He wanted Turenne. He wanted an heir.

'My lord?' Blue eyes glanced her way, as they plunged into a side street. 'Where is the Field of the Birds?' The device on Lucien's shield was a black raven, and the Counts of Aveyron had long been allies with the Counts of Champagne. It struck her that the tourney field must lie on Lucien's land.

A pulse throbbed near his scar. 'I hoped you hadn't heard that.'

They were walking between two rows of houses, and the gutter at the side was full of turnip peelings. Isobel lifted her skirts clear before speaking again. 'My lord, in the Abbey, you mentioned a tournament on the day after our wedding, I realise this must be the same one. Is the Field of the Birds part of your holding?'

'Yes.' His voice was dismissive. 'In his day, my father was patron of tournaments held at the Field of the Birds. I have had little to do with them.'

It was a puzzling response given Lucien's enthusiasm for tournaments and his success in the tourney field. And was it her imagination or was he avoiding her gaze? 'Why ever not?'

'Some years ago, I put my Champagne holding in the hands of a steward. He was running Ravenshold well enough. Until recently, I had no reason to visit.'

'There were other tournaments, I suppose.' She looked hopefully at him, but his face was closed. Unreceptive. 'I have never been to a tournament, my lord. At Turenne, my father's minstrel—'

His expression hardened. 'Isobel, a tournament is more than pretty ladies handing out favours to handsome knights. A tournament is a war-game.'

'Nevertheless, I should like to see one.'

'I don't advise you start at the Field of the Birds. I've heard it's badly regulated these days.'

'How so?'

'Since my father's time it has, so I hear, become… unruly. It will be messy, perhaps bloody. King Arthur and the Knights of the Round Table it is not.'

Isobel looked uncertainly at him. There was a darkness in this man's soul she could not account for. 'My lord?'

'Well, that is what you are expecting from a tournament, is it not? Deeds of valour. Quests.' He spoke abruptly. 'The tournament at the Field of the Birds is—well, it's war. If you want to play at being Queen Guinevere, you should wait for the Twelfth

Night joust at Troyes Castle. That should be more to your taste.'

Lucien's tone disturbed her. He was trying to put her off going to the All Hallows Tourney, but he would not succeed. It was well known that the Kings of France and England had voiced their disapproval of tournaments, but a champion of Lucien's status would not balk at the toughest of competitions. Was it possible that he was worried about her?

In truth, the Twelfth Night joust in Troyes sounded as though it would be much more to her taste. Unfortunately, the man who had stolen the relic was going to the All Hallows Tourney, Isobel would have to go too...

'If you are concerned for me,' she said softly, 'you need not be. I can look after myself. My lord, are the tournaments held in the Field of the Birds *very* dangerous?'

'So Sir Arthur—my steward—tells me. As I said, I have not attended one there in years.'

'Will you be competing? I would really like to go.'

Lucien dropped her hand. 'Isobel, I advise you to consider this discussion closed.'

'You *are* taking part!' She tipped her head back and met his gaze. 'No champion worth his mettle could fail to relish the challenge of a *real* tournament. If the competition is fierce, the prize money will be good. Where is the Field of the Birds?'

Blue eyes seemed to bore right through her. 'My lady, I see where you are heading and I will not have it. The wretch who took that relic will be looking out for you.'

'He won't see me. I will be discreet.'

Lucien snorted. 'I doubt you know the meaning of the word. Isobel, I forbid you to attend. I won't have time to watch out for you.'

'But, my lord—'

'Isobel, I do not wish you to attend. Do I make myself clear?'

Isobel heard obduracy in his voice, but she had met male obduracy before and knew what to do. She dealt with it in the way that she dealt with it when encountering it in her father. 'Yes, my lord,' she said, giving him a limpid look. 'Perfectly clear.'

Sister Christine met her at the convent gate. 'Lady Isobel, what were you thinking, tearing out into the town like that?'

With a bow and a thin smile, Lucien turned on his heel. The gate clanged shut and he was lost to sight. *I hope he sends for me soon.* Isobel had seen enough of the inside of a convent for one lifetime, and even the company of an obdurate man was preferable to a life lived behind convent walls.

The nun's silver cross was bright against her dark habit. 'My lady, I should warn you, the Abbess is most displeased.'

Isobel bit her lip—she liked Sister Christine, and it wasn't pleasant to realise that she had caused her trouble. 'Sister, please don't tell me you have been waiting here all this time?'

'Of course—I had to miss Office.'

'Oh, Sister, I am truly sorry.'

Sister Christine tucked her hands into the sleeves of her habit. 'You were out a long time; I cannot think what you were doing.'

Isobel opened her mouth to explain that Lucien had been with her every moment, but the nun shook her head. 'Don't tell me, tell Reverend Mother.' She gestured towards the Abbey church. 'You will find her in the Lady Chapel.'

Swallowing down a sigh, Isobel went into the church, pausing by the wooden screen that separated the Lady Chapel from the nave. The Abbess was sweeping up damaged fragments of stone, along with Elise and a couple of novices, and when she noticed Isobel, she thrust her broom at a novice.

'Lady Isobel, I realise you were shocked at the loss

of the relic, but you went into the town without your cloak. Without a maid. What were you thinking?'

'I am sorry, Reverend Mother, there was no time to fetch my cloak. And Count Lucien did act as my escort.'

'Apparently, you ran off at such a pace, you did not wait to see whether the Count had followed you or not. It is your good fortune that he did, although I am sure he must have been appalled by such unseemliness. Lady Isobel, you must learn to curb these impulses, and comport yourself with decorum. You cannot forget your status for a moment. Soon you will be the Countess d'Aveyron—you should not be running about Troyes like an unruly child. And most certainly you should not rely on Lord d'Aveyron to chase after you and see you safe.' Her nostrils flared. 'I trust you are unharmed.'

'I am.'

'Praise be. You are fortunate that Count Lucien is an honourable man. A less scrupulous one might have seized the opportunity to take advantage of you.'

Isobel stared at the cross on the Abbess's breast. *What would she say if she knew we followed the thief into a brothel? What would she say if she knew that Lucien—this honourable man—had seized on the chance to kiss me? In public. In the Black Boar.*

Isobel caught Elise's sympathetic gaze on her and resisted sending her a smile. Abbess Ursula was treating her like a naughty child, but she refused to be cowed. As the Abbess had said, she would soon be the Countess d'Aveyron.

'Reverend Mother, I ran from church because I saw the thief. I hoped to catch him.' The words tumbled out. 'He was lurking by the north door—stuffing something into his pouch. I swear it was the Limoges reliquary—I saw blue enamel, gold—'

'Be that as it may, it is not your concern. You should not have run out in so unladylike a manner.' Abbess Ursula turned to Elise. 'And as for you, you should have known better. Why did you not stop her?'

'My actions are my own, please do not blame Elise,' Isobel said. 'Reverend Mother, I am sorry if you think my behaviour was wrong.'

'You thought to catch the thief yourself.' The Abbess raised an eyebrow in so supercilious a manner that Isobel recalled her royal ancestry. She looked very regal. 'What if Count Lucien had *not* followed you? What if you had met with violence?'

'I was trying to help. Your Order has been good to me, I am especially grateful for the care I received at St Foye's.'

'You do not repay us by placing yourself in harm's

way. Viscount Gautier sent you here so we could keep you safe until your marriage. If anything should happen to you in the meantime, the reputation of our Order would be tarnished, perhaps irreparably. Who would send their daughters to us, if they came to harm?'

'My apologies, Reverend Mother.'

'And there are other concerns that in your haste you did not take account of...'

Isobel clenched her teeth. 'Yes?'

'By running off in so wild a manner you risked alienating Count Lucien. Did you see any sign that he was put off by your recklessness?'

Isobel did not know how it was, but Abbess Ursula's question evoked a vivid memory of a sensuous mouth pressing against hers, of a masculine arm winding possessively about her waist...

'Count Lucien gave no sign that he was alienated,' she murmured. *We crossed swords a little, but I do not think I alienated him.*

'You are blessed.' The Abbess made a sound of intense disapproval. 'The town fills with felons every year because of the fair. Which is why the Guardian Knights have been established. It is their duty to deal with miscreants, not yours.'

'Yes, Reverend Mother, I know. Count Lucien has explained this to me.'

'Has he? That is all to the good. We shall leave this folly behind us. In future, I trust you will think twice before indulging in such impulses. If God wills it, the relics will be returned. I have faith that He will also deal with the man who committed this sacrilege.' Abbess Ursula frowned at the ruined altar frontal, and turned for the nave. 'Sisters, follow me. Lady Isobel and Elise can finish the sweeping. And after that there is a yard or so of border on the altar cloth to be worked.' She held Isobel's gaze. 'I should like it as much as possible to be finished before you leave the Abbey.'

Chapter Five

The next morning, with no word from Lucien about moving out of the convent, Isobel had to assume the palace was fully occupied. While she waited to hear from him, she used the embroidering of the altar cloth to distract herself from worrying that, once again, Lucien had abandoned her.

The wind had changed overnight, and a brisk easterly was gusting over Troyes. Instead of sewing in the stronger light of the courtyard, she and Elise took refuge half in and half out of a small storage room in a quiet corner of the cloisters. There was no window, so they sat by the doorway with their cloaks about their shoulders and the blue altar cloth stretched between them. If she leaned forwards, Isobel could see the sky. Clouds scudded past like flocks of sheep.

Isobel was glad of the chance to talk quietly to Elise—she had much to learn and she sensed that

Elise could help her. However, a barrage of questions would not be welcome. She must tread carefully.

Elise, what brings you to this Abbey?

No, she could not ask that, that was far too probing.

As for the subject Isobel most burned to discuss—*Elise, what is it like to bed with a man?* It wouldn't be easy working that into conversation—she had only met Elise a couple of days ago. Even Lady Anna, whom Isobel had known for years, had shown reluctance to discuss her discomfort at what happened when a man bedded his wife.

Details had been scant. Isobel needed to know more. *What is it like? Does it hurt every time?* She had no idea why she supposed Elise might know the answer to that last question, save instinct. Elise was no innocent.

The nuns at St Foye's Convent, while elaborating on the wifely duties, had been silent on the more carnal aspects of marriage. It was not surprising. How could nuns who lived chastely know of such things? Carnal experiences were forbidden to them. The sisters had made up for their lack of experience in that area by speaking most eloquently on the importance of a wife denying herself. A wife must—they insisted—put her husband first in all things. Denial was their watchword.

When Isobel had asked her mother, Lady Maude, about what happened in the marriage bed, her mother had simply reiterated what the nuns had said. Lady Maude had gone out of her way to place a strong emphasis on duty. Duty.

Her mother spoke of duty; the nuns of denial. But being lectured on duty and denial didn't answer Isobel's questions. She must know everything. She had no wish to die in childbirth as her mother had done. More knowledge was *essential*.

Particularly since, having kissed Lucien, it was clear that she and her betrothed were attracted to each other. His touch made her weak. It made her think most unladylike thoughts. Before seeing him again in the Abbey lodge, Isobel had assumed it would be easy to keep him at bay. The kiss in the Black Boar had proved her wrong. It wouldn't be easy to deny him. That kiss... Surreptitiously, she fingered her mouth. The feelings Lucien had evoked—the thoughts...

Duty had been the last thing on her mind. And as for denial...

Was it possible that Anna's experience in the marriage bed would not be hers?

Smothering a sigh, Isobel glanced at Elise. Never mind that she was unused to broaching such matters, she would open on neutral ground...

'Elise, have you lived long in Troyes?'

'Only a few months, my lady.'

Isobel formed a couple of stitches and waited, hoping Elise would enlarge. When it became clear that Elise was not in a talkative mood, she tried again. 'What is it like when the Winter Fair begins in earnest?'

Elise's needle flashed as she worked the border. 'This is the first time I have been in Troyes at the close of the year, my lady. I imagine it becomes as busy as it does during the Summer Fair.' Briefly, she lifted her head. 'In the summer, the town is a bear garden.'

'It is hard to imagine it busier than it was yesterday.'

'It will be. At times the streets are almost impassable.'

Isobel made an encouraging noise, and watched Elise set a few more stitches. Then she said, 'When we have finished this section of cloth, I should like to go out again. There are quarters of the town I have yet to explore.'

That got her attention. Elise looked up, frowning. 'Is that wise, my lady? It is probably best to follow Abbess Ursula's advice and remain here, particularly with your father's escort at the barracks. It's not long until Winter's Eve. Once you are married

I am sure Lord d'Aveyron will give you all the escorts you need.'

Isobel rethreaded her needle with gold thread. 'I confess…' she spoke slowly, feeling her way '…to feeling apprehensive about my forthcoming marriage.'

Elise shot her a look and returned her attention to the altar cloth. 'You have been betrothed to the Count for some years. He is very personable, and far more reasonable than I had expected—'

Isobel went still. 'You have heard Count Lucien is unreasonable?'

Elise's cheeks went as bright as poppies. 'I… My apologies, my lady, I spoke out of turn.'

'If you have heard something, I should be grateful if you would tell me…'

Vehemently, Elise shook her head. 'I am sorry, my lady. I have heard nothing.'

The clouds shifted across the sky. Elise squirmed and finally met Isobel's gaze. 'About your marriage, my lady. I pray that all will be well. I have seen no sign of cruelty in Count Lucien.'

Isobel's eyes widened. 'No sign of cruelty?'

'Men can be cruel, my lady, and noblemen more than most,' Elise said, shrugging. 'They have power, and power breeds cruelty. All I am saying is that I have observed no sign of cruelty in Count Lucien.'

'I am relieved to hear it,' Isobel said frankly. Elise's remarks had knocked her back, strengthening her suspicion that Elise was no innocent. 'Until today, I hadn't seen Count Lucien in years. It has long been my fear that he mislikes me.'

'He mislikes you?' Elise's needle stopped pushing through the altar cloth, her voice sharpened. 'My lady, I doubt that is true. And even if it is, it has no relevance, since your marriage is a dynastic one. You should be pleased that your father, Viscount Gautier, was able to arrange such an advantageous match.'

'Naturally, I am very grateful.' Isobel forced out the words, though now she was actually talking about the fear that had been haunting her for months, inside she felt anything but grateful. She felt ignorant. How was she to learn about the physical aspects of marriage, when open discussion was frowned upon? Anna's dark hints had piled fear on fear. Isobel wanted reassurance, not only because she was afraid of what happened in the marriage bed, but also because of the consequences. Women died in childbirth every day.

'I should like to get to know Count Lucien before we are married.'

Elise gave her a tight smile. 'God willing, you will have years to get to know each other. In any case, Count Lucien is not a complete stranger. You met him at your betrothal. Surely you have seen him many times since then?'

Isobel found herself touching Elise's arm, seeking a reassurance that she suspected Elise was not willing to give. Elise responded pleasantly enough, but her manner was formal. *She is keeping her distance. Something—someone—has hurt her, and she is unwilling to trust me.*

'Until I arrived at the Abbey, the only time I met Count Lucien was at our betrothal. I was eleven, he…he was fifteen. Elise, I am afraid…afraid…' Isobel was appalled to hear her voice crack as she remembered her poor mother and her vain attempts to provide a male heir for Turenne. *The strain robbed Mama of her life.* Isobel was the only child to have survived. Attending Lady Maude's various lyings-in, she had stood by helplessly as her mother's face had distorted in agony. The screams had cut her to the quick. Lady Maude's death had left Isobel with a dread of childbirth. *I have to overcome my fears. I have to!*

'You are thinking of Lady Maude, I believe,' Elise said.

'I…yes.'

'Have you discussed your fears with the Abbess?'

Isobel stared at the rows of fluted columns that marched round the cloisters. 'I tried. The Abbess told me to put my trust in God. I can't help thinking that it's all very well for a nun, sworn to a life of chastity and prayer, to tell me to put my faith in God. It is not so easy when you have watched your mother's life ebb away.'

'What happened to your mother may not happen to you.'

Isobel stared blindly at the blue silk on her knee. 'I know that, of course, but...'

'Your fear lingers.'

Isobel gave a jerky nod.

Elise set another stitch before looking up again. 'There are ways to prevent conception, my lady.'

Isobel stared. 'I can see that you know them. Please, continue...'

'Some methods are better than others. My lady, if you wish to make enquiries, a local apothecary might be a good place to start. When you are married, you might find one and—' A soft footfall made Elise break off, two nuns had entered the cloisters. 'Later, I shall tell you later.'

Isobel leaned in to whisper. 'Do you know where to find an apothecary in Troyes?'

Elise nodded.

'You must show me, as soon as possible. This afternoon.'

'What about the Abbess?'

Isobel frowned at the nuns processing along the path, at the tall columns ranging around the cloister. 'I have had enough of being fenced in. Besides, I have other errands in town.'

Elise smoothed the blue fabric on her knee and resumed sewing. 'Oh?'

'I am curious about the tournament at the Field of the Birds. I need to know how to get there.' Fearing that Elise might refuse to accompany her if she knew Lucien had forbidden her to attend, Isobel decided to say nothing of that. Nor was she going to mention the stolen relic and her desire to find it and return it to Conques. Not unless she had to.

'The Field of the Birds?' Elise looked thoughtful. 'You might ask Count Lucien. His device—'

'Is a raven. I know. I forgot to ask him.' Isobel bent diligently over her needlework, ashamed at how easily the lie slipped past her lips. 'Elise, did you know that Count Lucien is a tourney champion?'

'I had heard something of the sort.'

Isobel heaved a wistful sigh. 'I've never been to a tournament.'

'Count Henry's holding a joust at Troyes Castle on Twelfth Night.'

Isobel shook her head. 'I am reliably told that will be a bland affair. The tournament in the Field of the

Birds is expected to be more exacting. More exciting. That's the one I want to see.'

'You want to watch Count Lucien. My lady, I advise you to wait for Twelfth Night. It's not for nothing that the King of France disapproves of tournaments.'

'It's a pity you don't know the way to the Field of the Birds, but no matter, I know where to ask.'

Elise gave her a long look. 'Why does that not surprise me?' she murmured.

The nuns sank on to a stone bench directly opposite, and one of them drew a psalter from her sleeve. They looked altogether too settled for Isobel's liking.

She pitched her voice low. 'Are they spying on us?'

Elise gave a small smile. 'I am not sure, but it looks that way.'

'We won't get out this morning then, not with them there. But later, I should like you to take me to that apothecary. Will you?'

'If you wish.'

'My thanks. At the same time, I can make enquiries about the way to the Field of the Birds.' Isobel frowned at the nuns. 'We'll wait until this afternoon when the sisters are in Office. As long as we are back before everyone gathers in the refectory for supper, no one will miss us.'

* * *

'That was easy,' Isobel said, swinging her cloak about her shoulders as she and Elise slipped through the gate by the Portress's Lodge.

'It may not be as easy getting back in,' Elise pointed out, closing the convent gate behind them.

'We can worry about that later,' Isobel said. She was half-afraid Elise would lose her nerve and change her mind about accompanying her, and she was determined to get to the Black Boar before that happened. 'First, I shall discover the way to the Field of the Birds, and then you can take me to that apothecary.'

They made their way up the narrow street in the direction of the market, wrangling half-heartedly with one another. Without being told in so many words, Elise had surmised that the Count would be displeased if Isobel attended the tournament at the Field of the Birds.

'I really don't know why I agreed to come with you,' she said. 'Lord d'Aveyron is bound to take this very ill.'

'You are doing this because you have become my friend,' Isobel said. 'And because I need your help.'

'I am not so certain you need anyone's help. I am confident you would manage without me. However, you should not be walking abroad on your own.'

Elise shook her head. 'My lady, you must take more care, innocence may not always be your shield.'

'What do you mean?'

'I mean only that you should be asking Count Lucien about the Field of the Birds. He won't like the idea of you roaming the town any more than the Abbess liked you riding out to Ravenshold.'

Isobel steeled herself to resist all arguments. And she refused to confess that the Count had already forbidden her to attend the tournament at the Field of the Birds. It was odd though, the more Elise insisted how unsuitable it was for a lady such as herself to think about attending without her lord's approval, the more keenly Isobel wanted to go. And not only because she wanted to watch out for the thief. Lucien's prowess on the tourney field was well known. She longed to see him in action.

As the Abbey de Notre-Dame-aux-Nonnains fell behind, her mood lifted. Troyes was filling fast, the population seemed to have tripled overnight, with merchants pouring in from all quarters. There were men in exotic damask tunics—the cloth woven with intricate patterns that Isobel knew must come from Byzantium and beyond. Girls swathed in silk from head to toe peered out at the world through dark, almond-shaped eyes. Dusky-skinned guards marched alongside pack animals. Mules brayed. La-

dies were carried through the narrow streets in lit-
ters, apparently more fragile than the Venetian glass
their husbands intended to sell. Hordes of people
swirled this way and that, chattering like starlings
in languages that were utterly alien.

Diving into a rush of townsfolk streaming down
the street, Isobel went with the flow until the sign of
the Black Boar was swinging overhead. The tavern
door was shut as it had been before, and the shutters were firmly closed. Black smoke floated out of
a louvre near the roof ridge. The door opened, and
a youth staggered out on a wild flurry of laughter.

'There!' Isobel was delighted to have found the
inn again. With the streets so full, it had crossed
her mind that she might lose her way. Beside her,
Elise had fallen ominously quiet. 'Elise, what's the
matter?'

'My lady, you…you are not thinking of going in
that place?'

Elise's eyes were startled. Shocked. Isobel felt a
pang of disquiet. From the outside, the Black Boar
looked much like many other wayside taverns.
Slightly squalid. The daub was falling away from
the lower walls, and it could have done with a fresh
coat of whitewash, but that closed door aside, there
was nothing to mark it out as a place where men
paid for anything other than food and lodgings…

Elise knows about the Black Boar.

'You know what this place is,' Isobel said quietly.

Elise caught her hand. 'I know it is no place for the future Countess d'Aveyron. My lady, don't go in. We would be far safer finding that apothecary.'

Lucien was riding towards the Abbey in the company of his squire, Joris. Count Henry's steward had informed him that a bedchamber overlooking the canal would shortly be free. The chamber would not be ready until tomorrow—the coming fair was to blame for that, the Count's palace was packed. At such short notice, Lucien counted himself lucky that decent lodgings had been found for his betrothed at all. And thanks to a sudden indisposition on the part of a cousin of the Countess of Champagne, a small solar was also available.

Isobel will be pleased.

Their horses picked their way between porters with trolleys and handcarts. Chattering housewives squeezed by with baskets over their arms. Scavenging strays wove in and out of the horses' legs.

Lucien was looking forward to watching Isobel's face when he told her about the apartment. He wanted to see those green eyes light up. *Much as she might feel affection for the nuns in the south, she had had enough of convent life.* He couldn't blame her.

He had almost reached the Abbey when he saw them. Isobel and Elise—the shy girl he had met at the convent—were sneaking out of the gate. Drawing rein, Lucien watched them drag up their hoods and scurry into the throng. *What are they up to?*

He waited until they had reached the end of the street before he dug his heels into Demon's sides. As he did so, he bit back a grin and reminded himself that he must take care, that women were not to be trusted. If he had learned nothing else from Morwenna, it was that. *Women are unreliable.*

'Who are those women, my lord?' Joris asked, following his gaze.

'The one on the right is my betrothed, Lady Isobel de Turenne. The other is her maid, Elise.'

Realising that he and Joris were somewhat conspicuous on their horses, Lucien dismounted and motioned Joris to do the same.

'We are following them, my lord? Why don't you hail them?'

Lucien shook his head. 'If I did that, I might never learn what she's up to.'

'Why don't you simply ask her, my lord?'

Lucien sent his squire a pitying look and pressed on. Joris had a lot to learn.

It soon became clear where Isobel was heading. It was hard to credit that a gently bred girl like Lady

Isobel de Turenne would knowingly return to the Black Boar, but he would swear they were heading that way. He had warned her off, and she was taking no notice.

'Stubborn,' he muttered, as they entered the square and the Black Boar came into view a few yards ahead. As he had predicted, Isobel and Elise were outside. 'She's a stubborn wench.' Isobel's tenacity left him surprisingly sanguine, more intrigued than angry. *What is she up to?*

Isobel and Elise were arguing. Lucien couldn't catch the words, but it didn't take a mind-reader to work out what the problem was. Elise was reluctant to enter. Elise had sense. 'And a good thing too,' he murmured.

'My lord?'

'Never mind.' Closing the distance between him and his stubborn betrothed, Lucien thrust Demon's reins at Joris. 'Wait here.'

'Yes, my lord.'

He reached the tavern moments after Isobel and her maid had slipped inside. Elise might have sense, but Isobel...

The inn fell quiet as he entered. The fug was worse than before. Smoke stung his eyes and caught at the back of his throat. Lord, what a place. The air reeked of boiled cabbages and garlic.

Isobel—his future countess, with her unwilling companion trailing after her—marched boldly up to the serving hatch. Sensibly, Elise had swathed her face with her veil, she looked like a girl from Araby. Not so Isobel. She tossed back the hood of her cloak, giving all who cared to look her way a clear sight of that open, innocent face.

Doubtless, Isobel thought she would be safe because she had done no wrong. Leaning against a wooden pillar, Lucien crossed his arms and prepared to wait. Isobel must be made to see that convent naivety was no protection, not in here. His bride-to-be needed to be taught a sharp lesson. The local girls would not take well to the arrival of two fresh and pretty rivals, and Isobel and Elise were drawing all eyes. *Thank God I saw them. They will want rescuing.* He was almost looking forward to it.

Isobel was speaking to the potboy—Lucien caught the gleam of silver as she pressed something into his hand. It flashed in on him what she was doing. Through the smoke haze, Lucien saw her lips move but customers were talking again, a low buzz of interest that drowned out what she was saying.

Lucien didn't have to hear her to know that she was asking about the coming tournament. *I told her not to attend. I was thinking of her safety and yet here she is, flouting my authority.* More and more of Isobel's character was being revealed with every passing moment. She was stubborn, she was foolhardy, and above all she was disobedient.

The ramifications of Lucien's hasty first marriage had shown him the importance of discipline. Of obedience. His father had never forgiven him for the dishonour he had done Isobel in marrying Morwenna. Since that time, Lucien had done his best to make up for his youthful inadequacies. He strove to conduct himself with honour.

He bitterly regretted that his father would not see that he was at last fulfilling his promise to Isobel. He sighed. It was a pity the bride his father had chosen showed such signs of waywardness. Lucien had expected that a lady, a convent-bred bride, would be above reproach. And here she was, in the town brothel, trying to bribe information out of a potboy.

Somewhere in the shadows to the right of the serving hatch, a woman—a bosomy redhead—let off a stream of invective. Her voice was coarse, and her words weren't fit for a lady's ears. Isobel turned towards her just as she charged out of the shadows.

Lucien wanted his second marriage to be an improvement on his first, and to that end, he must ensure Isobel recognised his authority. Marriage was all about authority. That was the mistake he had made with Morwenna, he had left it too late before asserting his authority. True, he had been little more than a stripling when he had wed her—Morwenna had been his senior by five years—but it had been a bad error. By the time he had realised his mistake, a pattern had been established and Morwenna had become too set in her ways to change.

That wasn't going to happen where Isobel was concerned.

As the redhead's magnificent bosom heaved, Lucien pushed away from the pillar.

The redhead looked belligerently at Isobel. 'Who the hell are you?' Her voice was sharp as a saw.

Isobel was such an innocent she smiled. 'You are speaking to me, *madame*?'

The redhead set her hands on her hips, her lip curled. 'If you are looking for work, you are wasting your time. We have enough girls. Good girls. Girls who know their business. You don't look as though you would know your way round a monk's—'

Lucien stepped into the light of a spitting candle and cleared his throat. 'Ladies, a word if I may?'

Isobel whirled round. Elise went white and ducked behind the potboy.

'Ladies, have you forgotten our appointment?' Digging into his pouch, he tossed a couple of pennies in the direction of the redhead and offered Isobel his arm. Isobel lifted her nose, but she took his arm. The redhead scrambled for the coins.

Elise was hanging her head in shame. Not so Isobel. No sooner had she stepped over the threshold than she snatched her hand from his arm. 'You followed us,' she said, eyes sparking green fire. 'You have no right.'

Lucien set his jaw. So much for thanks, did she not realise that the redhead had been on the point of tearing her limb from limb? 'You are my betrothed—that gives me the right. Particularly since you came here against my express wishes.'

Isobel set her hands on her hips in very much the way the redhead had done. 'You didn't tell me to avoid this place.' Her eyes lowered. 'Not in so many words.'

Taking her chin, he made her look at him. 'That is true as far as it goes, but you could have been in no doubt that I did not wish you to return. You had no male escort to protect you! And as for you enquiring about the tourney—that is flagrant disobedience.' He sighed. 'Incidentally, did you learn anything?'

Green eyes clashed with his, those cherry-coloured lips were tightly closed. Lady Isobel of Turenne was damnably attractive when she was angry. Lucien felt a powerful and extremely inconvenient urge to kiss her.

Aware that Joris and Elaine were watching them with some interest, he released Isobel's chin and once again offered her his arm. 'Come, my lady, we cannot quarrel in the street.'

Glittering eyes held his before she reluctantly put her hand on his sleeve.

Disappointment churned in Lucien's guts. In her own way, Isobel was showing every sign of becoming as inconvenient a wife as Morwenna had been. Where was the demure, obedient lady he had hoped for? He had come in search of her, wanting to bring her pleasure and somehow, they were quarrelling.

It is early days. I must not judge her too soon.

'I had hoped for a peaceful marriage,' he said. 'Are my hopes misplaced?'

Her mouth twitched, her expression lightened. *Mon Dieu*, she only had to look as though laughter was a breath away, and Lucien found himself warming to her. Morwenna had rarely laughed. Had that been part of the trouble? Morwenna had taken everything so seriously...

'Misplaced? I do hope not.' She looked sideways at him. 'You are not a tyrant, are you, my lord?' She gave Joris a measuring look. 'Are you Lord d'Aveyron's squire?'

'Yes, my lady.'

'This is Joris of Caen,' Lucien said, belatedly

performing the introductions. 'Joris, this is my betrothed, Lady Isobel de Turenne, and this is Elise of...?' He looked at Elise.

'Just Elise,' the girl muttered.

Isobel was making Joris blush with the power of her smile. 'Well, Joris? Is my lord a tyrant?'

'No, my lady, of course not, Count Lucien is the most considerate—'

Lucien clapped his squire on the arm. 'Enough, Joris. I'll give you the penny I promised after.'

'My lord?'

Isobel's laughter rang round the square, and Lucien found himself smiling. Laughter was indeed a great blessing. As long as his betrothed learned to control her waywardness, there was hope for his second marriage.

'Do you wish to return to the Abbey, my lady?'

'Do we have to? We were going to...' white teeth caught her lower lip '...going to find something to eat.'

'Don't the nuns feed you?' Lucien waited for her response, she had been going to say something else, he was sure. However, having caught her in the Black Boar, he could not think that her other business would be anything that need concern him.

'It is Friday, my lord.' Thick eyelashes swept

down, hiding her eyes. 'And I have been having sinful thoughts all day.'

Her choice of words—innocent, he was sure—none the less had his gaze dropping to her mouth. To her breasts. Heat sparked through his veins. 'Oh?'

'I have a strong desire for red meat.'

'I know just the place,' Lucien heard himself say.

Chapter Six

More people had poured into Troyes; the approach to the castle was jammed. Isobel realised they were fortunate to have horses with them. Horses proclaimed high status—particularly a black stallion like Lucien's. As they progressed up the street, the townsfolk fell back to let them by.

Preparations were in hand for the Winter Fair, and the market area around St Rémi's Church had sprung loudly into life. Jostling and noise came from all directions—hammers banged; cartwheels rumbled. A crate fell from a stall with a crash of splintered wood and several rounds of cheese rolled out. The sea of people swept past with the cheesemonger darting hither and yon, desperate to scoop up his wares before anyone else did. Hens squawked; feathers and straw floated on the wind.

Isobel wasn't used to such frenetic activity. And the noise! Life in the convent was quiet and orderly.

If it were not for Lucien and Joris marching on either side with the horses, she and Elise would be buffeted to bits. *I must get used to this. Real life outside a convent.* By the time they crossed the canal and entered the Jewish quarter, the crowd had thinned and Isobel could breathe—and think—again.

She shot Lucien a covert glance, her gaze flickering from his stern, unsmiling mouth to the way he held his charger's reins, controlling him with the lightest of touches. She had been pleasantly surprised by his forbearance in the Black Boar. He had accused her of disobedience, but thankfully he had not berated her in public. Was the storm yet to break?

It was obvious Lucien valued self-control. He might be disappointed in her, but a man like Lucien, a champion who had won accolade after accolade, would not stoop to brawling with his betrothed in the street. If chastisement was to come her way, it would likely come later, when they were in private. She had angered him.

A crumbling Roman wall appeared ahead, farriers and armourers were set up in its shadow. Furnaces glowed like dragons' eyes. The air rang with the clang of hammer on steel, and the tang of singed hoofs hung in the air.

Lucien led them around the castle walls to where

a pie stand was set up beneath a walnut tree. As the rich and tempting smell of beef reached her, Isobel's mouth filled with saliva. He had brought them to a pie stand?

'You wish to eat, my lady?' Lucien's stern mouth eased as he handed his reins to Joris.

Isobel's heart lifted. Lucien knew that he had surprised her, and she would swear he was trying not to smile. 'I would love to. I'm starving.'

This last was not strictly true. The sisters knew better than to starve the daughters and wives of their benefactors, but one effect of the restricted convent diet was that it had instilled in Isobel a hearty respect for red meat. Even on a Friday, when meat was forbidden.

'Four pies, if you please,' Lucien said, handing over the money.

They sat on a bench beneath the walnut tree, Lucien on Isobel's right hand, Elise on her left. The pies were hot. Isobel's tasted better than anything she had eaten in years.

'Good, eh?' Lucien said. 'Bartholomew bakes the best beef pies in Champagne.'

'Heaven,' Isobel murmured, surreptitiously wiping crumbs from her mouth.

A couple of leaves fluttered down from the tree.

Through a gap in the wall, Isobel saw a mill wheel. While she finished her pie, she watched it turning.

'Thank you, my lord, I was hungry.' She brushed off her hands, faintly embarrassed at the speed with which she had wolfed the pie. A priest was walking by, heading for the castle drawbridge. When he nodded at them, she grimaced. 'I hope he didn't see what we were eating, I don't want the sisters to find out about the beef.'

Lucien gave her a sharp look. 'They don't use the birch on you?'

'No. But there are…penances for various transgressions.'

He leaned back, studying her. 'Penances?'

'Minor transgressions require the repetition of certain psalms in church; it is similar to when one makes one's confession. Larger transgressions require more…stringent penances.'

'Such as?'

Elise shifted, she was staring at a leaf on the ground. 'Embroidering the altar cloth. Lady Isobel mislikes that most particularly,' she said quietly, not lifting her gaze from the leaf. 'Though it's not so bad at the Abbey.'

The way Elise kept her gaze on the leaf…it was as though she found it hard to look at Lucien. *Elise is shy, painfully shy.*

Rising, Lucien offered Isobel his hand. 'Rest assured, the nuns will hear no mention of meat pies from me,' he said. 'In any case, the sin is surely mine. If they find out, you can say I bought them, and for courtesy's sake you were forced to eat them.'

'Thank you, my lord.'

Lucien's fingers closed warmly over hers. When he had kissed her at the inn, Isobel had been unprepared for it, but she had liked it. She liked the contact now. Lucien's fingers were strong and capable, his nails were clean and cut straight across. There was nothing particularly remarkable about them, nothing to hint at how much she would enjoy their touch. He ran his thumb across her knuckles, and an echo of the shivery sensation she had felt in the inn feathered through her.

'I shall return you to the Abbey,' he said, tucking her arm into his and giving her one of his rare smiles. 'I was coming to see you when I saw you heading for the tavern. I wanted you to know that chambers will shortly be available at Count Henry's palace.'

Isobel's heart gave a nervous lurch. 'When will they be ready?'

'Tomorrow afternoon.'

Heart thudding, Isobel looked into his blue eyes.

So...it begins. From tomorrow, I will be entirely in your hands...

Her blood thrummed in her veins—she felt excited, she felt afraid. A husband had so much power over a wife. Isobel had waited many years to come to this crossroad, and she had always imagined that her father and mother would be standing with her. With her mother's death and her father's illness, that was no longer possible.

She knew remarkably little about Lucien the man. At times he seemed quite approachable—the kiss at the inn, the buying of the meat pies. At other times, he was stern and distant. She simply could not fathom him. *The great tourney champion. He is an enigma.*

He had followed her to the inn and waited for her to engage the potboy in conversation *before* he had announced his presence. Why? It was as though he expected her to condemn herself in his eyes; it was as though he was waiting for her to prove herself unworthy in some way.

'I shall prepare to move to the palace tomorrow then.'

His head dipped, and it struck her that he was watching for her reaction. 'If that is convenient.'

He expects me to be pleased. Thrusting her doubts

behind her, Isobel put brightness into her voice. 'Thank you, my lord, that will be…a relief.'

The Abbess was waiting at the convent gate.

'There you are,' she said, grasping Isobel by the wrist. Then she noticed Lucien, and released her as quickly as she had grasped her. 'Count Lucien!'

'Good day, Reverend Mother.' Lucien interposed himself between Isobel and the Abbess. 'Did my lady not inform you of our meeting to discuss our forthcoming marriage?'

Abbess Ursula gripped the cross at her breast and looked coolly at them. 'Lady Isobel said nothing of any meeting, my lord.'

'My apologies, Reverend Mother, I am sure you will forgive her. We had much to decide upon.' He looked down his nose at her. 'And now we are come to inform you of our plans. Lady Isobel will be taking her leave of you tomorrow.'

'Tomorrow?'

'Count Henry's steward has found chambers for her in the palace, they will be ready tomorrow. I see no reason why she should not move in then.'

The Abbess made a choking sound. 'My lord, I am afraid that will not be possible, Lady Isobel's maid has not recovered. I do not advise that an unmarried lady moves into the palace without her companion.'

Isobel felt Lucien stiffen.

'Reverend Mother,' he spoke softly, but there was iron in his voice. 'You are surely not suggesting that Lady Isobel will be at risk while she is under the protection of Count Henry?'

'Lady Isobel will need a maid.'

Isobel felt a tug on her skirt.

'Please,' Elise whispered, eyes fixed on Isobel. 'Take me.'

'I should like that,' Isobel said, looking at Lucien.

'Good idea,' he said. 'Elise shall accompany my lady to the palace.'

Abbess Ursula sniffed. 'My lord, I had hoped to have charge of Lady Isobel a while longer. There are certain…aspects of her character that require more…training. You are bound to have noticed them. I strongly recommend Lady Isobel remains at the Abbey until your wedding. That way we can improve her—'

'Improve her, Reverend Mother?' Lucien murmured, placing his hand on Isobel's. His thumb moved back and forth over her skin, in that subtle caress that unsettled as much as it reassured. 'What can you mean?'

'Lady Isobel is rather…wayward, my lord.' The Abbess paused. 'And we don't want history to repeat itself, do we?'

* * *

Lucien went still, but his mind raced. Abbess Ursula's effrontery—on two counts—briefly robbed him of speech. Isobel was unquestionably wayward. The sight of his betrothed standing up to that redhead in the Black Boar would live long in his mind. He was startled to feel his mood lift as he remembered. It was true that Lucien had hoped that his second wife would be quietly, sweetly biddable. Isobel was neither quiet nor biddable, but he was sure, with the right training…

'It is not for you to criticise my betrothed. Her time here is over.' It came to him that convent training would never work on someone like Isobel. She was as unsuited to life in a nunnery as he would be. Perhaps her early arrival in Troyes had as much to do with Isobel as it did with her stepmother—she was desperate to escape the convent.

As for Abbess Ursula's reference to Morwenna— how dare she! Isobel was bound to find out about Morwenna at some point, but Lucien had no intention of that happening until after their wedding. After he had honoured his promise to his father. *After we have had time to get to know one another.*

That last thought caught him unawares. Ruthlessly, he dismissed it. *We shall marry, and Isobel will choose one of my castles to live in. And then, apart from the children she will bear me, life will go on very much as it did before.*

In the aftermath of the first attack on Morwenna, Lucien had been forced to tell Abbess Ursula that Morwenna was his wife. Only the Abbess and a handful of his knights knew of his first marriage. Lucien had revealed his secret to the Abbess purely for Morwenna's sake. He had wanted to protect her, and he had known that the Abbess would be more inclined to squash rumours of witchcraft if she knew Morwenna was Lucien's wife.

Notwithstanding, Lucien had had many a sleepless night over the Abbess learning that he was married. If word had got out—the scandal would have rocked Christendom. A noble of Lucien's status was expected to marry *well*. Morwenna was not noble. She had been a minstrel's daughter and her illegitimate birth was against her. If Isobel's father, Viscount Gautier, had found out about the marriage, he would have accused Lucien—quite rightly—of breaching the terms of his betrothal contract. Not only would Isobel be lost to Lucien, but with her would have gone any hope of him having a real marriage.

I kept marriage to Morwenna quiet in the hope that Morwenna would become strong enough to survive an annulment.

That day had never dawned. Morwenna's mind

had become increasingly clouded and he hadn't had the heart to divorce her. He had lost himself in tourneying; flinging himself into the life of an itinerant knight; hoping against hope that one day Arthur would send a message informing him that Morwenna had recovered. The message had never come, and Lucien hadn't been able to bring himself to seek an annulment from a woman who was unable to fend for herself.

Several years had gone by with Lucien braced for the day when the Abbess would reveal his secret to the world. Rather to his surprise, that day had never dawned. The Abbess had kept her word; she had kept his shameful secret. As far as Lucien could tell, she had never breathed a word about his marriage.

Until now…

If Isobel learned about Morwenna too soon, her view of him would be coloured by that one terrible mistake from his past. A woman of her status would see his marriage to Morwenna as an insult. Isobel would have grounds to reject him, and the world would learn his shameful secret. His dishonour. And those years of striving to regain his honour on the tourney field would be as dust in the wind. It was too soon for Isobel to learn about Morwenna.

'Lady Isobel is my responsibility now,' he said, firmly. 'And I thank you for your care of her.'

Abbess Ursula inclined her head. 'Very well, my lord. May I wish you both well in your marriage?'

'Thank you, Reverend Mother.'

When the Abbess had gone, Isobel touched Lucien's arm. 'My lord, what did Reverend Mother mean about history repeating itself?'

His jaw tightened. 'It's not important. Forget it. You will soon be out of here.'

'For that I am grateful.'

Lucien lifted her hand from his arm and kissed her fingers. 'I shall bring porters and an escort at noon tomorrow. Until then, I bid you farewell.'

Count Henry's palace was but a short step away along the Rue Moyenne and across the bridge, so there would be no need for horses. As Lady Isobel of Turenne's betrothed came to escort her and she bade farewell to the nuns, the last notes of the noon bell rang out from St Peter's Cathedral.

It had rained earlier, and the cobbles gleamed with wet. It was cold, goose-bumps ran down her neck. Winter was fast approaching, but nothing could depress her spirits. Pulling up her hood, Isobel walked out of the Abbey and placed her hand on Lucien's arm.

At last, she was to have a taste of what life as the Countess d'Aveyron might be like. There would be no more penitential sewing for her, no more hours on her knees poring over her psalter. The man at her side would shortly be her husband.

Lucien's arm was steady as he guided her towards the palace. Strong. It was hard to remember her status and walk sedately. *I am free of convents for ever! Elise and I will have a set of chambers entirely to ourselves. There will be no more sharing a bed-chamber with other noblewomen; there will be no more jostling for the best place in bed.*

She kept her head high and tried not to look at Lucien. He was full of contradictions, and she had doubts about their future together, but she was eager for their marriage to take place.

Lucien in the flesh was not quite as she had imagined him. During the time when she had been awaiting his summons, she had decided he must be cold-hearted. Remote. A lord who would brook being questioned by no one. There were times when that seemed to be true. Clearly, he set much store in obedience.

He smiled but rarely. And yet—when he did smile, his whole face transformed. *I do not know how it is, but his smile touches my soul.* Isobel knew she could not set much store in a smile. Smiles came cheap. Usually. She did not believe that was true in Lucien's case. His rare smiles were to be treasured.

It was somewhat galling to learn that he could touch her with something as simple as a smile after abandoning her to the nuns for so long.

And then there was his serious, distant look…if it were not for that, she might insist that he told her why he had taken so long to summon her. *We shall have the rest of our lives together, I shall ask him later…*

Elise and Joris were talking behind them, something about the road being rutted by too many cartwheels. Isobel glanced back. Between them, they were ensuring the porters didn't let Isobel's travelling chests slide off the handcarts. Joris had Isobel's jewel box tucked under his arm. The jewel box didn't contain much—a string of pearls; a gold ring that had belonged to her grandmother; a few coins her father had given her for the journey.

Lucien's manner with Joris was invariably relaxed and easy. It was difficult to imagine him playing the tyrant with his men. He wouldn't need to.

Their procession passed a cloth merchant's, people were staring.

'That must be Isobel of Turenne,' one woman muttered. 'She and Lord d'Aveyron are to marry.'

The woman's companion—a pale girl of about thirteen—replied, 'What about the woman he keeps at Ravenshold?'

Isobel caught her toe in the hem of her gown. *The woman he keeps at Ravenshold?*

In a trice, her sense of optimism was gone, snuffed out like a candle. *Lucien has a woman. A woman he keeps at Ravenshold.* It would explain so much.

He glanced at her, doubtless wondering why she had all but tripped over her gown. A dark eyebrow lifted.

She risked a question. 'Did you hear those women, my lord?'

'What women?'

Heart in her mouth, Isobel shook her head and walked on. As they turned into the main street, leaving the Abbey behind, Count Henry's palace came into view.

Careful. This might not be the best moment to question Lucien about a lady-love. *He could yet reject me.* Isobel sighed, her years of waiting had scarred her, it seemed. Scared her. *I won't be bundled back to the Abbey...I won't.*

Isobel's time in the convent had not blinded her to men's baser natures. It was common knowledge that great lords often kept mistresses as well as wives. King Henry of England was notorious—despite his Queen, Eleanor of Aquitaine, being one of the most beautiful women in the world, King Henry had his Rosamund. And, if rumour could be relied upon,

King Henry had countless other mistresses as well. Why should Lucien be any different?

If Isobel hadn't been so focused on escaping the convent, this would—should—have occurred to her. *Does Lucien have a mistress?* It was a question that tied her stomach in knots, a question she could not ask him, not today. If Lucien had a mistress—and surely a handsome lord like Lucien might have any woman he crooked a finger at?—he might have grown fond of her.

The knots in her stomach tightened. She had been naïve. The girl's voice echoed in her head. *'What about the woman he keeps at Ravenshold?'*

Lucien had a mistress. That would explain his tardiness in marrying her, he had a *belle amie*. The questions kept on coming. *If Lucien keeps his lady-love at Ravenshold, surely he will settle her elsewhere when we marry?*

Does he love her? Does he?

By the time they walked under the archway into the palace courtyard, Isobel's mind was in such a ferment that she barely noticed her surroundings.

Vaguely, she saw there was space. Stables lay on one hand; horses were visible through an open doorway. A groom was sweeping up some rain-sodden hanks of straw. Several men-at-arms were on duty by the gatehouse, and across the yard smoke was winding through the roof of a bakery.

Count Henry's steward had told Lucien that the palace was full, but after the chatter and shove of the streets the courtyard seemed as quiet as the convent. High walls shut out the townsfolk; they shut out the noise and rush.

'This way, my lady.' Lucien indicated a door at the side of the main building.

My lady. Lucien's polite formality was beginning to trouble her. Was he using it to keep her at arm's length? Isobel racked her brains to try to remember whether he had called her 'Isobel' after finding her in the Black Boar. She thought that he had, but she could not quite recall…

A stairway curled upwards. Lit by unglazed arrow-loops, it was dark and draughty. They rounded one turn and another, coming to a halt by a studded oak door.

Lucien waved her in. 'This will be your solar, until I take you to Ravenshold.'

The solar was long and narrow. Tapestries covered every inch of the walls—making it look as though they were standing in a mythical forest. Rabbits frolicked in grassy clearings; maidens garlanded unicorns with flowers; ladies danced in and out of the trees. Two arched windows sat on either side of a stone fireplace, and—what extravagance!—they were glazed. The window seats overflowed with tasselled silk cushions. A fire blazed in the hearth.

'Goodness,' Isobel said, forcing pleasure into her voice. There was a hollow feeling in the pit of her stomach. 'This is very grand, my lord.'

The windows overlooked the canal. Barges were gliding past below, filled to sinking point with packing crates and barrels. On the other side of the canal, Abbey Church towered over the roofs and streets of Troyes.

Elise and Joris entered, followed by the porters. Elise dropped her bundle and disappeared through a curtained doorway in the panelling at the far end of the solar.

'Your jewels, my lady,' Joris said, handing Isobel her jewel box with great ceremony. Clearly he thought it contained a fortune. If only he knew.

'Thank you, Joris.'

'The bedchamber is at the far end, I believe,' Lucien said, blue eyes flickering briefly towards the curtained doorway where Elise had gone. 'I shall leave you to get settled.'

'Thank you for securing these chambers, my lord.'

Isobel was finally free of the convent. But—she studied Lucien's dark, scarred features—was she exchanging one form of imprisonment for another? 'My lord, will you be staying in the palace?'

The dark head shook. He was wearing his distant look. 'I have business at Ravenshold. When in town, I have quarters at the castle barracks.'

Isobel dug her fingers into her palms. It was hard—no, it was *impossible* to forget the woman he kept in his castle. 'My lord, I would like to see Ravenshold.'

'Later. It is not fit to be seen at present. Work is in hand to bring it to rights. When that is done, be assured I shall show it to you.'

Isobel's heart twisted. What he was saying was that his *belle amie*, whoever she was, was still in residence. He was not ready to be rid of her! Isobel looked into his eyes and gritted her teeth. *I will make you forget your mistress.* Somehow she hung on to her smile. 'I look forward to seeing you when your business permits, my lord.'

He was halfway to the door when he turned and retraced his steps. Giving her a lopsided smile, he bent to whisper in her ear. 'My lady, a small reminder...'

'My lord?'

'There are to be no more enquiries about the Field of the Birds. Since you will not be attending the All Hallows Tourney, there is no point. Is that clear?'

Chapter Seven

Unable to give him the promise he wanted, Isobel fiddled with the clasp on her jewel box. Was Lucien always so intransigent? Was it a foretaste of what marriage was going to be like—with her asking permission every time she wanted to do something, and with him denying her? Did he enjoy wielding power over her in this way? 'Perfectly clear, my lord.'

Lucien and Joris bowed and went out. When the crackling from the fire was louder than the footsteps going down the spiral stairway, Isobel went into the bedchamber. It was smaller than the solar, and dominated by a roomy bed with an oak headboard and carved bedposts. Pillows were creamy white; fluffy blankets were folded at the foot. A pair of coffers had been polished to a soft shine, and a row of wooden pegs ran along one wall. Elise was busily shaking out their cloaks and hanging them up.

Isobel set her jewel box on a shelf next to a candlestick and sat on the bed. From the way she sank into it, the mattress was filled with swansdown. 'Elise, do try this out. The convent pallets are beds of nails in comparison.'

Elise sat cautiously beside her, and prodded the mattress. 'What joy,' she murmured with a small smile. 'Not a straw in sight.'

'How many penances do you imagine the sisters would impose for sleeping on this?'

'An eternity of them?' Elise rolled her eyes. 'Doubtless they'd burn the bed, to avoid temptation.'

With a smile, Isobel took Elise's hand. 'We're going to like it here.' *And if Lucien did not have a mistress, I might like it even more...*

'Yes, my lady.' Elise rose. 'If you will excuse me, I shall unpack your belongings.'

'Not yet awhile, we have the rest of the afternoon. I need your counsel.'

'My lady?'

Their wedding was days away and Lucien had made no mention of whether he would see her before then. If the women she had heard in the street were in the right, he was keeping a mistress at Ravenshold. Isobel jumped to her feet, and began to pace. She walked to the window, and ran her hands over thickly-embroidered curtains which fell from ceiling to floor. Every stitch spoke of opulence, of immeasurable wealth. They were looped back with silver braiding.

Lucien leaves me in his friend's palace and goes back to his mistress at Ravenshold. How often does he share his bed with her? Will he do so tonight? Her nails were digging into her palms. Slowly, she uncurled her fingers. She should not care. She did not care. *Our marriage was never a love match. It is a matter of politics.*

'My lady, are you all right?'

'I am quite well, thank you, Elise.' *Apart from having doubts about my betrothed.*

Will he get rid of his mistress after our wedding, or will I have to endure the embarrassment of knowing that he has a rival hidden away at Ravenshold?

If only she had had leisure to study Lucien's nature. If they had met at regular intervals during the years of their betrothal, she would know if he was a man who would think nothing of humiliating his wife.

She straightened her back. She must count her blessings, matters could be very much worse. At least she was not in love with him. If she were, she would be heartbroken. She was not heartbroken. And Lucien was not all tyrant. Yesterday he had taken her part when the Abbess would have chastised her for leaving the Abbey without permission.

He had realised she was uncomfortable at the Abbey and had gone to the trouble of securing this apartment for her in Count Henry's palace. He had taken them to the pie stand when she had expressed a desire to eat meat on a Friday.

If only he had not forbidden her to go to the Field of the Birds.

'Elise, I'm going to that tournament.'

'The one after your wedding?'

Isobel nodded.

'My lady, is that wise? Count Lucien forbad it.' Elise's gaze was keen. 'Are you going out of spite?'

Something in Elise's tone caught Isobel's attention. 'Spite? Where did you get that idea?'

'The gossips in the Rue Moyenne.'

'You heard about his *belle amie*.' Isobel closed her eyes and wished the floor would open up and swallow her.

'My lady, I am sorry. I can see it must be upsetting.'

The words were sympathetic, and Elise reached out to touch her arm. Which made it all the more odd when it dawned on Isobel that Elise could be motivated by curiosity as much as sympathy. Of course, she had only known Elise for a couple of days. Now she thought about it, Elise was just as much a stranger to her as Lucien was. It was hard to read a person when one did not know them.

Striding to the window, Isobel pressed her nose to the glass. Across the canal, the roofs of Troyes crowded up against each other, a jaggedy patchwork of shapes and sizes. 'Elise, the man who stole the reliquary is going to that tournament, I refuse to miss it. It might be my only chance of finding the relic.' She had no wish to disobey Lucien so soon after their wedding, but that couldn't be helped.

'My lady, given Count Lucien's objections, I don't advise—'

Isobel made a chopping gesture and turned. 'Elise, my mind is made up, I am going. And I should be pleased if you would come with me.'

'*Me?*'

'If you don't care to come, I shan't hold it against you. I don't know how much you know about tournaments—I have never been to one myself—but they apparently begin with the newest knights testing each other's mettle. The early part of a tournament is known as—'

'The vespers.'

'You've been to one?'

'It was some time ago, my lady. I recall it beginning with the young knights warming up.' Elise came to the window, eyes anxious. 'I have heard that in recent years tournaments at the Field of the Birds have been…unruly. After Count Lucien resigned as patron, any semblance of order was gone. Tourneys at the Field of the Birds have become notorious. When the mêlée starts, the onlookers are one step away from becoming a mob.'

Isobel took this in with some surprise, she had no idea Elise knew so much about the Field of the Birds. 'Why didn't you mention this earlier?'

'I thought you would change your mind about wanting to go.' Elise stared at the bed, her expression unreadable. 'My lady, if you go without his blessing, I suspect it will be a struggle to find a good vantage point, let alone see that thief. And if you do see him, what shall you do?'

'I shall think of something.'

Elise shook her head. 'If the man realises you are watching him…my lady, you must take care. Can you be sure he will stop at thievery? He may be violent. And there's more to consider…'

Bemused at the flow of words from her hitherto quiet maid, Isobel waited.

'Even the best-regulated tournaments are dangerous. King Louis loathes them. Men get killed. The coming tournament will be fiercer than most. You may regret going.'

'Elise, I won't faint at the first sight of blood, if that is what concerns you.'

'I am sure you will not. But, my lady, knights are likely to be injured, Count Luc—'

'Count Lucien is hardly a novice.'

'No one is invincible, my lady. The Count's scar is testimony to that.'

'None the less, I am going.'

Elise scowled at a plaited rush mat by the side of the bed, muttering darkly about ladies with an unholy relish of blood sports.

'Elise!'

Elise bit her lip. 'My apologies, my lady, that was uncalled for, but I stand by what I have said. Tournaments can be brutal and bloody. I don't think you should go.'

'I have to, I owe a debt to the nuns at Conques,' Isobel said quietly. Given how helpful Elise had been in the convent, and how keen she had been to accompany Isobel to the palace, her present intransigence was odd to say the least. She had mentioned men dying, perhaps she was squeamish. 'Elise, you have made your objections plain. I will not chastise you if you do not come with me. But I most definitely need your help with finding that apothecary. I shall be needing those herbs. I take it you will not refuse me on that. Tell me, are there other ways to prevent conception?'

'The nuns kept you ignorant, didn't they, my lady?'

Isobel felt a flare of anger. What was the matter with Elise? Her tone couldn't be described as nasty, but nor was it pleasant. It was almost as though Elise knew Isobel was uncomfortable discussing this and was relishing her embarrassment. Her discomfiture. *I must be imagining it, why should Elise relish my discomfiture?* It made no sense, yet…

With a glance at the doorway—anyone might be in the solar beyond—Isobel lowered her voice. 'Are there other ways to avoid conception?'

'Yes, my lady, there are.'

'What are they?'

It was Elise's turn to glance at the doorway. 'There are a number of ways, my lady. None are infallible, but I believe the herbs work best.'

'Very well, you shall explain the other methods to me; I should like to know them. After that we shall visit the apothecary.'

'As you wish, my lady.'

'Today.'

'Yes, my lady.' Elise hesitated, chewing her lip. 'My lady, about the All Hallows tournament…if you are set on going, I will come with you. You can't go alone.'

'I could take my father's men as escort. Or...' Isobel tipped her head to one side '...I could follow the example of the Duchess of Aquitaine when she wished to escape notice.'

'My lady?'

'I could dress as a man.'

Elise's eyes went round with shock. '*No!* Oh, my lady, Count Lucien would take that very ill, you cannot go abroad dressed as a man. If you *must* go, I shall be pleased to accompany you. I hope you understand that I would have felt I was failing in my duties, if I had not made my objections known.'

'I understand,' Isobel spoke soothingly. 'Likely I would say the same in your shoes. You have to protect yourself.' If Elise had a humble background, it made sense for her to speak out in this way. She had no noble family to stand by her, and if she angered Count Lucien, she would need support. 'If anyone discovers we went to the Field of the Birds, I shall make it plain that I insisted that you came with me.'

'Thank you, my lady.' Elise gave her a soft smile, but her eyes remained troubled.

On the afternoon of Winter's Eve, the Bishop of Troyes officiated at the marriage of Lucien Vernon, Comte d'Aveyron, and Lady Isobel of Turenne. Isobel had not seen Lucien since the day he had brought her to the palace. A week had passed since then.

Their wedding took place in the porch of St Peter's Cathedral in the old town. As was the custom, the ceremony was simple and brief—a few words before witnesses, an exchange of vows, and a blessing.

The Count of Aveyron and his bride had been given use of the Great Hall in Count Henry's palace for their wedding feast. Thus, soon after their marriage had been blessed, Isobel found herself processing on Lucien's arm to her seat at the high table on the dais. To honour their alliance, Isobel was wearing a blue gown that matched Lucien's colours. Her veil was white silk, her circlet silver.

The Great Hall shimmered with light. Candles clustered on trestles and wall sconces. More light radiated out from the fire and from hanging lamps. The banners of the lords of Champagne swayed up in the rafters, metallic threads twinkling like stars.

At the far end, Isobel missed a step. A board bearing the familiar gold and red of the Viscounts of Turenne was nailed to the end wall as a backdrop. Her father's colours were framed by blue banners, emblazoned with Lucien's great black raven.

Her eyes misted. She shouldn't be startled to see her father's colours displayed so prominently; her marriage was political. She could never forget the contract had been forged between Lucien's father and hers. None the less, it warmed her to see the colours of Turenne linked so closely with the colours of Aveyron. She glanced shyly at her new husband, found observant blue eyes looking down at her, and smiled through the mist. Lucien produced one of his rare smiles and her heart swelled. Finally, the day she had waited for had arrived—they were married! She was determined not to dwell on her problems, not today.

At the table, Isobel shared a trencher with her husband. Their host, Count Henry, sat on her other side. The Count of Champagne was middle-aged and portly, and he sat like a king at his board. His wife, Countess Marie, was some years younger. A slight thickening about her waist suggested that she was with child.

She gave Isobel a refined smile. 'I wish you well in your marriage, Countess Isobel.'

'Thank you, my lady.'

'We shall have singing shortly,' the Countess told her. 'I have engaged one of my troubadours to perform for you.'

'That is most kind,' Isobel said. Countess Marie was the daughter of King Louis of France and his first wife, Eleanor of Aquitaine. Clearly, she shared her interest in music with her mother.

From the head of the table, Isobel looked out over candle after candle, over trencher after trencher, at what looked like half the nobility of Christendom. It was no surprise to see the aristocracy of Champagne sitting around the board, but lords and ladies from the Duchies of Aquitaine and Normandy were here too. Others had come from as far afield as Brittany. There were knights and lords from the Counties of Auvergne, Toulouse, Flanders...

Flames leaped in the huge fireplace, bathing faces with flickering light. The air held the tang of wood-smoke and the smell of roasted meats. The noise—chattering, laughter—was deafening and, as the festivities progressed, the clamour increased. A couple of jugglers began to perform in the space at the side of the table, and soon brightly coloured balls were criss-crossing overhead.

'They are too hasty, they will make a slip,' Lucien observed. 'I wouldn't mind betting a ball lands in someone's wine.'

Isobel had never seen him so relaxed. The stern lines of his face had eased—he looked years younger. And impossibly handsome. When his blue eyes crinkled up in amusement, he was devastatingly attractive. She smiled experimentally at him and when he immediately smiled back, her stomach knotted with an emotion she was startled to recognise as yearning.

'It seems very likely,' she said. 'I don't think I shall wager against you.'

After the quiet of a convent, her wedding feast was somewhat overwhelming. Lucien's presence at her side was a blessing. Until she had seen him waiting for her in the cathedral porch, Isobel had not realised how much she wanted this marriage. The emotions that had run through her had been telling. Uppermost had been undisguised pleasure at seeing Lucien again. He had not changed his mind and found reason for further delay. Naturally, she had wondered about the course their lives together would take, and about how soon she might persuade him to rid himself of his mistress. And last, but by no means least, there had been that disturbing thrill that had shot through her as he had taken her hand and raised it to his lips.

And here they were at their wedding feast. *We are married. After all the waiting, Lucien and I are man and wife.*

Lucien's friend, Sir Raoul de Courtney, waved for wine and servants rushed to serve him. The wine had been flowing for hours, the wine barrels in Count Henry's cellars must be fathoms deep. Waiting women scurried this way and that with as much energy as they had done hours ago; wine slopped from great clay jugs as they tripped over dogs lying in the rushes.

Count Henry was doing them much honour. The oval serving platters were so large it took two serving men to carry them. A boar's head and several haunches of venison filled the hall with the mouth-watering scents of roasted meats. There were dishes of roast duck braised in wine, and stuffed goose. There were apple dumplings, and sweetmeats that had come from the east...

'What are these?' Isobel asked, helping herself to a dried fruit and nibbling it warily.

'Those? They are dates,' Lucien said. 'Be careful, they have stones.'

'I like them.' Choosing another date, Isobel sighed, she was longing for a quiet moment to herself. This feast was too...too much.

'Tired?' Lucien's hand covered hers. His eyes glittered and he lowered his voice. 'We could retire.'

Blushing, Isobel gestured hastily towards the fire. 'I am fine, thank you, it is just that it is a little stuffy in here.' She was not as anxious about her wedding night as she had been—Elise had taken her to the apothecary's as she had promised. A small sack of herbs was hidden at the bottom of her jewel box. Isobel had begun taking them at once, and she prayed daily that they would be enough to prevent her getting with child. But recalling her friend Anna, she remained apprehensive. *How much will it hurt? What if I am a disappointment to him? I must make no mention of mistresses. I must not anger him, not tonight.*

She leaned close and her shoulder touched his arm. 'It is too soon to leave, my lord. Countess Marie mentioned a troubadour.'

He rolled his eyes. 'Lord save us, not Bernez?'

'The Countess didn't mention a name.'

'I hope it's not Bernez, the man drones on for hours.'

Isobel sipped at the wine, and passed the goblet to him. Whatever happened in the bedchamber, she wouldn't feel truly married until they were on Lucien's land. She was the Comtesse d'Aveyron. 'Will we be leaving for Ravenshold soon, my lord?'

Lucien's smile faded. 'Count Henry has said the apartment here—' he indicated the door leading to the spiral staircase '—is available for as long as we require it.'

Heart sinking, Isobel kept her eyes on his face and waited, alert for his slightest change of expression. 'We are to remain in Troyes? For how long?'

Was this his tactful way of telling her that although they were married, he would continue to see his mistress? She forced herself to keep smiling. Her face felt stiff. *I am not going to tolerate a mistress.* However, she was determined not to argue with him tonight. Not when tomorrow morning she intended following him to the All Hallows Tourney…

Down the board, a young knight was offering a sweetmeat to a blushing lady. The young man was quite the gallant; he was entirely focused on his lady. *That knight would deny his lady nothing.* She glanced surreptitiously at Lucien, and wondered if he would ever play the gallant for her.

'We must live in Count Henry's palace for a while, my lady,' Lucien was saying. 'I have neglected Ravenshold in past years.'

Noticing that 'we', Isobel felt hope bloom anew. 'In the past there have been too many tournaments, I suppose. Too many prizes to win.'

Thinking about the prizes that Lucien had won reminded her why they had married. *My value to Lucien lies in my dowry. It is a blessing that there is some liking between us, but I cannot allow the physical attraction that I feel for him to obscure the fact that for him my value lies in what I bring to him. The lands of Turenne. To Lucien, I am but another prize. Which reminds me…*

'My lord, about my dowry…'

'Mmm?'

'In his letter, did Father mention I was bringing a chest of silver with me?'

'He said something of the sort.' He looked thoughtfully at her. 'I don't recall it coming with us from the Abbey. Where is it?'

'The Abbess took it into safekeeping. It is locked in the Abbey crypt.'

'I am glad you mentioned it. Viscount Gautier won't want your silver to stay in the clutches of the church. I'll send for it first thing in the morning.'

Isobel found herself smiling at Lucien's careless irreverence. It was a smile that hid a painful burst of longing. *I want Lucien to want me for myself, not because I bring him a chest of silver and, on my father's death, the lands and revenues of Turenne.*

He took her hand, rubbing his thumb across her palm, making it tingle. 'There is something I wish you to know.'

'Oh?'

'I deeply regret that Viscount Gautier could not be here to witness our wedding, I know it must grieve you.'

'It does, but I have grown used to the thought. When I left the south it was clear that Father was too ill to travel. My lord, my father and I are not close—I can count the hours we have spent together on the fingers of one hand.'

'I am sure you exaggerate.'

'Only a little.' Isobel focused her gaze on a candle halfway down the board. 'Father wanted a son—he would have preferred me to be a boy.' The words had barely left her lips when she wished them unsaid. They were too revealing, too much pain lay behind them. On account of her sex, her father's love had been withheld from her. She could feel Lucien's gaze on her, and when she turned to him and saw understanding in his eyes, she felt as though the ground beneath her had shifted. For it was not pity she could see in those blue eyes, but sympathy— sympathy such as her father had never given her. Her chest ached.

'You do him proud, Isobel,' he murmured, giving her thigh a comforting squeeze. 'I am sure Viscount Gautier appreciates you.'

Lucien's perceptiveness unnerved her. Blinking rapidly, she prayed he had not seen her momentary weakness. Despite everything, she would have liked her father to have witnessed her wedding, just as she would have liked her mother to witness it. There were times when she felt the need of an ally. It was not like her to mourn for what she could not have, but she would have liked a sister or brother to support her today. Her escort was billeted in the nearby garrison, and though Elise had been on hand to help her, she had not known Elise for long. Poor Girande, the maid who had been her companion for years, was still languishing in the Abbey infirmary...

Lucien's hand remained on her thigh, warm and firm. His touch gave her the illusion that she was no longer alone. She was a married woman.

Ours is a political marriage. Lucien is marrying me for my dowry.

Lucien stroked her thigh, turned to Sir Raoul, and embarked on a discussion about erosion in the ramparts at Ravenshold.

Bless him. Her husband might not be the most gallant of men, but he had seen her distress and was giving her time to compose herself.

After a few moments, he turned back to her. 'Raoul can confirm that Ravenshold is in an appalling state. Raoul?'

Sir Raoul grunted agreement. 'Luc's not lying, Countess.'

'It is not fit for a lady, parts of it are practically in ruin,' Lucien added. 'I would prefer you to see it *after* I have put it to rights. That is why we will remain here at the palace.'

'My lord, I do not care about the state of Ravenshold.' Feeling more herself, Isobel touched his hand. 'It is your home in Champagne and I would far rather be there than lodged as a guest in Count Henry's palace.'

'You would?'

'Of course.'

Lucien looked at the hand she had placed on his, his expression a mix of puzzlement and surprise. When he interlaced his fingers with hers, a *frisson* of sensation shot through her. 'I shall think about it. My servants are in disarray thanks to an influx of knights who have arrived for the tournament tomorrow. Conditions there are very…spartan.'

'My lord…Lucien, have you any idea what life is like in a convent?'

A dark brow shot upwards. 'My lady?'

'Convents are spartan too, my lord. They are nothing like this palace. Some convents allocate cells to their guests—they are as stark as the nuns' cells. Others put visitors in lodges. Either way, the accommodation is cold and cheerless. Particularly when the vow of silence is imposed at night.'

'The sisters tried to make *you* keep the vow of silence?' His lips twitched. 'I can see that might tax you. Did they succeed?'

She gave him a quelling look, which turned his smile into an outright grin. 'Lucien, you have a wife now. It is my duty to share the burden at all your holdings, and that includes Ravenshold.'

'You would help me set Ravenshold to rights?'

'Yes.' Intercepting the look of alarm he shot at Raoul, she added hastily, 'Of course, I would not dream of interfering in military matters, but I am looking forward to taking charge of the household.'

For a moment, Isobel could swear Lucien's expression was one of pure bemusement. It was as though she had been speaking to him in a foreign tongue and he needed an interpreter.

'You wish to set Ravenshold to rights?'

'I am your wife, Lucien, your countess. I have been trained to manage your household, why is this so surprising?'

'It is your duty.' His voice was soft.

'Lucien, it is more than that. I *want* to help.'

There were undercurrents here that Isobel could not fathom. She lightened her tone. 'There is not enough to occupy me at the palace. Countess Marie has a battalion of servants running to satisfy her every whim. I only get in the way. I need to be *doing*, and I would far rather be doing for you, my husband.'

If Lucien had looked bemused a moment ago, he now looked definitely baffled. He exchanged glances with Sir Raoul.

'Told you,' Sir Raoul muttered, accompanying his words with the oddest of smiles.

Isobel stiffened. 'Sir Raoul told you what?'

'He mentioned he met you in Conques last year.' Lucien shrugged. 'He warned me you were a mouthy wench.'

Sir Raoul spluttered into laughter. 'Luc, you devil...my lady, I swear I never said anything of the sort, I—'

Lucien cut his friend short with a look as a cheer went up. Countess Marie's troubadour was up in the gallery.

Count Henry leaned forwards to claim Isobel's attention. 'Our trouvère will sing for you, Countess,' he said.

'Thank you, I am honoured,' Isobel murmured, politely lifting her eyes to the gallery.

Lucien gave a smothered groan. 'God save us, it is Bernez.'

Beneath the tablecloth, strong fingers tightened on hers. He moved their joined hands up and down her thigh, in long, languorous strokes that were more sensual than comforting. As the troubadour loosed several chords on his lute, Isobel thought she caught the words 'mouthy wench' again. Then the entire hall, including her husband, fell silent.

Chapter Eight

Lucien studied Isobel's profile as Bernez launched into song.

She wants to help me. Lord. Morwenna had never made such a suggestion, not even in the early days when she had been worming her way into his heart. Morwenna had only shown interest in her brews and concoctions. Lucien had long thought his choice of Morwenna as his bride had been down to ill luck as much as ill judgement. Another possibility now occurred to him. *Did Morwenna choose me because I was able to give her the space she needed in which to conduct her experiments?*

He glanced up at the minstrel's gallery. Bernez had a clear, sweet voice. The man played like an angel, his voice flowed out over the hall like honey, but there was no ignoring the fact that this was entertainment for women. Lucien gritted his teeth and braced himself to endure what promised to be a long and impossibly idealistic love story between a married lady and one of her husband's young knights.

Courtly love—what nonsense it was. As if a healthy man would be content for long in a chaste relationship! Such stories were popular at the Champagne Court. And from the starry expression on his wife's face, it was clear that Countess Marie was not the only one to adore them.

Like her mother, Queen Eleanor, Countess Marie actively encouraged troubadours; her corridors and halls were full of them. Countess Marie's ladies swooned over their stories, doubtless whiling away their time flirting with Count Henry's household knights, just as the ladies did in the ballads. On the surface, the flirtations appeared harmless. But how many married ladies were using the pretence of a flirtation with a young and handsome knight to shield a real affair? Countess Marie was a rare jewel—she would never stoop so low.

Would Isobel? Lucien wanted to trust her, he wanted children with her. And a man needed to know his children were…well, his. Today, the minstrel's story was about unrequited love. As Lucien listened, it was a challenge to keep the sneer from his face. *Can a man ever trust a woman?*

The old guilt filled him. Once Lucien had realised Morwenna's true nature—volatile, uncertain, a flickering candle—he had ceased to bed her. For a while, he had been chaste, holding to the sacredness of marriage, even if that marriage had been based on trickery—on lies, and greed, and lord knew what else. After a couple of years, during which time he had lived like a monk, cynicism had set in.

He had begun to take lovers. Not many. Lucien had enough self-awareness to accept that for him the marriage bond should be sacred. But there had been lovers. One had been a married woman with the sense to be discreet. There had been one or two girls on the tourney circuit. He had taken pleasure, he had given pleasure.

And every time, guilt had hung over him like a Doom.

No more, he thought, stroking Isobel's thigh, and edging closer so that he might breathe in her perfume. No more guilt.

Isobel is my wife.

His heart lifted. Lucien felt—he frowned—the feeling was unfamiliar and difficult to analyse. He felt carefree. Most unlike his usual self. He had not felt this way in years.

Not everyone was paying Bernez the lute player quite as much attention as the Countess Marie. While Lucien had been lost in thought, muted conversation had sprung up about the board. Diners at the top end of the table were discussing the fate of the Queen of England.

Relations between King and Queen had soured after Queen Eleanor had sided with her sons against her husband, going so far as to encourage her sons in revolt against their father. The Queen had been on her way to join her sons in Paris when she had vanished. No one knew her whereabouts, or even whether she was alive or dead. It was a subject that hung on many people's lips.

'Anyone had word on Queen Eleanor?' a knight seated to the left of Raoul asked.

Lucien frowned. The man was loud, and his question a trifle tactless given that their hostess, Countess Marie, was the Queen's daughter. Countess Marie had not seen her mother for years, none the less…

One of the squires leaned in. 'I heard King Harry seized her.'

A grizzled knight scowled. 'Where's your proof? King Harry is very tight-lipped.'

'Do you blame him? It won't advance his popularity in the Aquitaine if he admits to imprisoning his wife.'

Raoul's neighbour shrugged. 'Aye, but it is their son Richard, who…'

The conversation flowed this way and that, and

Lucien's new Countess turned to him, her green eyes bright with interest. Her veil fell forwards and a breath of summer came his way—honeysuckle. Honeysuckle and roses. With it came a sensual tug of attraction. It was so strong he ached. *Isobel is quite the most desirable woman in the hall.*

'My lord,' Isobel whispered, giving Countess Marie a sidelong glance. 'It can't be pleasant for the Countess not to know where her mother is.'

'Don't concern yourself. Countess Marie has not seen the Queen since she married King Harry.'

Isobel tipped her head to one side and her silver circlet caught the light. 'That does not mean she is not upset by the Queen's disappearance. Politics might have kept them apart, but they are mother and daughter. There must be a bond between them.'

'Must there?'

She frowned. 'You are too cynical, my lord. Do you know what has happened to Queen Eleanor? Can the King really have imprisoned her?'

Lucien picked his words with care. Ever since the Queen's disappearance in the spring, the world had been talking of little else. Queen Eleanor was known to be difficult; she had surrendered the reins of power in the Aquitaine with great reluctance. And then she had committed that most terrible of sins— siding with her sons in open rebellion against her husband. 'I only know what everyone else knows,' he said. 'The Queen was on her way to join the princes in Paris when she vanished.'

'King Henry must have her,' Isobel muttered. 'Who else would dare?'

Privately, Lucien agreed, no one else would dare.

Small fingers dug into his arm. 'You don't think he would kill her?'

Lucien shook his head and kept his tone confidential. 'Lord, no. As a wife, she must drive King Henry to distraction, but I doubt even he would go that far.'

'He had that churchman killed. What was his name?'

'Becket.' Lucien grimaced and glanced about him. 'Isobel, it is not wise to speak so boldly in public. King Harry has friends here. Besides, I am sure the Duchess is safe—wherever she is.'

'I doubt one could feel safe in a prison.'

Lucien felt his face go hard. 'Do you?' In effect, that was what he had done to Morwenna, imprisoned her. It had been for Morwenna's good, and he had been within his rights as a husband, but that did not alter the fact that he had imprisoned his wife. He forced a smile. 'He is punishing her. It is a husband's right to chastise his wife.'

'We are speaking of a Queen!' Indignation sparked

in Isobel's eyes. 'A woman who was the Duchess of Aquitaine in her own right!'

Lucien raised an eyebrow. 'She is particularly intractable. Many would say she deserved to be confined.'

At his side, Isobel seemed to freeze. She gave him a haughty look. 'Is that your view, my lord? Would you lock an intractable wife away?'

When Raoul's head turned sharply towards them, Lucien could have kicked him. 'You will never know the answer to that, will you, little dove?' he said. 'Because I am sure you would not be so foolish as to turn into an intractable wife.'

She sat very straight and what her reply would have been, Lucien could not say, for at that moment a serving girl approached with a tray of sweetmeats. 'More dates, Countess?'

Isobel gave the girl a distant smile. 'Thank you.'

Lucien accepted a handful of dates himself. Thankfully, the arrival of the sweetmeats seemed to have lightened the mood. When his wife's eyes turned back to his, hauteur had been replaced with thoughtfulness.

'My lord, I cannot imagine what it must be like for Queen Eleanor to be a prisoner after the privileges she has known. How can she tolerate it? And how can he—her husband—behave in such a way?'

'Rebellion is no light matter. One might just as easily ask how could she—his wife—have behaved in such a way? At the least, she needed reining in.'

'Reining in?' Isobel's voice was sharp. 'We are talking about a woman here, not a horse.'

Conscious of the Countess of Champagne sitting feet from him, Lucien kept his voice low. 'At what point does rebellion become treason?'

Isobel's pretty cherry-coloured mouth thinned. Lucien was on the point of saying something along the lines that if Eleanor had respected her husband's judgement, imprisonment would not have been necessary when he had second thoughts. Isobel was reacting most vehemently on behalf of a woman she had never met. Why? *I will not find that answer tonight, not while sitting at our wedding feast.* Yes, it was his wedding night, and the loveliest woman in Champagne was his.

Tonight of all nights, he would be a fool to insist that imprisonment was actually a light punishment for a queen who might be accused of treason.

Tonight I will bed my wife, and there will be no guilt. There will be no anger. There will only be pleasure.

Lucien had planned their retreat from the Great Hall. He had no wish to fall victim to the traditional bedding ceremony, and had arranged that Sir Raoul, his steward Sir Gawain, and Joris should position themselves at the bottom of the stairwell. Their orders were simple. They must hold back any revellers who thought to continue the evening's entertainment by plaguing him and Isobel on their wedding night.

After the last notes of the interminable ballad died away, Lucien nodded at Raoul and thanks to his offices he was able to lead Isobel from the dais without molestation. The door at the bottom of the stairwell slammed behind them, cutting off noise from the hall. Candles shivered in wall sconces. As Lucien ushered Isobel up the curling stairs, the shadows wavered and jumped.

At the top he held the door open for her. '*Mon Dieu*, I thought that man would yowl all night.'

'Yowl, my lord? I enjoyed it.'

Lucien bit back a reply he knew she would find cynical, and led her into the solar. 'It was pretty enough,' he conceded. 'All very poetic. But it's not real.'

'What do you mean?'

'The feelings the lute player was singing about are transitory. They don't last. You can't build empires on passing feelings.'

'You don't believe in love?'

'If love exists, it is not a feeling. It is a decision.'

'Like an arranged marriage?'

'Just so.'

'How very…practical you are, Lucien.'

Long blue skirts trailed across the boards as she approached the glowing warmth of the fire. Lucien was left with the distinct and uncomfortable feeling that he had disappointed her.

After the fluster and chaos of the Great Hall, the quiet in the solar seemed unnatural. Small sounds were loud. The swish of Isobel's skirts. The crackle and spit of the fire. A jug of wine and two goblets sat waiting on a side-table. Glass lamps glowed in the corners. There was a slight gleam on the polished boards by the curtained doorway—candles had been lit for them in the bedchamber.

'Where's your maid?'

Elise stepped out from behind the screen and came to stand in the shadows. Head low, she curtsied. 'Here, *mon seigneur.*'

Lucien frowned—he was beginning to find the girl's self-effacing diffidence irritating. 'You can look at me, I won't bite.'

Elise's eyes widened and she gave him the briefest, most reluctant of glances. 'Yes, my lord. Is…is there anything you need?'

'No, thank you, you may leave us.'

Dropping another hasty curtsy, Elise fled.

'What's the matter with that girl? She's yet to look me square in the eye.'

'She's shy. She's not used to being in the company of a great lord like yourself.'

Lucien grunted and pushed the maid from his mind. He was feeling uncharacteristically uncertain of his ground. He wanted Isobel—what red-blooded man would not?—and at last they were alone. Oddly, he felt absurdly uneasy and he could not think why. Except...

It flashed in on him that his previous wedding night had been less than happy. In truth, it had been a disaster. Lucien had been young, green, and utterly in love. He had been stunned when Morwenna had revealed her true colours. Morwenna had begun by telling him that she was not pregnant after all, that he had married her for nothing, and that his wits must have been touched for him to have believed her. And when the boy that he had been had protested that he did not care, that he loved her anyway, Morwenna had laughed in his face and—

'Lucien?'

With Morwenna's mockery ringing in his ears, Lucien found himself back in the present. His first wedding night had been the precursor of years of unhappiness. However, it was not Morwenna who was standing before him, gently touching his hand.

'Please pour yourself some wine,' Isobel murmured, her hair brightened by fire glow. 'I shall retire. I do not need long.'

I do not need long. Sensible, forthright Isobel. Desirable Isobel.

No guilt. There will be no guilt.

She gave him a gentle smile and turned to the screen. Her silk veil trembled as it flowed out around her.

Her veil is trembling? His heart turned to lead. *She fears me?*

With a concerned frown, Lucien took a deep breath and went to find out.

Isobel had pulled off her silver circlet and set it on a coffer when Lucien's shadow fell over her. Catching her hand, he raised it to his lips.

'Since I dismissed your maid, I should offer you my services.'

'Thank you.' Isobel's heart was racing. She was certain he must feel how she was shaking. 'I don't think there's any point in my denying this—I am nervous, my lord.'

'Lucien,' he reminded her. 'And there's no need for nerves.' With a smile, he reached for the pins and ties on her veil. 'You can be at ease.'

He draped her veil over the coffer. Cupping her cheek, he drew her close and kissed her. 'You see?

We have done this before,' he muttered, voice deepening.

With a shy laugh, Isobel took his shoulders, angling her mouth to give him better access. 'And this,' she said, speaking into his mouth, 'we have also done this.' She could taste spiced wine on his tongue—cinnamon, honey...

Thank goodness I have taken those herbs...

'But I have not done this in your company,' Lucien said. Slowly, he reached for her girdle and unfastened it. Her girdle slid to the floor.

Isobel's breath caught. A large hand enclosed her breast, stroking gently through the fabric of her gown.

'Nor have I done this, although I have longed to.'

'You have?' Isobel pulled back and looked deep into his eyes. Lucien's pupils had dilated, and his smile was as warm—as *gentle*—as a new bride could wish.

Gentle? She curled her fingers into his tunic as she remembered the day Anna had come running back to St Foye's Convent after her wedding. She could not forget Anna's tears as she had spoken about what happened between a man and his wife in the marriage bed. 'There is much we have not done...'

His lips twitched. 'True.'

'Come on then...' Taking him by the hand, she

pulled him to the bed. 'Best get on with it. Quickly, Lucien.'

His eyes were startled. 'I thought to take it slowly, so as not to alarm you.'

'You are my husband. Do it quickly, do everything quickly.'

'Isobel, there may be pain—'

'So I have been told. All the more reason for you to get it over with swiftly. I will be happier when I know how bad it's going to be. Doing new things makes me nervous. Especially this. Quickly, Lucien.'

'You assume it's going to be bad.' He shoved his hand through his hair. 'Isobel, you unman me.'

Pushing bedcovers aside, Isobel lay back against the pillows and held out her hand. 'I am sorry, Lucien, I have much to learn. I thought you would be pleased to do it quickly. It is just that I am...' she bit her lip '...*very* nervous.'

Lucien braced his arms on either side of her head, and looked down at her. His eyes were soft as a summer sky. 'My Countess,' he murmured. 'My sweet and innocent Countess. Perhaps you will feel better if I enlighten you. Women can enjoy the act of love.'

Isobel looked at him in disbelief. She enjoyed his kisses, but the full act of love? No. Such a possibility had never occurred to her. No one had mentioned enjoyment—not the nuns at Conques, nor her mother, nor Anna. Further, her mother had died in childbirth, which only went to prove that not only was the act of love in itself to be feared, but also the consequences...

Shaking her head, she pushed all thoughts of the sachet of herbs lying in her jewel box to the back of her mind. 'Men enjoy it, women merely submit.'

The mattress rustled as he took his place beside her. 'I am telling you the truth, Isobel. Women can enjoy it. You enjoy our kisses, do you not?'

'Ye-es.'

Doubt was written all over Isobel's face. Lucien could see she wanted to believe him; he could see her struggling with whatever nonsense the nuns had stuffed into her head. 'Some women love it,' he added.

'What women? You mean fallen women? Does your mistress love it?'

He sighed, lifted one of her hands and held it in front of her, so she could watch as their fingers interlaced. 'I have no mistress.'

Her brows snapped together. 'No?'

'Isobel, in the past I have been more sinner than saint. I have had lovers. No longer.'

Her frown deepened, and he had the distinct sense that she did not believe him. 'Did they enjoy it?'

'So they said.'

Her mouth turned down. 'Fallen women. Ladies are expected to submit.'

'That's the nun in you speaking, it's not the real you. Isobel, I have to tell you that enjoyment is not confined to fallen women. Women from all walks of life are capable of enjoyment.'

'But, Lucien, the nuns said—'

'Were the nuns speaking from experience?'

'I...no. No, I don't suppose they were. My friend Anna though... Anna married recently and she told me...' She hesitated, shaking her head. 'It sounded dreadful.'

'Her husband hurt her?'

'Very much. She hated it, and—'

'How well did Anna know her husband before they bedded?'

'Not well. They had a brief betrothal. I doubt she saw him more than I have seen you—' She broke off, flushing.

'You must not fear me. I shall be at your command and shall stop the moment you give the word.'

'On your honour?'

He smiled. 'On my honour.' Releasing her hand, he teased out a strand of blonde hair, and drew it across her breast. With the tip of his forefinger, he started at her crown and followed the strand down its length, travelling down the side of her head and neck, over her collarbone and across her breast…

His kept his touch light. Beneath it, her breast tightened. She was understandably nervous. A virgin. But—Lucien did not think he was deluding himself—his new wife desired him. Blood quickening, sensing that she was relaxing, he gradually increased the pressure, closing his hand on her. 'You like this?'

'Mmm.' She tugged at his tunic, pulling at him until he lay half over her.

Given her fears, Isobel could not desire Lucien as much as he desired her. He ached with want. Even more so when she gave a faint moan and her eyes flickered to his mouth.

He cleared his throat. 'Isobel, I would have you confess it—you are not frightened of me.'

'I am not afraid of you, Lucien. Only the act. And…'

'And?'

'The consequences.'

'We shall take it one step at a time. Trust me.'

Her hair flashed gold in the candlelight as she nodded. 'I will. When you have done it, then I will know. Quickly, Lucien. Do it quickly.'

Small hands worked at his belt and threw it aside. They dipped beneath his tunic and undershirt. When they found his skin, Lucien almost lost control. He had not lied to her, in the years since he had married Morwenna he had had lovers. But he had desired none as much as he desired Isobel.

'My golden girl,' he murmured.

Then his golden girl did something she had not done before—she shifted and pulled her skirts up over her hips. Lucien's mouth went dry. She was slim and white, and that smooth, summer-scented flesh inflamed him. Intriguing shadows seemed to promise endless delight. Shared delight. Impatient as she, hard as stone, he fumbled blindly at her skirts, thinking to draw her gown over her head.

'No time,' she muttered, arching up to join her mouth with his. 'Quickly, Lucien, quickly.'

Desire was a dark fire in his veins. Lucien was beyond arguing. He was beyond taking care, beyond anything except the driving need to have her. She wanted him quickly, she could have him. Busy hands were at the ties of his chausses, stoking the fire. Tugging, pulling—pushing aside his chausses and braies. Slender fingers closed over him and he jerked at her touch. She was eager, was his golden girl.

When he returned the compliment, touching her in that intriguing shadowy place, testing, teasing, she whimpered and writhed. After a few strokes, he let out a sigh. Without question, she wanted him.

With a groan of relief, Lucien positioned himself and gave a quick, hard thrust. Her skirts were bunched about her waist, and her eyes were intent on his. A line formed between her eyebrows. He controlled the urge to move and cleared his throat. 'It hurts?'

She shook her head, and waves of golden hair rippled out over the pillow. 'It feels rather…strange.'

Carefully, he found a rhythm.

Her eyes closed. 'Oh, that's…' her husky laugh surprised him '…different.'

'Mmm.'

Small fingers dug into his shoulders. She turned her head and pressed a kiss to his forearm, a tiny, almost insignificant gesture. It was too small a gesture, surely, to have something shift so powerfully in his chest?

He swallowed. 'Isobel.'

She looked beautiful beneath him in their marriage bed. Her cheeks were flushed and her green eyes never left him. Her golden hair lit up the bedchamber. *She* lit up the bedchamber.

'Lucien,' she muttered.

Already she was matching his rhythm. It felt so

good that at this rate she would soon have her wish—
he would not last long. He reached between them.

'*Oh!*' Her shocked, shy moan had the tension
winding tighter. 'That's...'

'Different?'

'Mmm.' She gave his arm a gentle bite and drew
her head back. 'You can...' she was panting as much
as he '...take it more slowly, if you like.'

He did not think he could. Not with her breath
coming faster at his every touch. Not with her mouth
dotting his arm with kisses.

Suddenly it was over. She tightened around him
and her eyes went wide. She gave a fluttering sigh.
Capturing her mouth with his own, Lucien's world
convulsed into delight. *Different indeed.*

Their breath steadied. A brief silence fell. Isobel
slid her fingers into his hair and let out a slow sigh.
'That was...'

'Better than expected?'

A light laugh sent something that felt like joy
flooding through him. Joy. Who would have thought
it?

'Very much so.' She was playing with his hair and
his scalp warmed at her touch. 'Next time you are
interested in trying that, Lucien, I think we should
take it more slowly.'

'You do, do you?' Joy. It was a strong feeling.

Unsettling in its unfamiliarity. Confusing. Lucien reminded himself it could have nothing to do with Isobel personally, not when they had yet to become familiar with each other. It was far too soon for him to feel affection for her. He felt this way tonight be-cause…because…this was the first time he had lain with a woman since Morwenna's death. It was also the first time since his marriage to Morwenna that he had been able to enjoy a woman without the ac-companying burden of guilt.

'Mmm.'

With a grin, Lucien tightened his hold on his wife's warm, lissom body. Freedom from guilt was as strong as any love potion; he was coming back to life already. He should not be. He ought to con-trol himself. It was the tournament tomorrow and he had undertaken to officiate. He needed rest.

Hell burn it, this was his wedding night…

'Isobel?' He kissed her neck, inhaling deeply. *Iso-bel.*

'Mmm?'

'If you wish, we could try it more slowly.'

'Now?'

'Now.'

Chapter Nine

Darkness. Isobel woke slowly. The candles had blown out, and there was movement on the other side of the wooden screen.

'Lucien?' she called, stretching languorously.

With a rattle of curtain rings, Elise appeared, rushlight in hand. 'It's me, my lady. You asked me to wake you early because of the tournament. Count Lucien has already left.'

The All Hallows Tourney! Isobel bolted upright. How could she have forgotten?

Elise lit the candles, ducked through the curtain, and returned with a wash-bowl and ewer. She put them on a coffer. 'You still intend to go, my lady?'

Isobel felt a pang of guilt. 'Yes.' She should feel happy. Happy and relieved. Lucien had told her that women could take pleasure in the act of love, and he had proved the truth of his words last night. She had taken pleasure. More than she had dreamed possible. Why had no one thought to tell her that losing one's virginity need not be all pain? Why had no one mentioned that joining with a man might startle her with its beauty?

She grimaced. All of which made it doubly hard to go against Lucien's wishes. She couldn't forget that the man who had given her pleasure last night was the same man who had left her languishing in a convent for nine years. One night of bliss couldn't put that right. And yet…

I don't want us to be for ever fighting. She sighed. Nor did she want a husband who was going to ride roughshod over her wishes. *Would it have killed him to let me attend the tourney today?*

'Are you all right, my lady? Do you need assistance?'

'Assistance?'

'Did the Count hurt you?'

Isobel drew her head back. Elise's question verged on presumptuous, given she was not a trusted family retainer. She reached for her shawl. 'My lord did not hurt me in the least.'

'Not at all?' Elise's voice was harsh. 'You are quite well, my lady?'

What was wrong with Elise? She looked most put out, as though Isobel's reply had disappointed her in some way. 'Yes, thank you.'

Elise muttered under her breath.

'Elise, whatever is the matter?'

'You bedded him,' Elise said, in a flat voice.

Isobel stiffened. 'Elise, you are impertinent. Lucien is my husband.'

Elise did not seem to have heard her. 'I hoped you might refuse him. I thought you were angry at the wasted years, and the fear of pregnancy. I thought the dangers of childbirth weighed heavily on your mind. Have your fears gone?'

Isobel drew her shawl tightly about her shoulders, attention arrested by that hard edge in Elise's voice. Where was the timid girl Isobel had been so relieved to meet in the Abbey? 'Elise, whatever's the matter? You know I am Lucien's wife. You know that a wife cannot deny her husband. That's why we visited the apothecary.'

Elise stepped right up to the bed. 'Did he force you?'

'Force me? Heavens, no,' Isobel answered, blushing.

Elise stared at her. 'My lady, you will have to take the herbs every day.'

'I know.' Pushing back the covers, Isobel got out of bed. Regret swept through her. How could she forget that? She was deliberately thwarting Lucien, who she knew wanted heirs. But Lucien was not the one who had to give birth. He might not be so keen on getting heirs if he had attended a woman's lying-in. He might not be so keen if he had seen her mother die.

Lucien had relieved her mind on one aspect of marriage, but she doubted he would ever rid her of her fear of childbirth.

Shortly after dawn, when the mists were rising from the surrounding vineyards, Lucien Vernon, Comte d'Aveyron, rode on to the Field of the Birds. He was fully armed. Chainmail weighed heavy beneath his blue tunic and cloak, and his black stallion was tricked out in a blue silk caparison that swirled with every step. Lucien guided him into position near a cluster of pavilions at the end of the lists. The pavilions were his and to mark this they, like Lucien's tunic and Demon's caparison, were blue.

Lucien was not taking to the field until later, but already excitement was coursing through his veins. This time the usual anticipation he felt at the beginning of every tourney was mingled with not a little astonishment.

Thoughts of Isobel were hard to chase away, and they were somewhat distracting. His new wife. His new and very desirable wife. He could see her in his mind's eye—she would still be lying in bed at the palace. Her cheeks would be flushed with sleep, and her hair would be fanning across the pillows like gold silk…

With an impatient sound, he thrust the image to the back of his mind. *Focus, Luc, focus.* This was neither the time nor the place for distraction. Lucien had expended much energy on mastering the skills necessary to become a successful knight, and much time acquiring the experience to become a champion. He would not lose focus.

The whole of Champagne was apparently fascinated by his return to Ravenshold and his marriage to Isobel. Even though Lucien was not the official patron of this tournament—Lord Glanville now held that privilege—in the past few days over a dozen knights had ridden up to the Ravenshold gatehouse. They had begged to join his team—the Blues. They had assumed that Lucien's return and his marriage meant that he would be taking up his father's mantle and that tournaments held at the Field of the Birds would once again be patronised by the Count d'Aveyron. After his disastrous first marriage, Lucien had been happy for Lord Glanville to take over responsibilities as patron. Lucien himself had visited Ravenshold too rarely to be relied upon. Which was why, until today, he had never led a team on to the Field of the Birds.

This morning, however, it felt as though the old times had returned. Hosting the knights at Ravenshold as his father had done. Feeding them, watering them. After so long fighting on his own account, Lucien had been startled—and touched—by the support he had received. Perhaps, next year, he might play the patron in earnest.

He would have a word with Count Henry and see if they might reach an agreement. It made sense that Count Henry should hold lighter tournaments in Troyes, whilst Lucien hosted the more testing events at Ravenshold. As far as most knights were concerned, the more gruelling the tournament, the better. This wasn't simply because fighting in the fiercest tournaments offered more in the way of practice. As he himself knew, for the seasoned and successful warrior, there were fortunes to be won. Vanquished knights paid ransoms to their captors.

Not that Lucien fought for the prize money—he had never needed to. He had fought to forget about Morwenna. He had fought to forget about the wedge his first marriage had driven between him and his father. It hadn't worked. However many honours came his way, however many prizes he won, he had never been able to rid himself of the guilt. His marriage to Morwenna had driven his father to his grave.

Focus, Luc, focus.

Lucien didn't want deaths today, no one did. This was a military exercise, not a slaughter. Which was why he had clapped his helmet on and mounted up even before his blue standard had been hoisted over his pavilion. He might not be the official patron of this particular tournament, but he would do his utmost to ensure that lives were not lost.

'The ground is soft,' he said, grimacing at Raoul de Courtney. In light of the sudden forming of the Blues, Sir Raoul was acting as his second-in-command. Like Lucien, Raoul was up and mounted. His helmet rested on his pommel. Raoul and Lucien would remain at hand in case tempers flared during the vespers.

Beneath him, Lucien's stallion stirred and shook his great head. Lucien leaned forwards to pat his neck. 'Steady, boy.' Demon champed on his bit, his breath puffing out like dragon smoke in the cool morning air. Demon relished a tournament as much as Lucien, and he was picking up on the nerves of the younger knights and squires who were bawling to each other as they ran hither and yon. Last-minute repairs were being made to harness; spare helms and mail coats were being unearthed; there was much jostling about the whetstone. Across the lists, their opponents, the Reds, were making similar preparations.

Raoul frowned at the field. 'Too soft?'

'It's hardly surprising, given the season. Likely it will pass muster. Untried knights must be warned to take care. I'm going to make a trial pass to judge for myself.' Lucien glanced at the marshal, waiting for the signal that would send him charging into the lists. 'I'm glad we're in the same company today.' He put a smile in his voice. 'Wouldn't want to unhorse you again.' Raoul drew his head back. The two were fast friends, but Lucien knew that memory of that last tournament rankled.

'*Mon Dieu*, find another song, Lucien. You didn't unhorse me, it was a faulty stirrup.'

Lucien shook his head. 'Keep saying that, my friend, and maybe in time you will come to believe it.'

The mist clung like wisps of gossamer to the dips in the land. Squires milled around the lance-stands, pale-faced and sweaty with dread. Townsfolk were streaming up the road from Troyes—the stands along the edge of the field were starting to fill. A furious hammering spoke of a battalion of carpenters making last-minute alterations to the benches at the far stand. Dogs barked. Rooks circled overhead. There was a smell of fresh bread and cooked meat. Vendors were crying their wares—pies and pastries, flasks of wine...

It couldn't be all play. How could it? Cavalry officers must try out real lances. They must take part in fights where steel was honed to a bright edge—in tournaments like this where the jousting was more than mere theatre to please the ladies. There were still rules, of course, these out-of-town tournaments followed regulations. None the less, the brutal truth was that with newly dubbed knights taking to the field, anything could happen. Tempers might fray. There would be bloodshed. There might even be a death or two.

Behind his helmet, Lucien grimaced. He wasn't the official patron today, but given his family connection to the place, he had taken it upon himself to ensure there was as little bloodshed as possible. Given that he had declined to take part in proceedings here since his marriage to Morwenna, he was surprised at how strongly he felt. *No one must die here today.*

Lucien hadn't wanted Isobel here because he found her distracting. Lord, the woman was distracting even when she was not present.

People were pressing against the rope barriers stretched along the lists. Merchants and villagers for the most part. A veil fluttered, a child laughed, and the crowd parted as two girls pushed their way to the front. They stood out on account of their clothes. People seemed to be deferring to them, as if they knew they were not ordinary girls. Lucien squinted through the slit in his helmet and his blood chilled.

Isobel! Elise. For a moment he was too taken aback to feel anger, though he knew that would come. *Isobel disobeyed me.* He held Demon steady, alert for his signal from the marshal. He watched his wife, anger balling into a tight fist in the pit of his stomach. *How dare she?*

Isobel and her maid stood out among the peasants and merchants. Isobel, hair barely concealed by a delicate wisp of a veil, was gut-wrenchingly beautiful. Her cloak was dark-green and lined with fur. Beneath the cloak, Lucien glimpsed a sea-green gown that clung lovingly to every curve. Her body… Lord, she should not be walking abroad in that gown. He could see why she had waited to leave the Abbey before wearing it; the fabric hugged every sinuous curve and showed off her slender waist. In that gown, his wife was, quite simply, an incitement to sin.

Isobel is my wife! Does she have no escort? Lucien couldn't tear his eyes from her. She should know better than to flaunt herself in such a way. People knew exactly who she was. They would wonder why she was not sitting on his stand. And there she stood, gazing about her with that straightforward, confident gaze he was coming to know—completely oblivious of the impression she was giving. *She looks as though she is the plaything of a prince.*

Lucien swore. Duty held him. At the other end of the lists, the marshal was speaking to a knight in the Reds, the order for him to test the ground had not been given. Anger gave way to anxiety. Isobel's gown and body might be an incitement to sin, but her face was that of an innocent. She leaned out against the rope with her usual open, honest expression, and turned to search the crowd. He shifted his head to keep her in sight through the slit in his helmet. She was looking for someone.

'That blasted relic-stealer,' he muttered. 'God, but she's stubborn.' *Stubborn. Disobedient. Beautiful. And far too vulnerable.*

'Did you say something?' Raoul said.

Lucien gestured across the lists towards Isobel. Her maid looked pale. She seemed conscious of the dangers. However, when did Elise not look nervous? 'Over there. Do you see them?'

Raoul made that choking sound that bordered on laughter. 'I didn't think Lady Isobel was planning to attend?'

Lucien grunted. The phrase *lambs to the slaugh-*

ter jumped into his head, and it would not shift. These out-of-town tournaments were not usually the province of gently bred women. *They should have brought an escort. Where are her father's men?*

More uneasy by the moment, Lucien wondered if Isobel was carrying a purse. Not that that signified; her cloak was fit for a queen—a cut-purse might attack her for the cloak alone.

And she imagined she was hunting a thief?

Elise frowned at Isobel. Across the lists, Lucien watched her lips move.

'My lady, we ought to leave,' Elise said for the tenth time.

'I can't see him, do you think he's changed his mind about coming?'

'Thieves are not known for their reliability, my lady.'

Isobel flung Elise a look of exasperation. 'The man is here, I know it; we just have to find him. I gave the potboy in the Black Boar a handful of silver and he swore the thief would be here. That boy would have betrayed his mother for less.' She huffed out a breath. 'Our luck might change if we work our way round to the other side of the lists. The thief will be desperate to get the relic off his hands, and where better to find a buyer? Half the nobility of Champagne is here. Let's look nearer the pavilions.'

Elise linked arms with her, as though to pin her in place. 'It's not safe. My lady, it's bad enough that you have flouted Count Lucien's wishes, but to be chasing after a thief—I know you have been bored and restless at the Abbey, but this—it's sheer folly!' She paused, eyes clouded with concern. 'We ought to go back to the palace. If Count Lucien sees you…'

Isobel stiffened. 'Count Lucien cannot command my every move.'

'Can he not? He might strike you—'

'Strike me?' Isobel gave Elise a startled look. 'Why on earth should you think that?'

Elise gave her an odd look. 'How much do you know about him, my lady? Count Lucien is a warrior, trained to get his way by force of arms. Now you are married, he is within his rights to punish you. Many men hit their wives.'

'This is nonsense, Elise. I am confident Count Lucien will do me no harm.'

'Are you?'

Isobel held down a flare of irritation. 'Yes, I am.' With a sigh, she caught Elise's hand and ducked back into the crowd. Too many people were blocking her view, she was determined to work her way round to the red pavilions. 'Have you seen his lordship?'

'Not yet.'

Since Lucien's device was a black raven on a blue field it followed that the blue pavilions would be his. Isobel would leave those till last. Her gaze wandered back to the knights gathered under Lucien's colours. The wind was in the wrong direction, and the raven on his standard was lost in the folds of the cloth. She couldn't see him. Ah! There he was in the middle of the field, next to Sir Raoul. She would give that area a wide berth...

She pointed. 'He's over there.'

'Look the other way, my lady! He'll see you!'

'Elise, please be calm. No one has seen us, we were only at the rope for a moment.' She lightened her tone. 'Just think how pleased the nuns will be when the relic is returned.'

'Abbess Ursula says prayer will bring it back to them.'

Isobel made an impatient noise. 'Prayer has its place, Elise, but action is needed if we are to retrieve the relic.' She smiled. 'I have spent much of my life in the company of nuns, and kind though they are, they live too much with the angels. You and I are made of more earthly stuff. We shall give it another half-hour, and if we haven't seen our man by then, I promise we shall return to the palace.'

* * *

Lucien glared through his visor. 'Isobel's trying to melt into the crowd. Blast the woman. I warned her I was too busy to attend to her today. She's shaping up to be as ungovernable as Morwenna.'

'Lovely though, don't you agree?' Raoul jammed on his helmet and fastened his chin strap, muttering something that Lucien could not catch.

Even across the field, Lucien saw the instant Isobel clutched at her maid. He followed the direction of her gaze. *Holy Virgin, she's found him!* Or rather, the thief had found her. The man must have slept in a hedgerow for the past few nights—he was unshaven, his hair hung down in greasy rat's tails, and his clothes looked as though they had been fashioned from sacking. They were filthy. He was filthy. And he'd seen Isobel.

The man's reaction removed any faint hope that he might not recognise her. He jerked his hood down and started forcing his way towards her through the crush by the rope. Lucien glimpsed a grim face and the flicker of steel. Ice shivered through him.

He knows she could convict him.

Elise screamed.

Isobel! Duty forgotten, Lucien dug his spurs into Demon. He thundered towards the rope, and the crowd scattered.

Someone cried, *'Knife! Beware!'*

Isobel and Elise were scrambling away from the thief when Isobel tripped and went down.

Elise shrieked. *'My lady!'*

Lucien's heart was in his mouth. He had five yards to go...four... Demon powered over the rope and Lucien hauled him to an earth-shaking standstill. The thief slipped like an eel into the crowd.

Isobel was sprawled in a muddy patch, her skirts a green froth about her knees. Her veil had slipped and mud from Demon's hoofs was splattered on her forehead and bodice.

Lucien whipped off his helmet. Wide green eyes stared up at him. She was white as snow.

'Lucien?'

'My lady, are you all right?' Elise said, hovering over her.

Isobel held Lucien's gaze. Her breasts were rising and falling, and hectic spots of colour burned in her cheeks.

'You are unhurt, my lady?' Lucien was on his knees at her side before he had thought. In a quiet corner of his mind, he noted with surprise that his heart was pounding as though he were in the midst of a mêlée.

'I...' She looked affronted and pushed down her skirts. 'He had a knife!'

Lucien felt his tension ease. If Isobel was well enough to be affronted, she was unharmed. He felt a powerful urge to shake her. By deliberately flouting his orders, she had put herself in harm's way. 'So I saw. My lady, if you could but have waited, I would have helped you retrieve the reliquary.'

'I had to come.' She was searching the crowd. 'I heard the thief was here, and—'

He swore under his breath. 'My lady, you placed yourself in danger. I believe I mentioned that I could not assist you today.'

'You are busy. I understand.'

Something in her tone grated, she sounded more aggrieved than seemed possible, given the relic did not belong to her. Was there more on her mind? Or was this simply the anger of a spoilt woman, upset because she had been ordered not to attend?

He gritted his teeth. If his second marriage was to succeed, Isobel would have to learn who was master. At least she was unharmed. Inside, a small voice murmured that perhaps he should have explained why he was not in a position to help her today. But Lucien had never been in the habit of explaining himself to anyone.

'My lady, thanks to your folly, I was forced to desert my post.'

Silence. Those great, green eyes simply looked at him.

'Isobel, I will help you in your quest to retrieve the reliquary, but *not today*. Today I am occupied.'

'The tournament, I understand.'

'I find myself in the position of unexpectedly fielding a team.' Leaning back on his haunches, he indicated his pavilion. 'Several knights have sought hospitality at Ravenshold in recent days.'

Nodding, she brushed mud from her gown.

'Allow me.' He reached out to brush a fleck from her cheek, wryly aware that no amount of mud spatter could obscure her beauty. His heartbeat had not yet settled, which led him to an uncomfortable realisation. He didn't want anyone to hurt a hair on her head—the thought made him distinctly queasy. 'You are certain he did not touch you?'

Giving a small headshake, she allowed him to help her to her feet and shook out her skirts. 'I thank you, my lord, I am unharmed. My lord, I should like to—'

He stopped her with a gesture. Her spirit was strong, but at this moment she resembled a rose with ruffled petals, a delicate rose. 'I only have a moment. My lady, since you are here, you will retire to my pavilion. And that is not a suggestion, it is an order.'

Her eyes flashed. 'I am not one of your soldiers.'

Lucien allowed his gaze to rest for a moment on her mud-spattered bodice. 'No, you are my wife.' He spoke softly through gritted teeth. 'You are my Countess. And as such you not only owe me your obedience, you owe some respect to your title. I should like you to behave in a suitable manner. My pavilion is the large blue one with the raven on the—'

'Lord d'Aveyron,' Isobel cut in, voice dry as dust. 'I learned your colours years ago.'

With a slight headshake, Lucien continued. 'I will send Joris to fetch you. He will find you refreshments. Stay with him until I can escort you back to the palace. Elise?'

'My lord?' Elise's voice was scarcely above a whisper.

'See my lady remains where it is safe.'

Elise bobbed him a curtsy. 'Yes, Count Lucien.'

'My lady, might I suggest that you consider wearing something less…ostentatious when you next go abroad.' Lucien touched the purse hanging at Isobel's belt. 'You might also consider wearing less plump a purse. And you must take an escort.'

'I did bring an escort!'

'Then where the devil are they?'

Her nose went up. 'Tethering the horses.'

'One of them should have remained with you, the Countess d'Aveyron should be accompanied at all times.'

Her nostrils flared, though when she replied it was mild enough. 'I thank you for your advice. My lord—'

A trumpet blast cut her off, and Lucien heard his name. The marshal was summoning him to test the ground. *Hell.* 'Wait here,' Lucien said, preparing to mount. 'Don't think about moving until Joris gets here.'

Chapter Ten

Joris escorted the Countess d'Aveyron and her maid to the entrance of the blue pavilion. The wind was playing with the Count's standard—one gust had the raven flashing into view, the next had it vanishing again.

'One moment, my lady.' Joris looked anxiously at Isobel. 'My lord said I might find you seats in the stands, provided you accept my company. There's something I must do for him first.'

'Very well, Joris.'

'You—forgive me for asking, my lady—' the boy went red '—but you will wait here?'

Isobel smiled. 'Rest assured, Joris, we shall not stir.'

Joris ducked into the pavilion. Isobel could hear talking inside—some discussion about armour…

'No, Sir Geoffrey,' Joris said. 'Your mail coat is

far too short. Count Lucien has said you may borrow his, it will protect your legs.'

A second voice, presumably Sir Geoffrey's, replied, 'My thanks, Joris, but I am wearing my own armour. The Count's is too heavy, I'm used to mine.'

'But, Sir Geoffrey...'

The good-natured wrangling continued, and Isobel took stock of the tourney field. Straw targets were lined up in the centre of the main ground; two quintains stood to the side, near one of the lance-stands. Lucien was the only knight presently on the main field—with no one blocking her line of sight, his colours were instantly recognisable. He was cantering towards a knight stationed by the marshal's box, his charger's caparison rippling like waves.

Isobel's chest ached. Her husband was the very image of a chivalrous knight. He had been so swift to ride to her rescue. She bit her lip. He had also been swift to order her about. She should not be surprised. That was what men did. But it was disappointing. *There he is, so handsome. So strong. My perfect tourney champion. And he orders me about as though I were his squire.*

Sighing, Isobel thought of the songs that had delighted her at Turenne and in the Great Hall last night—the ballads the trouvères carried from hall to hall. They were full of romance. And—she frowned across the field—they were peopled with chevaliers who treated their ladies with respect. *Lucien looks the part, but he does not have a romantic bone in his body.*

'We are fortunate with the weather, my lady,' Elise said. 'I do not think it will rain.'

Isobel glanced at the sky. The wind was slowly pushing the clouds to the west. A stand of oaks on the edge of the forest had a flock of rooks rising and falling above them—their cawing was faintly audible over the whinnying of horses and the chatter of townsfolk. There was an air of expectation, the tension was palpable.

It was then that she saw it. A blur of movement at the edge of her sight, a glimpse of brown. It was no more than that. Goose-bumps rose on the back of her arms. A hound running behind the pavilion? Or a person? A person who was hunched over, so as to make themselves small?

She nudged Elise. 'Did you see that?'

'My lady?'

The sun, wintry and pale, poked through the clouds. 'Something…someone…I am not sure. Elise, I think the thief—'

Elise gave an abrupt headshake. 'The Count all but rode him down! He'll surely stay well clear.'

'I hope so. To be safe, however, we had better join

Joris.' Gripping Elise's hand, Isobel stepped into the pavilion.

The conversation came to a halt and three startled pairs of eyes turned their way.

Joris dropped a coat of mail on to a trestle with a heavy chink. 'Is all well, my lady?'

The trestle was bowed beneath its load of arms and harness. A basket of medicaments—bandages and pots of salve—sat beneath it. *They are prepared for all eventualities*. More goose-bumps formed.

'I am not sure. I thought I saw…something. Joris, I think you should summon Count Lucien.'

'My lady.'

Joris hurried out, and the knight stepped forwards. As yet he was but lightly armed in a leather gambeson.

'Sir Geoffrey?'

Nodding, he bowed. 'You must be Lady Isobel.'

Isobel nodded. Sir Geoffrey looked impossibly young, for all that he had a breadth of shoulder and air of strength that should serve him well in the coming tournament.

'It is a pleasure to meet you, my lady. I am one of Count Lucien's household knights. You saw something that concerned you?'

'A thief.' Isobel rubbed her forehead, her head was beginning to pound. 'I think.'

'A *thief*?' Sir Geoffrey's smile faded.

'You may have heard about St Foye's relic? It was stolen from the Abbey Church.'

'The town is talking of little else.'

'Sir, someone is skulking about at the back of the pavilion. If it is the thief, and I cannot swear to it, he is not likely to be playing the Good Samaritan.'

Sir Geoffrey snatched a sword from the trestle. 'I'll take a look.' He glanced at a boy, presumably his squire. 'Harry, stay with the ladies.'

'Yes, sir.'

Sir Geoffrey's squire—a baby-faced child—stood very straight. His small hand fastened round the hilt of his dagger.

Isobel listened while Elise clung to her hand. Snarls and yelps spoke of a dogfight nearby. She heard a hoot of laughter, and the cawing of the rooks at the edge of the forest. Sir Geoffrey's progress round the pavilion was marked by the subtle chink of spurs and a faint shadow moving across the canvas. No, *two* shadows...

Isobel heard a muffled exchange, then a voice, raised in anger. *'Fool!'*

A chilling grunt was followed by a long, bubbling groan. Someone choked out a name. *'Clare!'*

Elise was crushing her fingers to the bone, but Isobel barely noticed, she was transfixed by the shadows on the pavilion wall. The blue canvas bulged as something fell against it and dark colour bled through. The colour of pain. Of death? *God, save us.*

Elise opened her mouth and screamed.

Isobel shook herself free, grabbed the basket of medicaments, and dashed outside.

Lucien drew level with his pavilion and threw himself off Demon. It was no good telling himself that a woman's scream was designed to chill the blood, that it was designed to summon help. This scream nearly stopped his heart.

Is that Isobel? Is she safe?

Almost tripping over a guy-rope in his haste to reach her, Lucien followed Joris's pointing finger and ran round the back. He took the scene in at a glance. *'Jesu!'*

It was ugly. A body lay on the grass. *Geoffrey!* Isobel was kneeling in front of him. Her head was bare—she was pressing her veil to a wound in Geoffrey's neck. Her gown was smeared with blood, as was the tip of her golden plait.

Time seemed to stop. The basket Lucien recognised from the pavilion sat untouched at Isobel's side. Her cloak was gone—no, not gone, there was a wad of green under Geoffrey's head. Out of the chaos in his mind, relief briefly took precedence. *It is not Isobel's blood, Isobel is unharmed.*

Lucien turned his attention to Geoffrey. The lad's eyes were glassy. Unfocused. *Too late. We are too late. Geoffrey has gone.* There was too much blood. A section of his pavilion looked as though it had been daubed with red paint…

It was Elise screaming. The noise was as sharp as a blade, and it was attracting an audience.

'Enough, Elise!' he snapped.

Elise stumbled off, whimpering.

'Joris?'

'My lord?'

'You and Harry…take Geoffrey into the pavilion. Get help if you need it. Isobel…' Her long eyelashes glistened with tears. Heart in his throat, guts in a tangle, for Geoffrey had been one of his most promising knights, Lucien held out his hand and softened his voice. 'We can help Geoffrey best in the privacy of the pavilion.'

She pushed to her feet, white-faced. Despite the gore on her gown and her blood-dabbled, uncovered hair, she held on to her dignity. 'Yes, my lord.'

In the pavilion, arms and harness were swept from the trestle and it became Sir Geoffrey's bier.

'He's gone,' Isobel murmured, voice dazed. 'I was too slow.'

Lucien squeezed her hand. She was in shock. Truth to tell, he was in shock, he had been fond of Geoffrey. 'It wasn't your fault. That wound—look—the knife hit an artery. Impossible to staunch—Geoffrey was lost the moment the cut was made.' Releasing Isobel, Lucien went to stand over Geoffrey. 'Geoffrey was unarmed?'

'He had his sword,' Isobel said.

'Where is it?'

'Here, my lord.' Ashen-faced, Harry handed it to him.

Lucien turned the sword over. The blade was clean. Shiny. Puzzled, he frowned. 'He didn't use it.'

'No, my lord.' Harry's voice cracked.

When Isobel went over to the boy and put her arm about him, Lucien felt a pain in his chest. She and Harry were of the same height. *Isobel has a good heart. And she held her nerve far better than that useless maid of hers.* Speaking of which...

'Where's Elise?'

'I don't know, my lord.'

'Joris, find her. Then take three men and escort my lady and the maid back to the palace.'

'Yes, my lord.'

Taking Isobel by the shoulders, Lucien looked

down at her. 'Go with Joris, I want you away from here with all speed. I will join you when I have seen to Geoffrey. Don't wait up though, if I finish late, I shall be bedding down in the barracks.'

Isobel had supper before the solar fire, half-heartedly spooning down some mutton broth Elise had brought up on a tray. When night began to steal the colours from the ladies and unicorns on the wall-hangings, she realised it was time to retire. Lucien hadn't appeared. It wasn't surprising. Dealing with the aftermath of Geoffrey's death was bound to take time.

While Elise hunted out fresh candles, Isobel went into the bedchamber and looked out the window. The glass had a grey tinge to it that seemed to suit twilight. Outside, in the more prosperous streets near the palace, the torches were lit. Yellow lights were flickering into being in windows and door-ways. Cooking fires would be banked for the night but none the less, wood-smoke hung over the town like a pall. Elsewhere, dark shadows were forming, sooty wraiths that crept along the canal and the dips between roofs.

A solitary pigeon beat its way across the darkening sky. Isobel watched the pigeon, throat tightening, and sent up a silent prayer for Sir Geoffrey. Poor boy, he had been so young. *God grant that he rest in peace.* Unhooking the silver curtain ties, Isobel closed the curtains.

A faint knocking floated over the panelled screen. By the sound of it, someone was outside the solar door at the top of the stairs. Elise, trimming the wick on a candle, met her eyes.

'See who that is, would you, Elise? If it is Count Lucien, you may admit him. If it is anyone else, please explain that I am about to retire for the night.'

'Yes, my lady.' Leaving the candle, Elise went through the curtained doorway.

Isobel found herself staring with some puzzlement at the candles. Elise had left them all behind her. The only light in the solar was fire-glow—she must have good eyes not to take a light with her. With a shrug, she sat on the edge of the bed and pulled off a shoe.

Footsteps approached. Heavy, booted footsteps. Not Elise. Dropping the shoe, Isobel came to her feet. She was facing the door as Lucien walked in.

Lucien bowed. He was wearing a black tunic, liberally embroidered with gold about the neck and cuffs. The tourney champion of earlier had been transformed into the courtier—a stern-faced courtier with an intriguing scar on his temple. He was tapping a beribboned scroll against his thigh.

'I would not have disturbed you so late, my lady, but a letter has arrived from Turenne, and I thought you would like to receive it.' Looking very formal, he held out the scroll. 'Can you read, or do you need help?'

'I can read.' Isobel took the scroll, the seal was unbroken. 'You have not opened it?'

'Since it is from your family, I thought you should be the first to look at it.'

'Thank you.' Isobel stared at him for a moment, his manner was distant, but she could not help but be warmed by his consideration. Many husbands, she knew, would think nothing of reading their wives' correspondence. She broke the seal. The letter had been written by a scribe; she glanced at the bottom to see who had sent it.

'It is from your father?'

'No, it's from my stepmother, Angelina.'

She began to read:

My dear Isobel,
I send you greetings and blessings, and pray that you are in good health. Your father has instructed me to write to you so that you may share in our great news. We are happy to tell you that I am with child.

God willing, the baby will be born in January—

Isobel found herself staring at the word January. *January.* Angelina was to have a baby in January!

These tidings were bittersweet. For as long as Isobel could remember, she had longed for more family. She had always wanted a brother or sister—partly to ease her mother's distress, and partly for herself. Her years at the convent had been marked by the making and losing of friends, as other girls first arrived at St Foye's, and then returned to the world to be married. Isobel had yearned for someone with whom she might feel a particular bond, a bond that would last.

If Angelina comes safely to term, I shall have more family!

Angelina was younger than her mother. Stronger. There was every reason to hope that she might be swiftly and safely delivered of her child. In January.

Her eyes prickled.

'Isobel?' Lucien touched her arm. 'Is it ill news? You look very pale.'

A brief, bright flash of joy ran through her. *I am to have a brother or sister!*

'Isobel?'

'One moment, my lord, I have not finished.' Quickly, she read the rest...

Isobel, you should also know that a cloud remains over Turenne on account of your father's continuing poor health. He is weak and finds breathing difficult. I have asked the villagers to pray for him, and beg that you do the same. I am holding to the hope that our good news will lift his spirits and strengthen him.

Please know that your father talks of you often. Know also that we send you and Count Lucien our good wishes for the future. May you receive all blessings...

'Well?'

Isobel skipped the closing salutations and rolled up the scroll. 'My stepmother writes to tell me that my father remains weak. She is hopeful of a recovery.'

'I am relieved there is hope.' He hesitated. 'When the letter arrived, I feared for the worst.'

It was on the tip of Isobel's tongue to explain that Angelina was with child, but even as she opened her mouth to do so, she was engulfed by a torrent of doubts.

Lucien believes he has married an heiress. If Angelina has a daughter, that will remain the case as I will be the older daughter. But if Angelina has a son, my brother will inherit. I will have brought Lucien nothing. Nothing save a chest of silver pennies.

Desolation was a sick churning in her gut. This letter from Turenne had transformed her world. If

Angelina bore a son, Isobel's value as a bride would be greatly diminished.

I don't want to tell him about the baby...

She stiffened her spine. Lucien had married her because she was an heiress. She wanted him to value her in other ways, but during her years in the convent she had come to see that as far as Lucien was concerned, her value rested solely on the lands she would bring him. Had he kept her waiting in case her mother was brought to bed of a boy, a boy who would have deprived him of the lands of Turenne? *When Mama died, and Lucien learned of Father's weak health, he must have thought my position as heiress was secure. Only then did he summon me.*

Isobel might wish otherwise, but she must fact the truth. Lucien valued her for her lands. Take away her lands and what was left? Nothing.

It was vital she learned to please him. *I must become invaluable to him in other ways. I must strengthen the bond between us.*

She would tell him about the child eventually. In the meantime, she would teach him to love her, as she was beginning to love him. *I am beginning to love him? No!* Her fingers tightened on the scroll as she looked up at him, aghast. She could hardly have shocked herself more. *I do not love him. It is affection I feel for him. Affection.*

Guilt coiled like a serpent inside her. Somehow it made it worse that she should realise she was growing fond of him at the same time she decided not to tell him about Angelina's baby. *I cannot tell him, he might seek a divorce. I must win him before he learns of the baby...*

Lucien squeezed her hand. 'Isobel, are you unwell?'

He sounded as though he were speaking from afar, though in truth he was so close she could see the dark flecks in his eyes.

'I am well, my lord, thank you.' Isobel's mind was in chaos. She must find some way of bonding him to her. No sooner had the thought formed than the answer leaped into her mind. *Give him a child. Give Lucien an heir.* Briefly, she closed her eyes, as the image of her mother straining to give birth rose up before her.

'Good. I thought perhaps…after seeing Geoffrey…' He gave her hand a slight shake. 'Isobel?'

She opened her eyes, he was watching her closely, a line between his brows. 'I am well, my lord,' she repeated. 'Thank you for your concern.'

With a brusque nod, Lucien went to the window. Pushing back the curtains, he tapped the glass and gave the frame a slight push, as though checking it was secure.

Isobel thought of the sachet of herbs, tucked away at the bottom of her jewel box. *I shall have to stop taking those herbs.* Her stomach knotted. Fear was cold inside her, but if she gave him an heir, the bond between them would be irrevocable. *I shall have to give him a child.* The knots twisted. *If I can. Holy Mary, help me.*

Lucien let the curtain fall back into place. 'My apologies for not coming sooner. I had business with Count Henry.'

'I understand.' Isobel did not know how it was, but Lucien seemed larger when standing in her bed-chamber than he had in his armour on the tourney field. Realising rather belatedly that he was staring at her bare foot, she hastily rearranged her skirts to hide it.

'You were getting ready to retire,' he said, smiling crookedly.

Isobel's cheeks burned. *I shall have to give him his heir.* 'Yes, I was. Didn't Elise say?'

'Elise? We passed in the solar, she went down-stairs.'

'Elise has left the apartment?'

'Mmm.' Lucien took her hand, and wove his fingers with hers. 'She muttered something about fetching warm milk from the kitchens.'

'She must be hungry. I didn't ask for milk. My

lord, she'll be coming back. When I thought you were staying at the barracks, I asked her to sleep with me in here.'

He nodded. 'That is as well, I only came to bring you the letter. Much as I regret it, I cannot stay.'

'Unfinished business at the barracks?'

'Yes.'

'I understand.' The words slipped out easily, hiding her concerns. *Whatever he says, he must blame me for his knight's death. Is he regretting our marriage already?*

A candle flared. Lucien's eyes were very black and he had a look on his face, a look she had seen before. He had looked at her in that way in the inn before he had kissed her; he had looked that way last night. *He still wants me.* That at least was something. Isobel edged back till her calves hit the bed. She was embarrassed at the thought of Elise walking in on them, yet she knew that bedding with Lucien was as good a way as any of bonding him to her. The herbs she had already taken might prevent her from getting with child for a while, but he seemed eager to lie with her again.

The power of the herbs will fade. How soon might I conceive if I stop taking them from now on?

'You saw Count Henry, my lord?'

Lucien nodded, his fingers playing with hers,

making her stomach swoop. 'Mmm.' He raised her hand to his lips, lingering over the kiss.

Isobel's heart skittered. She glanced towards the solar. 'Di…did you tell him about Sir Geoffrey?'

Her question removed the warmth from his expression and he released her hand on a motion of assent. 'Naturally. He was very shocked.'

'Not as shocked as you,' she said softly. 'You had a fondness for him.'

He stared at her for a moment, eyes bleak, and gave an abrupt nod. 'So I was. Geoffrey was a good lad. He began as my squire.'

'Before Joris?'

Another nod.

Recognising that Lucien was wrestling with a deep emotion and was concerned not to show it, Isobel waited.

'I met him at Troyes Castle a few years back,' Lucien said. 'He came from a humble background, but he had a way with horses that had won him a place at the stables. I liked the look of him and Count Henry said he wouldn't miss him, so I took him on. Geoffrey trained hard. He was set on earning enough at the tourneys to support his mother.' He shoved his hand through his hair. 'His mother is ailing—she lives here in the town. I returned Geoffrey's armour to her this afternoon.'

Isobel knew the sad tradition. When a knight was killed in combat, if his armour was not taken as booty, it was generally returned to his family. Of course, Sir Geoffrey had not died in combat, but Lucien would uphold the tradition. Armour was expensive, and many a family had been beggared by a son with ambitions for knighthood. At present, Geoffrey's mother would undoubtedly be too grief-stricken to acknowledge the armour's return. Later, however, she would surely welcome it—if she was short of money, she could sell it.

'That must have been hard, my lord.' Lucien's answering grimace was testimony to the truth of her statement. 'Did you tell his mother how he died?'

'Skirted around the truth a little. Wanted her to be able to think of him as a hero.'

There was a hollow place where Isobel's stomach should be. *This is my fault. If I had not told Sir Geoffrey about the thief, he would be alive this evening.*

'There's a girl too,' Lucien added.

'Sir Geoffrey was married?' Dear Lord, he had looked so young. Was he already a father? Were there children who had been orphaned because of what she had said to him? If she had obeyed Lucien's command to stay away from the All Hallows Tourney, his knight would be alive.

'Not that I know of. But there was a sweetheart,

someone was hovering in the yard at the back. I heard a sob or two.'

'A sister, perhaps?'

'Yes, there is a sister, she's just a child. Someone else was with her.'

'Oh dear,' Isobel said, quietly. 'Perhaps I should visit them. My lord, I feel terrible about this. It is my fault.'

'I grant that I ordered you not to attend, but I fail to see how Geoffrey's death lies at your door.'

'In the pavilion...' she bit her lip '...I told Geoffrey I thought I had seen the thief. It was on my instigation that he went outside.'

'Isobel, one person is responsible for Geoffrey's death—the man who cut his throat.'

'My lord, if I had kept silent...' Tears stung in her eyes. 'Why did it have to happen?'

A warm hand cupped her cheek. 'It is *not* your fault.'

'Nevertheless, I should like to meet Sir Geoffrey's family.'

'To apologise? Isobel, I don't think that's a good idea—'

'I shall be tactful. I won't say anything to cause his mother more distress, but I should like to visit her. I might be able to...help.'

'With money?'

'Yes.'

'I have seen to that already.'

She covered his hand with hers. 'I am glad. However, I should like to visit them. The girl you heard… My lord, if she was Geoffrey's lover, there may be a child.'

Lucien stared as what she said sank in. 'Very well. If you take care what you say to his mother about the manner of Geoffrey's death, you may visit them after the funeral.'

'Thank you.'

Turning away, Lucien scowled at the entrance. 'Where the devil has that woman of yours got to? Is she milking the damn cow herself?'

Isobel lifted a shoulder, though in truth she had been wondering why Elise was taking so long. 'She will be back presently, I am sure. My lord, did you tell Count Henry about the theft of the relic?'

He nodded assent. 'Count Henry has promised his Guardians will investigate.'

'His Guardians? Oh, I remember, the knights who patrol Champagne.'

Reaching for her, Lucien pulled her towards him. Isobel tried not to notice how her pulse jumped. She tried not to notice how much she enjoyed being in his arms. *I don't want him to set me aside.*

Lucien's body was warm against hers, but his eyes

were preoccupied, resting on something behind her. 'The Guardians were established after attacks on merchants in previous years. Some had lost merchandise, others their lives.'

Isobel made a sympathetic noise. 'Sad to say, there are brigands everywhere.'

He glanced at her. 'I feel shame to have to tell you, Isobel, but many of them are knights. In good times they live off the money they can make at the tournaments. They hire themselves out as mercenaries. In bad times...'

'They prey on the merchants. Lord, what a world.'

Lucien nodded. 'Merchants make easy pickings. Even the wealthiest is not going to have much in the way of an escort.'

'Surely the Guardians cannot patrol every road in Champagne?'

'They watch the main thoroughfares. Count Henry wants his fairs to thrive, and for that to happen, merchants must feel confident that they and their goods are safe. After what happened today, Arthur is thinking of taking the oath and joining their company.'

'Arthur? Is he another of your household knights?'

The dark head shook. 'Sir Arthur Ferrer. I forgot you have not met him. He was steward of Ravenshold until recently. He has finished his term with me.'

'And the tournament today? What happened—was it cancelled?'

'I withdrew to bring Geoffrey home, and it went on without me. Raoul took command of my team.'

He stared broodingly down at her. 'I was thinking of joining the Guardians myself for a while,' he said.

It struck Isobel that since he was a Count in his own right, he would not find it easy to be answerable to Count Henry. *He is very proud.* She looked back at him, into his eyes.

'I won't rest until Geoffrey's murderer is brought to justice.'

Chapter Eleven

A twist of Isobel's hair lay on her breast. Lucien touched it with his forefinger. *Spun gold. And soft as silk.*

Their eyes met, and Lucien became aware of a constriction in his chest. It was anxiety. Anxiety for Isobel. The idea that a ruthless killer was on the loose in Troyes was bad enough, but more to the point was his concern for Isobel. She could identify the man.

'I thank you for trying to help Geoffrey,' he said, hoping she could not read the rest of his thoughts. The murderer knew Isobel's face. He knew she suspected him of stealing the relic. Was he out for her blood?

'Anyone would have done the same.' Her voice cracked. 'I only wish it could have been of use.'

'You did well,' he said softly, rubbing a golden strand between thumb and forefinger.

Isobel had done more than well. Tears were welling in her eyes now, but at the time she had kept her composure. *Morwenna would have panicked.* For all that Morwenna affected knowledge of the healing arts, she would have been more likely to shriek and run in the opposite direction than kneel at Geoffrey's side and attempt to stem the flow of blood.

Isobel's expression was sombre. He couldn't leave her like this. And if her maid didn't return, he wouldn't be leaving at all. He didn't want her to be on her own, it would be an easy matter for the thief to find where she was lodged. It would not be so easy to gain access to Count Henry's palace, but if the man was determined enough, anything was possible. He lifted a brow, trying for lightness. 'And lest you were thinking of acting against my wishes again, I thought I should tell you, there will be no more tournaments at the Field of the Birds until next year.'

Her smile was sad and she didn't look surprised. Geoffrey's death had shocked her; and she was worried about her father. That letter from Turenne could not have come at a worse time...

'Count Henry and I are of one mind on this,' he went on, hoping to lift her spirits. 'The present patron, Lord Glanville, is kicking up a fuss, but no matter. Next time a tournament is held at the Field of the Birds, it will be more stringently regulated as it was in my father's day. Lord Glanville has been too lax. Next year, the Guardians will be involved and I am to be patron.'

'Is it costly to host a tournament?'

Lucien shrugged. 'I can afford it, and Count Henry would prefer me to be in charge. Lord Glanville is, shall we say, less likely to cooperate with the Guardians.'

'I see.'

'In the meantime, if you can face the idea of a tournament after today, Count Henry has reminded me about his Twelfth Night Joust. You will be invited. Count Henry's tournaments are less challenging. More sedate.'

'Lances will be blunted, my lord?'

'Indeed. It is only fair to warn you that Count Henry intends to crown you Queen of his tournament, in honour of our marriage. You will be awarding the prizes.'

'Me? Goodness, that is an honour.' Her expression lightened. 'Thank you, my lord, I should enjoy that. Will you be competing?'

'Most likely.' Lucien frowned at the door. 'Where is that girl? Don't tell me she's found a sweetheart already?'

'Elise? Heavens, I hardly think so.'

'She had better hurry, I'm not leaving until she returns.' Lucien moved closer. Close enough to feel her warmth. He had not witnessed what had happened behind his pavilion, but Harry had told him. Had the thief tracked her there? Had Isobel been the real target rather than Geoffrey?

Another possibility, and one that was just as unpalatable, was that Geoffrey had been involved with the thief in some way. Lucien hadn't discussed this with anyone, not even Raoul. Could Geoffrey have been acting as the thief's agent?

Until today, Lucien would have taken an oath that Sir Geoffrey of Troyes was honest. Until today, he'd been certain that Geoffrey could no more act dishonourably than fly. True, Geoffrey's mother was ill and in need of costly medicines, but Lucien would never have imagined that Geoffrey would resort to underhanded means to find money. Not Geoffrey. *Not one of my household knights*. Lucien could not be sure, but it seemed far more likely that Geoffrey had been killed because he had been barring the way to Isobel.

Isobel is in danger.

He found himself gazing at her, top to toe, as though to memorise her features. He could not fathom it, but the more he saw of her, the more beautiful she seemed to become. She was more wilful than he had expected her to be, more of a handful and yet…

In some inexplicable way, the sight of Isobel seemed to loosen knots inside him that he had not known were there. That direct green gaze, so candid, so intelligent, seemed to offer something he had never looked for in a wife. A true partnership. It was very beguiling.

He checked himself. What was he thinking? He needed no one but himself. He must not forget that he had once found Morwenna beguiling. In those far-off days, he had been an innocent himself and completely inexperienced with women. Morwenna had taken him in. She had flattered him and had bedded him with the intention of making him fall in love with her. *Morwenna gulled me. She used my naivety against me. I was a fool then. But I am naïve no longer.*

Lucien wasn't about to be burned twice. Isobel must be kept at arm's length. That had been, he recalled with a frown, his plan all along. He had thought to marry her and keep her safe at one of his castles while he continued doing the rounds of the tourney circuit. In between tournaments and overseeing his lands, he would visit her and they could go about the pleasurable business of getting an heir…

Yes, life was going to be so much better with Isobel to come home to. *My wife.* She had grown into the most feminine of women. He let his fingertips explore her cheek, enjoying the way her skin darkened in the candlelight as much as the softness, the warmth. He leaned in and the fragrance of honeysuckle and roses caught at his senses. As long as he guarded his heart, there was no reason why he should not take pleasure in his marriage.

'I am a lucky man,' he murmured, dropping a swift, testing kiss on her mouth. Already her beauty was a trial to him. She was irresistible. So very beddable.

Her eyelashes lowered, her blush deepened. He pulled back, caught a slight sigh and...

Irresistible.

'Oh, the devil,' he said, gathering her fully into his arms.

He heard another little murmur. His tongue sought the warmth of her mouth as the scent of summer weaved about him, heady as spiced wine. Her eyes were closed, her head was tilted up to his, and that lovely body pressed close. There would be pleasure in his second marriage. As long as he remembered to keep his heart out of it.

She slid her hand up his chest, and wound her arms around his neck. Amazingly, his legs weakened, as they had not done with a woman in years. Yes, it was all very promising.

Except that her veil was in the way. Even though he had sworn not to touch her that way tonight—she was overset—Lucien longed to tear it off and loose her hair. She drew back and he noted with satisfaction how breathless she was, how her breasts strained against her bodice…

Blushing like a rose, she gestured at the bed. 'My lord, have you changed your mind about tonight?'

If she did but know it, that husky voice was an invitation to sin, but there were shadows under her eyes. The strains of today were showing, only a beast would bed her tonight. He shook his head. 'You need rest. Sleep well. Elise will be waiting outside, I shall send her in.'

'Thank you, my l…Lucien.'

Lucien had left his cloak on a chair in the solar. There was no sign of Elise. With a sigh, he retrieved his cloak and softly retraced his steps to the curtained doorway.

Wrapping himself in his cloak, Lucien settled down across the threshold of the bedchamber, and resigned himself to an uncomfortable night guarding his wife. Elise would simply have to step over him when she finally returned from whatever tryst she was keeping. Stupid wench. Isobel deserved better.

* * *

The cold made for a quick disrobing—Isobel had goose-bumps everywhere. Unpinning her veil, she slung it on a hook. She slipped out of her gown and loosened her braid. It was clear that Lucien must harbour some anger against her for disobeying him. Otherwise he would have joined her in bed. She knew he wanted her.

It is lust. He lusts for me.

Was it possible to build a marriage where the husband felt little for his wife but lust?

Lord, she was tired. Too tired to think. Likely it was as well that Lucien had gone, because she doubted she had the energy to pleasure him tonight. Briefly, Isobel wondered whether to remove her undergown before deciding against it. Winter was here and no mistake, the bedchamber was cold. Damp must be seeping into the palace from the canal. No matter. There were plenty of lambswool blankets. When Elise came back, they could warm each other.

Isobel pinched out her candle, left one burning for Elise, and slipped between the sheets. As she did so, she heard a soft thump in the solar. She snuggled under the covers and rubbed her arms to warm them. Elise had returned. She fell into a half-doze.

Time slipped by. And then more time. Elise did not join her.

Muzzy with fatigue, Isobel sat up. 'Elise? Is that you?'

Something rustled and from the other side of the screen, there came a low, but distinct curse. 'Hell.' The voice was male.

Was Lucien still here? Half-asleep, she stumbled out of bed, snatching up a candlestick on her way. It was solid iron, a weapon, if need be. She tiptoed to the entrance. 'Elise? Lucien?'

The gloom in front of her shifted and took solid form, a man stood between her and the fire. Heart in her mouth, she clutched the candlestick to her breast.

Her eyes adjusted to the firelight. 'Lucien!' She sagged with relief. 'Holy Mother, I thought you'd gone. You scared me.'

He prised the candlestick from her. Lucien's scar was made sinister by the shadows in the solar, his features looked stark in the firelight. He was all lines and sharp angles. His jet-black hair; the square jaw; that furrow between his brows as he looked down at her—all combined to form the image of a man who made no compromises. His eyes glittered.

I married this man. I must give him children.

'I intended to, but Elise did not return,' he said curtly. He looked extremely put out; it could not be comfortable on the floor. And she was keeping him from his business at the castle.

'I don't need a nursemaid. You didn't have to stay.'

He gave her a crooked smile. 'No?'

Her gaze was held by the scar on his temple, something about it fascinated her. Stepping up to him, she pushed back his hair—thick hair, so thick—and touched it with her fingertips. His eyes darkened, he went very still.

'Lucien, where did you get this?'

'Some witless woman tried to brain me with a candlestick?'

'No, truly…you didn't have it when we were betrothed. Is it a battle-scar?'

His smile faded. 'You might call it that.'

Something in his tone warned Isobel that further questions were not welcome. When his eyes drifted down and his expression turned to one of appreciation, she realised her hair was hanging about her, in some disorder after burrowing under the bedcovers. Hastily bunching it together, she pushed it over her shoulders.

'No need to do that,' he said, softly.

Heat washed over her. She was clad only in a light shift, a shift that revealed more than it concealed. And Lucien was smiling at her bare feet.

Hastily she retreated. She did not stop until she was back by the bed and the straw matting was harsh beneath her feet. Lucien came after her. Thank the

Lord, there was only one candle, he wouldn't see her blushes. She was not used to being married and his smile had a distinctly wolfish edge to it...

He replaced the candlestick on a coffer, shed his cloak and pulled her close. 'Elise is busy trysting; why should we not do the same?'

Isobel's mouth was dry, and her senses heightened. She was fighting with the urge to lick her lips—afraid he would notice. Lord, no, she wanted him to notice. *Holy Virgin, don't let him see how he attracts me.* She could feel so much more of him when clad only in her undershift. His body felt leaner, stronger. More male. It was not frightening but it was disturbing. Tonight there was that about him that was almost predatory. 'Lucien, please...'

'Relax. I have told you that I shall spare you my attentions tonight. Tonight, I seek simply to offer you comfort.' His hand closed possessively over her breast, gently cupping her.

Comfort? Isobel's breast tightened. She wanted to press herself against his palm. The ache in her belly told her how much she wanted—needed—to intensify the contact.

He nuzzled her cheek. 'Comfort, and perhaps a few kisses. Isobel, you're cold. Let me warm you.'

His kiss was as gentle as his hand. As seductive. It was a kiss that made her hunger for more—it had her gripping his shoulders and sliding a hand round the back of his neck. She twisted in the hope that he would see that she was giving him better access to her breasts. Recklessly, part of her wanted him to take advantage of her.

'That's it,' he murmured. 'Trust me. Show that you trust me.'

The remark struck a jarring note and she drew back. Lucien's eyes were black in the light of the candle, but the sensual spell was broken. She could never trust him, not completely. What about his mistress?

'Trust you? What can you mean?'

'Trust me. Let me into your bed.' He brought his lips to her ear, warming it with his breath. 'Tonight, Isobel, we shall simply give each other comfort.'

Isobel hesitated, wondering if it was comfort he sought from his lover. It was painful to think about his *belle amie*, but she couldn't help herself. She had meant to ask him about it earlier, but Sir Geoffrey's death had pushed it from her mind.

'Lucien, you are my husband,' she said, taking a deep breath. 'You must know I shall never deny you, but there is something…'

A dark eyebrow lifted. 'Yes?'

'Tell me about your mistress.' The chamber was

poorly lit, but Isobel could see she had caught him off guard.

'My mistress?' He looked utterly perplexed, completely bemused. 'What mistress?'

'The mistress you keep at Ravenshold. Your *belle amie*.'

'There is no mistress at Ravenshold,' he said.

Isobel stared blindly at the bed. What now? She could hardly accuse him of lying. One did not need the wisdom of Solomon to realise a marriage that began with the wife accusing her husband of keeping a mistress was not going to be easy.

Stupid, stupid. I should have kept my mouth shut.

But Isobel couldn't keep her mouth shut. It was a flaw in her soul and it had caused much strife with the nuns in Conques as they had tried to eliminate it. Over the years, her inability to hold her tongue had brought her many penances. But however many penances she was given, she remained outspoken. Silence wasn't her way.

'Men have mistresses, Lucien. I am not naïve. I have heard you have a *belle amie*.'

Amazingly, his mouth eased into something that could have been amusement. He leaned a hip against a bedpost and folded his arms. 'You have? That is passing strange, since I don't have one.'

She wished she could believe him. There he

stood—champion of a thousand tourneys, confidence and arrogance in his every line. The truth hit her like an arrow, and her heart sank. *He has had lovers, many lovers, in the years since our betrothal.*

'Some women...' she waved vaguely in the direction of the streets below '...I heard them talking.'

'Talk,' he muttered, shaking his head. He gave her a direct look. 'Aren't wives taught not to plague a man with mention of his mistress?'

'I am aware of the conventions, my lord.' She swallowed. 'Well-bred ladies are expected to ignore what their husbands get up to outside the marriage bed. And I am sorry if I anger you, but I think I should warn you that in this respect I do not think I am capable of making a good wife.'

'Oh?'

It was pin-drop quiet in the bedchamber, the only sound Isobel could hear was the slight flurry of her breathing and his. Somewhere on the other side of the canal, a door slammed. In the distance, a man was laughing. She lifted her chin. 'In fact I think I will be a very bad wife.'

'How so?'

She clasped her hands together and the words poured out. 'I was happy to marry you, my lord. Even though you have shown so little interest in me over the years.' The scar on his temple seemed to stand out more starkly than before, but she swept on. 'I have always been happy at the thought of marrying you. But I cannot stomach the thought of you having a mistress. I—'

'Isobel, I don't know who you heard, but they were mistaken. I don't have a mistress. I've had casual lovers, that I'll not deny. But no mistress, I swear it.' Pushing away from the bedpost, he took her hands. 'Isobel, there is no *belle amie* at Ravenshold.'

He shifted, and broad shoulders blocked out the candlelight, his dark head was angled towards her. Her husband. Her thoughts twisted round each other in her mind. Conflicted. Uncomfortable.

Lucien could not know it, but since Isobel had been a child and they had been promised to each other, all her girlish longings and desires had been focused on him. She was coming to see that the man she had imagined did not exist. Like a troubadour, she had imagined perfection. She had been hurt and angered at his tardiness in summoning her, but that had not stopped her from fabricating all manner of reasons for the delay.

He had a county to run.

He was set on winning every tournament in Christendom, so he could amass more prizes and trophies than any other knight...

Hurt pride had been her shield. It had prevented

her from seeing that the image she had constructed of him might not match reality. She had idealised him, and the anger she had felt at their delayed marriage had blinded her. Lucien might have had another cause for delaying. *He has had many mistresses and there is one, perhaps, whom he loves.*

There was a bitter taste in her mouth. The man looking down at her was handsome and strong, but he was also real; he had flaws. Was the mismatch between the dream Lucien and the real man large or small? Only time would give her the answer.

He looks to be the soul of honour, but is he lying? Noblemen kept mistresses. The Church did not condone it, though they could not stop it. Isobel's own father, Viscount Gautier, had a woman in Turenne whom he visited every week.

I should not have idealised him.

Men took lovers. As Isobel understood it, ladies who took lovers were less common. Ladies of breeding were expected to keep themselves for their husbands for the simple reason that men must know their bloodlines were pure. There must be no cuckoos in the nest.

She imagined that once a bloodline was secure a lady might be free to take a lover, but she had not been out of the convent long enough to know if that was actually the case. The nuns simply avoided uncomfortable topics. There were many frustrating gaps in her education, but one thing was certain. Men didn't suffer the same constraints as women. It might not be fair, but fairness was beside the point.

The purity of the bloodline was everything.

Minstrels sang of courtly love. In the songs she had heard at her father's hall, lip-service was given to the idea of equality between the sexes. In the *chansons* of the *trouvères*, ladies flirted with their knights, giving them favours to carry with them into the lists. In return the knights would worship their ladies. They would go on quests for them. The relationship would remain chaste and pure. In the ballads.

'Isobel, what thoughts are going through that head of yours?'

She moistened her lips. 'I am trying to believe you.'

Lucien says he has no mistress and when he speaks, the truth seems to shine from him. Isobel could be deluding herself; the desire to believe him was agonisingly strong. She did not want him to have a lover—she had never thought about any man but him. Their marriage was scarcely a day old, and the idea that Lucien might take his pleasure elsewhere made her sick with…with what? Dread? Jealousy?

A strange smile was playing about his lips, as though something she said had pleased him. Or amused him.

'My lord, are you laughing at me?'

His lips curved into one of his rare, heart-stopping smiles. Before she knew it, he had set his hands at her waist and pulled her up against his chest. 'I find you utterly delightful. Isobel, I never thought to confess this so soon, but I deeply regret the years we have spent apart. Believe me, there is no *belle amie* at Ravenshold.' He cupped her cheek with his hand, and the smile was gone. 'Lord, Isobel, you are freezing. Come along, get into bed.'

'Aren't you going back to the barracks?'

'No longer. Into bed with you.' The wolfish smile was back. 'Never fear, much as I am tempted, I shall not force myself on you.'

Isobel shot him a sharp look, read only the truth, and allowed herself to be helped into bed. After she had settled, he pulled the covers over her.

'I shall speak to that woman of yours in the morning,' he said, walking round to the other side of the bed. 'She must be made aware of her duties.'

'Elise didn't train as a maid.'

'That is obvious.' Lucien sat down and the bedropes creaked. He pulled off his boots and tossed them on the matting. It was extraordinary, but his manner was—almost—companionable. When he was lying under the covers at her side, he propped his head on his hand to study her. 'We shall sleep now, wife. Sleep and...' smiling, he inched closer '...comfort each other.' Finding her hands, he began to chafe them.

She glanced towards the entrance.

'Forget about Elise. Your useless maid is busy elsewhere. Relax. We shall sleep, that's all. Sleep and keep each other warm. Don't move.'

He shifted and blew out the candle. Darkness covered them.

The bed-ropes creaked and his body was back against hers. He guided her head to his shoulder and his arm went round her. After a lifetime of sleeping with other women, she had to confess his large body was blissfully warm.

Somewhat self-consciously, Isobel rested her hand on Lucien's waist and tried to relax. Relaxing next to a powerful male body, the one that attracted and intrigued her over all others, was not easy for a convent-bred girl.

Tentatively, she inhaled his scent. *This is Lucien, my husband.* He smelt very male—a hint of musk and spices told her the soap he used was costly and likely imported. He smelt of wood-smoke. Mainly, he smelt of warm man. She had enjoyed joining with him yesterday, but none the less, it was reassuring to know they could give each other comfort in this companionable way too. Not that a man like Lucien would ever really need comforting.

Feeling him press a kiss again to her brow, she smiled into the dark. She liked being held in this way. She liked the warmth. *I am with Lucien.*

His *belle amie*, if he had one, was not here.

I am with Lucien.

Her thoughts drifted and blurred one into another.

There was a tightness in the back of Lucien's throat that he could not account for. He ached with wanting, was ready to take her, but she would not welcome him tonight. Geoffrey's death was not the first death she had witnessed. Isobel had seen her mother die and today's events could not but remind her of that.

He contented himself with stroking her hair. *I cannot take her, not tonight.*

Lucien thought—hoped—there was liking between them. He would build on that. Isobel had revealed some resentment at having been, as she thought, ignored for so long. It was hardly surprising. Now they were married he could explain everything. He would tell her about his disastrous marriage to Morwenna. He would explain why he had not set Morwenna aside despite repeated demands from his father that he do so. His first marriage had been disastrous. His second—the marriage his father had planned for—had to be better. *We shall have children.*

Lucien's mind was at war with itself. It was not a feeling that he was familiar with. From the moment Isobel had walked into the convent lodge, his instinct had been to be open with her. However, circumspection was necessary. It would not have been wise to make a clean breast of things until after their marriage. And now?

Isobel might have accepted him in her bed, but the trust between them was wafer thin. Trust. He must build on that. He would—the thought was intriguing—woo his wife.

If he made his confession about Morwenna too early, Isobel might refuse to give him heirs. He had not behaved honourably. A noblewoman of Isobel's standing would be deeply insulted to learn that her betrothed had been married at the time of their betrothal. As for Isobel's father—Viscount Gautier would be outraged. If the news didn't kill him, he would be well within his rights to order Isobel back to Turenne and that would be the end of their marriage.

No, it was best he delayed confessing about his dubious past until *after* he had wooed her.

I want her. Lucien shifted uncomfortably. He was throbbing. Hard with desire. He had wanted her since the day she rode to Ravenshold. *Isobel would drive any man into a frenzy of need.* Need? Lucien felt a prickle of unease, and dismissed it. Not need. This was desire, plain and simple.

Morwenna had taught him that beauty was only skin deep. It was not—he fingered the scar at his temple—a lesson he was likely to forget. What attracted him most to Isobel, what made him want to keep her, was when she had so artlessly confessed that she did not think she would find it easy to stomach him having a lover.

Isobel doesn't want me to have lovers. Her admission warmed him. Why that should be, Lucien had no idea. Morwenna couldn't have given a fig what he did. Isobel was turning out to be very different.

Isobel doesn't want me to take lovers. It was a pity she had heard the gossips, though he only had himself to blame for that. He had kept his shameful marriage so quiet, what was the world to assume but that the woman he had kept at Ravenshold had been his mistress? Very few people knew the truth. Raoul. Poor Geoffrey. Joris. A handful of others.

Isobel gave a quiet sigh as he stroked her hair.

Roses and honeysuckle. *Mon Dieu*, it was going to be a long night.

He was going to woo her. Then, when he knew he had truly won her, he would tell her about Morwenna. Isobel was worth hanging on to.

He smiled into the dark. Besides, who knew what would happen if his wooing proved successful? If he won her, Isobel's behaviour might change. She might become the easy-going, biddable wife he had hoped for.

Isobel? Biddable? His smile faded. He couldn't put his finger on it, but the idea of him having a biddable wife was not as desirable as it had been. No matter. It surely wouldn't hurt to woo her a little.

But one thing he would never do was open his heart to her. Not even when he had told her about Morwenna.

Chapter Twelve

Lucien Vernon, Count d'Aveyron, had been running from dawn to dusk. In the morning he had led conferences—war councils, of a sort—with Count Henry's Guardian Knights. He organised patrols. He briefed knights on the importance of finding Geoffrey's murderer and of bringing him to justice. In the afternoon, he had ridden out to Ravenshold with his recently appointed steward, Sir Gawain. The castle must be restored to its former glory as speedily as possible.

Lucien had planned to be back in Troyes by mid-afternoon, but by the time he and Joris rode through the city gates, the shopkeepers were lowering their shutters for the night. Torches and lanterns were lit, and along the way, yellow light was seeping through cracks in windows and walls.

Trotting smartly through the town, Lucien drew

rein outside a goldsmith's. The shutters were fast, but this particular goldsmith—Joseph—had an excellent reputation for honesty and fair dealing. If Lucien could buy from him, he would.

'Wait here with Demon, Joris.'

'Yes, my lord.'

Lucien rapped on the door. 'Joseph? Joseph Goldsmith? Open up, will you?' He feared it might be some days before he was free to see his wife, but when he did see her, he did not wish to be empty-handed.

The shutter opened a crack, a shadow moved inside. 'Who is there?'

'Lucien Vernon.'

'Count d'Aveyron?'

'The same.'

Bolts grated and the door opened. 'Welcome, my lord.' Beaming, the goldsmith gestured him inside. 'I heard you had married. May I wish you a long and happy marriage.'

'My thanks.' Lucien found himself returning Joseph's smile as he bent his head and entered the darkened workroom. Through a half-open door, firelight glinted in the room beyond. Lucien had been smiling all day and he could not account for it. No, that was a lie; he could account for it. He was smiling because of his wife. Because of Isobel. The wife who, despite his apparent neglect of her, valued him enough to want him to be faithful to her.

'You wish to buy something for Countess Isobel?'

At Lucien's nod, Joseph lifted a strongbox on to the counter and set a lantern next to it. He gave Lucien a measuring glance. 'Your wife makes you happy, my lord. You will want a special gift.'

'No doubt. Have you anything that might suit?'

Joseph unhooked a bunch of keys from his waist and unlocked the strongbox. 'You are in luck, my lord. One of my best traders came in yesterday. He has contacts in the East, and he tells me that this belonged to an Indian princess.'

The pouch Joseph extracted from the strongbox fit easily into his palm. It was made of rose silk. Placing it reverently on the table, Joseph untied the drawstring and inched the lantern closer.

'If you wish, you are welcome to examine it outside, my lord. Although I do not think there is much daylight left.'

Isobel did not see her husband for some days. Each day Joris brought word-of-mouth messages—excuses for Lucien's continuing absence. The excuses varied:

My lord is in late conference with the Guardian

Knights tonight. He asks me to tell you he will be sleeping in his quarters at the barracks.

My lord has business at Ravenshold. He sends his apologies, but he will be back too late to sup with you.

My lord is meeting with Count Henry...

The messages might vary but the outcome was the same.

Lucien is avoiding me.

Isobel had liked to think that they had reached some measure of understanding. Thanks to the passion that had flared between them on her wedding night, she had thought to bind him to her by giving him an heir. But if Lucien was never with her, how was that to happen?

Days shortened and the nights grew longer, and Lucien kept his distance. Isobel bitterly regretted attending the All Hallows Tourney. *He holds me responsible for Geoffrey's death. Will he ever forgive me?*

While Isobel waited for her elusive husband to honour her with his presence, she prayed for her father's health. She prayed for her stepmother, that she should be brought to bed of a healthy child. She tried not to dwell on her own fears of childbirth; they served no purpose. Particularly since, if Lucien deigned to approach her again, her duty was clear.

* * *

There had been no message on the day that Lucien finally appeared—Isobel had given up hope of seeing him this side of Christmas. It was late and she was abed watching Elise unlace her gown, when she heard the clack of the solar door. Quick footsteps crossed the solar and someone rapped on the carved screen.

Lucien pushed through the curtain, and her heart gave a little leap. His blue surcoat was blazoned with his black raven, which told her he had likely been closeted with Count Henry. Striding to the bed, he took her hand and kissed it. Elise reached for her cloak and scuttled out.

'My apologies for not sending a message today, my lady,' he said, shoving his hand through his hair. 'I expected to be here sooner.'

Turning away, he began to strip himself. Belt, surcoat, tunic, shirt, boots...

Isobel lay back on the pillows, and willed herself to relax. *I must not expect miracles, Lucien will not be an easy man to win.* She watched Lucien disrobe, and tried to judge his mood. He had a very fine form—her gaze was transfixed by the way his arm muscles flexed as he moved. The moment he caught her eyes on him, his skin darkened.

Hiding a smile, she folded her hands primly on

the bedcovers. If he didn't want her to look at him, he could always put out the candles. She was glad though that he had not. There had been no opportunities to study a man's body at St Foye's Convent, and Lucien's intrigued her.

He had the perfect knight's body. And to her eyes, the perfect body for a lover. One glance and you knew you were looking at a champion. He carried no excess flesh. The skin of his back was burnished by candlelight, light which revealed the play of strong shoulder muscles as he shed his clothes. And one or two scars she had not noticed before. His clothes piled up messily on the floor.

Why did the width of Lucien's shoulders make such a fascinating contrast with his narrow waist, with his long legs?

When he was naked, he turned to face her, smiling crookedly. Her cheeks burned. Lucien might never mouth the pretty sentiments of the knights in the *chansons* but, thank Heaven, he was eager to bed with her again. If he harboured any resentment against her, it did not look as though it was going to affect his performance as a lover.

He cleared his throat, extracted something from the jumble of clothes, and joined her in bed.

A warm hand caught her chin. His kiss was light and gentle. She smothered a moan as more kisses were feathered across her face. His kisses had kept the glamour of their wedding night, her body was melting—she ached to be one with him. When his tongue slid over her lips, she pressed closer, opening her mouth on a murmur of pleasure she could not have suppressed if she tried.

He broke the kiss, eyes dark, hair rumpled. The rumpled hair was her fault, she realised, somewhat belatedly. She had been running her fingers through the thick, dark strands. *I love his hair.*

'I brought you a gift,' he muttered, pressing something into her hand. 'Wanted to give it to you days ago, but I…' He shrugged and leaned back on an elbow. 'No matter. I hope it pleases you.'

A rose-coloured pouch? Smiling, Isobel made a show of feeling it. It was round in shape—no, not round…

Fingers trembling, she loosed the ties. A brooch! Her mouth fell open. A crescent moon lay in the palm of her hand, a crescent moon that had more sparkle and shine than a winter morning. If she was not mistaken, those starry stones were diamonds, tiny gems which contained every colour of the rainbow.

She looked up to see him frowning at her.

'You don't like it?'

He had seen her surprise and misinterpreted it as

dislike. 'Lucien, it's exquisite. I love it.' Resting her hand on his arm, she pressed a kiss to a lean cheek. 'This must be worth a king's ransom.'

Strong arms reached for her and drew her to his chest. 'I can afford it, little dove.'

'You must have done well at the tourneys this year.'

'Well enough.' Blue eyes looked into hers. 'Isobel, I am not short of revenues. If I were, there is no way I would be contemplating hosting half the knights of Christendom at next summer's tourney. The Field of the Birds must be made safer, and that will come at no little cost.' He gave her a puzzled look. 'The Ravenshold estate is but one of my holdings. Surely your father has told you? I have lands in Normandy and the Auvergne...I am not a pauper.'

Isobel gazed up at him, as an unwelcome thought lodged in her mind. Naturally, she knew Lucien had extensive lands, but by his own admission Ravenshold had been badly neglected. She had wondered if poor revenues had been the cause. If her assumption was wrong, it must mean that Lucien was a poor overlord. Was the neglect at Ravenshold due to its lord having turned his back on his responsibilities?

Have I married a wastrel? A man who only has thoughts for what happens on the tourney field? Can he not see that a neglected holding would soon lead to reduced revenues? To disgruntled retainers and unhappy tenants?

Lucien kissed her nose and that musky masculine scent—already beguilingly familiar—wound through her senses. It seduced her into silence, but it did not stop the thoughts. If Lucien was a wastrel, she would soon discover it. If he was so obsessed with tournaments that little else mattered, that might work in her favour. He would surely welcome a wife who could handle the day-to-day running of his estates. *If I do not conceive, I can at least help run his estates...*

He was nuzzling her neck, measuring her breast with his palm, absently toying with a nipple. 'If you don't like the brooch, I shall get something else.'

Isobel closed her fingers over his gift. 'I love it.' A sensuous warmth was transferring itself from Lucien's body to hers, a warmth which worked insidiously at her thoughts, blurring them one into another. *He is so handsome. I want him. It is too soon to judge him.*

He nibbled her ear. 'The goldsmith tells me it comes from India. It belonged to a princess.'

Isobel stroked his shoulder. 'Where's India?'

'In the East, far beyond Byzantium. I am not certain, but I think India is beyond Persia.'

Drawing back, Isobel opened her fingers and stared at the brooch. 'It glitters so.'

He grunted and shifted. The bed-ropes creaked.

Reaching out to put the brooch on the side-table, Isobel blew out her candle. When she turned back, strong arms were waiting for her and it was all too easy to slide into them. It was all too easy to dismiss unwanted thoughts about a husband who was obsessed with tourneying. It was even easy to stop worrying about whether or not she would be able to give him an heir…

This attraction may not last for ever. While it does, I want to enjoy it.

Lucien was not in the habit of changing his mind. Habits, however, were not set in stone. In the morning, as he eased himself out of bed so as not to disturb his wife, he paused to gaze down at her and found himself contemplating a change of plan.

She looks like an angel.

The thought had his chest squeezing painfully. Isobel was no angel. Reaching out, he touched a strand of golden hair. Isobel was impulsive. Isobel was proud and disobedient and wilful. She talked too much. She knew what she wanted and had no qualms about going after it. And she expected faithfulness in her husband.

Moving to the window, he looped back the curtain and a shaft of early light fell softly on to the bed. On the side-table, the brooch glistened. Lucien was pleased she liked it—he had never spent so much on a woman in his life. And until Joseph had shown him the brooch, he had no thought of doing so. He gave a rueful smile. Joseph knew his business. No sooner had Lucien set eyes on it than he knew it was Isobel's.

Absently, Lucien rubbed his breastbone with the heel of his hand and reached for his clothing. He had changed his mind about waking his wife. Just as he had changed his mind about not wanting her at Ravenshold until it had been properly restored.

He dragged on his tunic, and fastened his belt. 'Isobel?'

Long eyelashes lifted, and she sent him a sleepy smile. Her smile should be outlawed, in a heartbeat a heavy pulse was throbbing in his loins. If only he had not arranged to meet Count Henry that morning...

'Good morning, Lucien.'

Her voice was husky. Yet more temptation. 'It's time we left the palace.' Frustrated desire made his voice curt. 'Get your maid to pack up your things.'

'We're leaving?' Eyes bright, she sat up. He tried

not to look at her breasts. 'We're going to Ravens-hold?'

He nodded. 'This afternoon. Joris will bring you an escort and some pack animals.'

'I have my own men,' she reminded him softly.

'Arrangements will be made for them to accompany you.'

She looked thoughtfully at him. 'You will permit me to assist in restoring your castle?'

'So it would seem.'

Isobel was out of bed in a moment, all delicate white limbs and flowing hair. Entirely forgetful of her nakedness, she hugged him to her. 'Thank you! You won't regret it, Lucien, I swear it.'

Reaching up, she pulled his head down to hers and gave him a kiss that left him breathless. Lucien lost himself in the kiss. In the feel of her skin—silk moving sensuously against his palms. In her scent—heady, alluring...

She should be outlawed.

He was wondering whether there might after all be time for them to take their joy of each other again, when something shifted at the edge of his vision. Elise. The girl was shrinking into the shadows by the curtained entrance.

Reluctantly, he pulled away. 'Cover yourself, Isobel, we are not alone.'

Isobel wound a blanket about her. Her lips were rosy from kissing, and the way she was looking at him... Lord.

'Joris will be here in four hours,' he said. 'Is that long enough?'

'Yes.' A small hand emerged from the blanket and touched his. 'Thank you, Lucien.'

Somehow, he extricated his hand from hers. He made his way out of the bedchamber, across the solar, and down the winding stairs. It seemed a long way to the Great Hall.

At first, Isobel was energised by Lucien's change of heart. As she washed and dressed, her heart was singing.

He trusts me! He was ready to allow her to move into his castle. This was her chance to show him that she could be a help and not a hindrance, and as long as she didn't interfere in military business, she was confident she would win his approval. Her kitchens would rival those of Countess Marie, and her guest chambers—well, perhaps they might not match this apartment—but she would transform Ravenshold. The bedchambers would be warm and welcoming...

The morning passed in a dizzy whirl.

'Elise, first we shall pack my gowns and veils in that painted chest.'

'Yes, my lady.'

'After that, I should like you to enquire as to the whereabouts of Countess Marie. I must thank her for her hospitality.'

'Yes, my lady.'

Elise dug into her clothes-coffer to make room for some gowns and Isobel went to put the brooch in her jewel casket. It was too good to wear today. She caught sight of the sachet of herbs at the bottom and it was as though a shadow fell over her. She had been deceiving Lucien, and whilst she had stopped taking the herbs, her conscience pricked her. In procuring them without his agreement, she had done him great wrong. Lucien had married her to beget an heir. Naturally, he wanted her dowry too but, setting that aside, he wanted a son.

Noblemen need sons. I was not ready to give him one. I will try though, I really will try...

The old fears weighed heavy on her heart. Lucien was sharing her bed because of his need for an heir. It was true that he took pains to ensure that the act of love was as pleasurable for her as she hoped it was for him, but that did not mean he felt affection for her. And much as she was willing to try for a child, she knew she was not ready for childbirth. She might not manage to conceive, and if she did, she might die as her mother had done.

Lucien has a mistress. The thought came out of nowhere. Since their marriage Isobel had tried not to dwell on Lucien's mistress. Her husband had bedazzled her with charm; he had bedazzled her with his body. She glanced at the rose-silk pouch. He had bedazzled her with his gift too, divining that she needed to be wooed after the years of neglect.

She went still. Or was the brooch a bribe—a bribe to make her forget about his mistress? *How does one forget something like that?*

'Count Lucien has a mistress,' she muttered, closing the jewel box. She was reticent about mentioning this again to Elise, but the words slipped out.

Elise turned questioning eyes on her. 'My lady?'

Her throat was tight. 'At Ravenshold. My lord has a *belle amie.*'

Elise scooped an armful of gowns and veils from the pegs on the wall and carried them to the bed. 'This upsets you, my lady?' Her voice was matter of fact, as she began smoothing out gowns. Her eyes were sharp. Watchful. 'Many wives would consider that a relief. If Count Lucien has a woman nearby he will not be disturbing you so often. There will be less chance of you becoming great with child.'

It would disturb me far more if Lucien did not disturb me!

Isobel's throat worked. She hadn't told Elise that

she had changed her mind about wanting to conceive. To hide her confusion, she picked up a veil and folded it into a neat square. Her fear of childbirth had dominated her for as long as she could remember, and Elise knew it. If she confessed that she had changed her mind, Elise would think her quite mad. She must turn the subject.

'Elise, before we leave Troyes, we mustn't forget to visit the Abbey. I need to see whether Girande has recovered.'

Elise froze. 'And if she has?'

'She will come with us to Ravenshold.'

Elise's mouth set in sullen lines. 'You will have no further need of me. Are you thinking to dismiss me?'

'I won't dismiss you.'

'You don't need two maids, my lady.'

'That is true, but by all accounts there is plenty to do at Ravenshold. It has been a masculine domain for too long.' *Apart from Lucien's mistress.* Isobel lightened her tone. 'There are bound to be tasks that suit your talents. At the apothecary's I noticed how knowledgeable you are about herbs. I would be pleased to have your help in planning an herb garden.'

'Just mind you don't leave me at the Abbey gates. I would hate to be dependent on convent charity.'

Isobel smiled. 'Elise, there is no need to worry. If you wish to continue in my service, I shall ensure it.'

Elise's eyes filled. 'Bless you, my lady.'

Chapter Thirteen

The sun was falling into the west in a coppery blaze when Isobel and her party clattered into Ravenshold bailey. Isobel's maid, Girande, had recovered enough to accompany them, and the three women—Elise rode with them—were surrounded by an escort large enough to do honour to a queen. Half the men were Viscount Gautier's, the other half answered to Lucien.

Isobel didn't know what to expect at Ravenshold. Disorder, certainly. Lucien had been frank about the run-down state of the place. Disorder didn't frighten her; she would welcome the chance to show her colours. *I can set his castle to rights.* But would she have to deal with a mistress too? She was less certain how she would handle a mistress. *He told me there was no mistress...*

Russet-coloured leaves fluttered across the yard like butterflies—a great drift of them hugged the base of the keep. At first glance, the buildings running along the bailey walls didn't look too ramshackle, although a low, thatched one had an alarming dip in the roof-ridge. The stables. Smoke was curling through the roof of a cookhouse. But it was the two round towers that dominated. Isobel was craning her neck to study them when there was movement in the stable doorway. Lucien.

Face lighting when he saw her, he strode across, brushing hay from his tunic and chausses. 'Isobel, you must see this.' He reached up to help her dismount.

Isobel put her hands on his shoulders. Lucien's tunic was threadbare and dirty—in several places it was ripped. She widened her eyes, this was the first time she had seen him look anything other than knightly. 'You have straw in your hair, my lord.'

Blue eyes met hers, they were shining with pleasure. 'New foal. Couldn't resist helping with the birth. Come and see.'

His delight was catching. Shaking her head at his clothes—he looked like a groom rather than a count—Isobel allowed him to draw her into the stables. The foal, a beautiful chestnut, was sitting in the straw in the last stall, watched over by her mother. A pair of large, liquid eyes turned their way.

'What a sweetheart,' Isobel breathed. 'Was it an easy birth?'

'It seemed so.'

If only women gave birth as easily as animals.

As Lucien smiled down at the foal, he wove his fingers with hers. Isobel's heart clenched. The way he habitually entwined his fingers with hers was most endearing. But she should not read too much into it; at best it was an ambiguous gesture. She would love to think that the gift he had given her signalled that she was more to him than a route to the lands of Turenne, but she had to be realistic. She was just another prize to add to his collection. She stared for a moment at their linked hands, an ache in her breast. For many people such a gesture might convey affection, but in their case it symbolised possession.

He believes me to be heiress to my father's lands. And so I am, unless Angelina gives Father a boy. I should tell him. I must warn him about the coming baby...

The words simply would not come.

The foal had him entranced. Covertly, she studied his profile. She had noticed before that his entire face was transformed when he smiled. He looked young and carefree. Devastatingly attractive. Was this a side of him that he showed to his mistress?

His mistress. Isobel managed to return his smile. Surely a man so enchanted by the birth of a foal, would not force his wife to endure the presence of a *belle amie* at Ravenshold? Had the woman been dismissed? Or had he found a cottage for her in that village they passed on the road?

His smile stabbed at Isobel's heart. 'Come, my lady, it is time to show you your new home.' His voice became dry. 'As you shall see, the work is likely to keep us busy until well after Christmas.'

As they sat at the table waiting for their supper, Isobel paused to reflect wryly on the truth of his words. In its present state, the hall at Ravenshold was a far cry from the Great Hall in Count Henry's palace. All afternoon, Isobel had been trying not to make comparisons, but it was a hard task. Evidence of poor stewardship and neglect was there at every turn.

Above them, Lucien's standard sagged in the rafters, so smoke-blackened that it was impossible to tell that it must once have been blue; the raven was lost in grime. The hall fire hissed like a thousand snakes, and it smoked. Unfortunately it didn't smoke badly enough to drive out the smells. Must. Decay. Beneath their feet, the rushes had not been renewed.

Surreptitiously, Isobel toed them with her shoe. Her nose wrinkled. What a filthy, squalid place.

'Isobel? What's amiss?'

She flushed—she had been trying to conceal the depth of her distaste. 'The rushes,' she murmured. 'There are bones in the rushes.'

'Quite likely.' Lucien shrugged.

Her husband was a mystery, a riddle she couldn't work out. Didn't he care that Ravenshold was practically derelict? He had plenty of revenues, so what could she think but that he had been neglectful? Her tourney champion was, it seemed, an irresponsible and feckless overlord. She took a deep breath. Like all knights, Lucien loved his horses, so she would start by mentioning the stables.

'My lord,' she spoke softly, 'you did mention that Ravenshold was in some disrepair, but I must confess I am shocked.'

Blue eyes looked steadily at her. 'I warned you.'

'So you did. You will have noticed how the timbers in the stable roof have gone. It needs a complete rebuild.'

'I am aware of that. We have no seasoned wood. Some half-wit has been using it as fuel. I have it in hand.'

'Oh?'

'Count Henry has offered some seasoned timber, it's arriving tomorrow.' Lucien glowered in the direction of the door that led out to the cookhouse. 'Where the devil is our meat? The sergeant knows you are dining here tonight.'

Even as he spoke the door opened, and Isobel heard the sergeant shouting. She exchanged glances with Lucien and the door closed again. No one came in.

Isobel slid the bread platter towards Lucien. Her visit to the kitchen had been most enlightening, though with Lucien in a hurry to show her everything, she had done little more than be introduced to the cook, who was, in reality, one of Lucien's sergeants. Loath to issue orders until she had taken the man's measure, she had said little. She needed to know she had Lucien's full backing first.

Lucien ate three pieces of bread. The fire hissed and smoked. Lucien drummed his fingers on the table and swore under his breath. Isobel was on the point of going to investigate when the cookhouse door swung wide and a boy—she could swear she had seen him in the stables earlier—came in.

'Chicken,' she said, brightly, as a roast chicken slid precariously on its platter before being thumped on to the table in front of them. Yes, the boy had definitely been recruited from the stables; he brought with him a distinct whiff of horse. 'How lovely.'

'At last, I'm starved.' Lucien took up his knife and soon several pieces of breast were neatly arranged on their trencher. Very neatly. He was such a mystery.

An image of Lucien, colours flying as he cantered the length of the tourney field on his immaculately caparisoned charger, flashed through Isobel's brain. Except for when he was playing midwife to one of his mares, he was so fastidious in his person. Yet Ravenshold was falling into ruin…

Against the odds, the chicken looked perfect. It smelt delicious—particularly once the stable boy had retreated, taking the stink of horse with him. Isobel could smell onions and thyme. Her mood lifted. Lucien's sergeant could cook. This was good, wholesome fare and her mouth was watering.

Lucien moved the best piece towards her.

'My thanks. Lucien?' She cleared her throat. 'Do you give me full authority in the domestic sphere?'

He swallowed, and for a moment she thought he was not going to reply. When he finally spoke, his voice was clipped, and his eyes guarded. 'You are my countess. Do as you will.'

Lucien left Ravenshold at dawn. Lying in a half-slumber while he pulled on his clothes, Isobel caught the words, 'Count Henry…Guardians…patrols…' before tumbling back into sleep.

When she next awoke, she lay in bed, thinking. It had been a relief to discover that Lucien's bedchamber had a fireplace. It was also clean, even if the furnishings were simple. Lucien's travelling chest sat next to hers. It was battered and scratched and had seen much service. *I shall have it repainted.* The blankets on the bed were perfectly serviceable, but Isobel had found one or two moth holes. *Those will have to be darned.* She was already planning other improvements. A blue coverlet. New linen for the sheets...

There was so much to be done. Today, she was going to comb through the castle from rooftop to cellar. She pushed aside the thought that she might find traces of Lucien's mistress; she was simply sizing up the task in hand. If she could restore Ravenshold to its former glory, Lucien would come to value her for something other than her lands. And if, in the meantime, she became pregnant, he also would value her for the heir she would give him. She didn't have long. Because soon, God help her, she would have no choice but to tell him that Angelina was with child.

Girande was fully recovered and eager to resume her position as Isobel's personal maid. This left Elise with nothing to occupy her, so Isobel took her with her as she did the rounds of the castle. They began in the bailey.

'Where first, my lady?' Elise asked.

The sky was clear. Elise was smiling, the sullen fearful girl of the day before had vanished. Isobel wondered if she had imagined her.

'You seem happy,' Isobel said.

'Oh, my lady, I am. I had no wish to throw myself on the mercy of the sisters.'

Isobel was pleased to have been able to help. She had not found life easy as she waited for Lucien to claim her, but she had always had her status. The nuns would never have starved her. Isobel suspected that there had been periods in Elise's life when she had not known where her next crust would come from.

'I am hopeful we shall become friends,' Isobel said. 'And one day, you might tell me how you came to find yourself at the Abbey.'

Elise's smile faltered. 'Yes, my lady.'

'This morning, we shall simply learn the lie of the land. Whilst we are doing that, I am hopeful of finding something that interests you. If not, there is bound to be plenty of needlework in a castle this size. Let's start on the battlements—it strikes me we shall see the layout best from there.'

They crossed the bailey, and were passing under

the shadow of one of the towers when a strong-limbed young man ran up. He was one of the knights Lucien had introduced the previous night. He had wavy hair the colour of ripe wheat and soulful brown eyes.

'Good morning, Lady Isobel.'

'Good morning, Sir…Gawain, is it not?'

'Aye, my lady, Gawain Steward.' He gave them both a little bow. Elise blushed. 'Count Lucien bid me to say that should you have any questions, you should apply to me. Although I must warn you, I have not been long at Ravenshold and the role of steward is new to me. I may not have all the answers.'

Isobel smiled at him. 'We are going to inspect the battlements, sir, and then we intend to explore.'

'If I may, I should be honoured to guide you,' Sir Gawain said.

'Thank you.'

With a flourish, Sir Gawain gestured towards a stairway that lay against the curtain wall. 'After you, my lady.'

At the top, Isobel paused to cast her eyes over the range of buildings huddled in the bailey. 'The hall and west tower I know already, since my lord has made the west tower his own. And that building down there is the stables,' she said, eyeing the sagging roof timbers. 'My lord showed me the new foal yesterday. I take it the building to the left of the stables is the smithy?'

'Aye, my lady. And the smaller building, the one near the west tower with smoke seeping through the vents, that's the bakehouse.'

'Thank you, Sir Gawain.' As Isobel scanned the yard, she frowned. Something was missing, no castle was complete without an armoury. Where was it? Her attention was drawn to the easternmost tower. 'And the east tower? Does that house the armoury?'

'Why, yes, my lady. The guardhouse takes up the ground floor, the armoury is above it.'

'And the upper floors?'

Sir Gawain cleared his throat, and though he continued to hold her gaze, it came to her that his stance was wary. 'I am not sure, my lady. I expect they are used for storage. I have not been above the armoury myself.'

The east tower, unlike its twin on the western side of the bailey, was completely shrouded in ivy. Weeds were growing around the base and, if Isobel were not mistaken, in cracks in the masonry at the top. 'The arrow-loops are choked with creeper.'

Sir Gawain flushed. 'I noticed that. The creeper will be attended to, my lady.'

'When we have finished up here, I should like to see the armoury.'

'It will be my pleasure to show it to you.'

Isobel stared a moment longer at the eastern tower, and shivered. The ivy had a stranglehold on the masonry, and some of the weeds at the base were so large, they must have taken root years ago. No part of Ravenshold was in prime condition, but the eastern tower had a particular air of abandonment. Of sadness. 'Are those brambles?'

'They too will be removed.'

'And the leaves. The bailey can't have been swept in a decade.'

Sir Gawain's lips twitched. 'As my lady commands.'

Giving the eastern tower a last glance, Isobel turned to look over the battlements towards the village. Praise the saints, here, all was in order. The field strips were clear of stubble and the earth was ploughed over, ready for winter. The vines had been neatly pruned. On the other side of the road was a small orchard, the grass beneath the fruit trees had been smoothly scythed. The contrast between the order outside the curtain walls and the disorder within was marked.

'Sir Gawain, it would seem that in my husband's

absence, his vassals have shown more diligence than the castle servants.'

'That appears to be true,' Sir Gawain said, carefully. 'Which reminds me, my lord asked me to tell you that tomorrow he is recruiting servants from the village. He wondered if you would care to join him in selecting them.'

'Thank you, Sir Gawain, I should be pleased to.'

Isobel gazed out at Lucien's land, and Sir Gawain stepped back to exchange words with a guard on the boardwalk.

'Dereliction,' Elise murmured. 'Complete dereliction.'

Elise was staring at the eastern tower, her expression arrested. Isobel followed her gaze. Doubtless Elise was referring to the weeds, the brambles, the drifts of leaves. Isobel didn't have the heart to chastise Elise for her insolence; any fool could see that Lucien's neglect of Ravenshold was shameful. It was odd though—the neglect seemed to be completely at variance with what Isobel had observed of his character.

His love of tournaments must be to blame. If he had directed all his energies towards the tourneys, he might have ignored his other duties. What about his other lands? Were they in the same state as Ravenshold? Could he not delegate? Sir Gawain struck her as being a responsible man. If Sir Gawain had only just been appointed steward, he was not to blame for conditions here. Who was Sir Gawain replacing? Whoever they were, they had been worse than useless. None of which spoke well of Lucien's ability to judge character.

'You will certainly be needing more servants, my lady,' Elise muttered. 'Other than a couple of stable-hands who Count Lucien seems to have taken on as pages, I've not seen any worthy of the name.'

Isobel climbed on to the parapet. They were almost above the gatehouse, and through the machicolations she could see the road below them.

'My lord has been occupied with the tourneys, Elise. Also, I believe his other holdings may have claimed his attention.' *At least, I hope they did. Dear Lord, don't let his other castles be as run-down as this one!*

Elise gave her a straight look. 'Lord d'Aveyron has been absent from Ravenshold for too long.'

Isobel bristled. 'You overstep the bounds, Elise; that is not for you to say.'

'I am sorry, my lady, I speak as I see.' Elise's eyes seemed to bore into her. 'And I see that you are already half in love with him. Take care, my lady, take care.'

'What can you mean?' Isobel's skin prickled as,

back on the boardwalk, Sir Gawain slapped the guard on the shoulder and started in their direction.

Elise leaned in. 'Take care, my lady, that is all. The Count is not what he seems.'

The Count is not what he seems?

And then Sir Gawain was back at her side, and Elise flushed and effaced herself in her usual manner, and Isobel had no opportunity to question her about her cryptic remark. Half her mind listened to Sir Gawain describing how Lucien had recently altered the span of time men sat on watch at the gatehouse. The other half was occupied in thinking about her husband.

Am I in love with him? She did not feel as though she was in love. In truth, Isobel did not know Lucien well enough to be in love with him. There was one sense in which they seemed to be ideally suited— in the bedchamber. Otherwise…

I hardly know him. He is a tourney champion with more prizes to his name than any other knight in Champagne. He allows Ravenshold to fall into rack and ruin, apparently without a qualm. He has great charm, charm he has no doubt employed to good effect over the years. He has admitted he has had lovers.

Isobel thought back to her arrival on the previous day, Lucien's charm had been much in evidence then. She had seen it in the easy manner in which he had greeted her, taking her straight to see the new foal. Was that all that had been—charm? Or was there more to it than that? Could it signify a growing bond between them? If only that were so. She was not in love but she did want him to like her.

Lucien does like you. A bond is forming between you. His delight in the foal was genuine and he wanted to share it with you.

On the other hand, she might be wrong. The bond might exist only in her mind.

Brow puckering, heavy of heart, Isobel cast her gaze over the weed-choked base of the tower. The brambles looked like tangled black wire. Impenetrable.

She sighed. If Lucien was not the man she had hoped for, she must make the best of it. She was his wife. She should count her blessings, and blessings there were…

He is gentle in bed, his touch is a joy—he has obviously had far too much practice at loving women. She grimaced. She would find out about his *belle amie* if it killed her.

In her mind, she conjured the image of a glittering diamond moon. *He is generous.* Another image flashed before her—of Lucien charging, pennon streaming, into the lists. *He is a great tourney champion.*

A gust of wind lifted the edge of her veil, and her skin chilled. *Elise said Lucien is not what he seems—what can she mean?*

Through a machicolation, there was movement. A girl in a moss-green cloak and grey gown was walking towards the gatehouse. Vaguely, Isobel was conscious of the girl hailing a sentry, but Sir Gawain was claiming her attention.

'My lady?'

'Sir?'

Sir Gawain embarked on a discussion about the crops which flourished best in the fields outside the curtain wall. Isobel nodded as he pointed out the neat rows of vines; the orchard; the villeins' field strips.

'You see that line of trees on the horizon, my lady?'

'I see them.'

'Just beyond the trees lies the Field of the Birds.'

'I had not realised it was so close to Ravenshold,' she murmured.

Sir Gawain leaned against a merlon, and launched into an account of the annual tournaments that in Lucien's father's day, the Lord of Ravenshold had hosted. Her husband wasn't the only knight in Ravenshold to be obsessed with tourneying; Isobel couldn't get a word in. At length, Sir Gawain came to a halt with a rueful grin, perhaps realising that his lord might not thank him for drawing his Countess's attention too forcibly to Ravenshold's past glories.

'My apologies, my lady, I talk too much.'

'Not at all, sir. I see you share my husband's interests.' Isobel turned to the stairs. 'I should like to see the armoury next.'

They were crossing the courtyard when Isobel noticed a fenced area behind the east tower. She could see shrubs and trees. A garden! And as far as Isobel could see, the garden was a far cry from the wasteland at the base of the east tower where ivy wrestled with bramble in the fight for survival. That bay tree had surely been pruned. Someone tended these plants.

'One moment, Sir Gawain, I must see that garden.'

'Of course. I shall wait for you here, my lady. I know nothing about gardens. Solène will answer your questions.'

'Solène?'

'Solène tends the herb garden.'

A pathway ran between the eastern tower and what looked like a storehouse. Isobel walked down it with Elise at her elbow. Herb beds were cut into a grassy area behind the tower, with hazel hurdles marking the boundary.

At this hour, the beds lay in the shadow of the eastern tower—a rosemary bush was rimed with frost. The beds were clear of weeds. The roses and lavender had been pruned, and the herbs harvested. A robin was pecking about in some straw that had been strewn over various plants to protect them from winter.

'Elise, I had thought to ask you to establish an herb garden, but there is no need. Thank Heaven, someone in Ravenshold understands her work,' Isobel said. 'Where is she?'

Elise indicated a thatched hut at the end of a grassy path. 'Perhaps she is in there, my lady?' Kneeling by the path, Elise bruised the leaves of the rosemary and sniffed her fingertips. 'This would be good in the kitchen.'

'Indeed it would,' Isobel said, going towards the hut.

As Isobel approached, the hut door opened. Solène, for this must be she, was some years older than Isobel. Dark eyes looked out from a face weathered by hours spent out of doors. Her hair was grey and thin. Plaited. And her hands—with their short, soil-engrained nails, and enlarged joints—were unquestionably the hands of a gardener. She was wearing a simple brown gown that was frayed at the hem.

'You are Solène?'

The dark eyes looked at her with curiosity, the skin around them creased. 'Aye, I am Solène. Who might you be?'

'I am Isobel of Turenne, now wife to Count Lucien.'

Solène's mouth sagged. '*Wife?* You are his *wife*?'

Thinking Solène might be hard of hearing, Isobel raised her voice. 'Yes, I am Countess d'Aveyron.' She gestured at the tidy herb beds. 'You must work hard to keep this garden in order.'

'Aye.' Solène's gaze flickered to Elise and returned to Isobel. 'Can I help you, my lady?'

'Not at present. Today I am learning my way around. Later I hope that you will supply herbs for the kitchen. I am also hoping you will be able to tell me whether my lord keeps a store of medicaments at Ravenshold.'

Solène gave a sharp bark of laughter. 'Not he. The other lady did, God save her, but her herbs will have lost their virtue. You will want fresh ones.'

'The *other* lady?'

Solène went white and backed towards the door of the hut. 'Tomorrow, my lady. We can talk tomorrow. Herbs for the kitchen, yes, I shall see to that.'

The door closed with a crack and Isobel found herself staring at a knot in the wood.

His other lady. Isobel had found the proof she was looking for. A wave of nausea swept through her. Lucien had lied. Her perfect, handsome knight had lied.

Chapter Fourteen

His other lady? Solène was talking about his mistress. *His other lady.*

Disappointment had turned Isobel's bones to ice. She felt brittle. Fragile. She had begun to trust Lucien, had begun to believe that he would not lie to her, and that he had spoken the truth when he had sworn that he did not have a mistress. But here was Solène, a long-time inhabitant of Ravenshold, mentioning another lady.

The Troyes gossips had known the truth of it. *Where is she? Has he sent her away?*

Haunting questions. Questions that remained with her as she walked through a haze of hurt to where Sir Gawain awaited them at the foot of the tower. Questions that lingered at the back of her mind as Sir Gawain escorted them into the guard-house on the ground floor. Elise did not speak, and Isobel stood with a fixed smile on her face as she was introduced to the guards. She hoped she said the right thing. The men's names escaped her. They said they were pleased to meet her, and she said that she was pleased to meet them—at least she hoped she did. They had good, honest faces.

'And now, my lady,' Sir Gawain said, gesturing at the stairwell. 'You wish to inspect the armoury?'

'My thanks, I do.' Isobel moved in a daze towards the twisting stair.

Lucien lied about his mistress. This should not upset me—I must remember ours is a political marriage. She repeated the words like a litany several times in her head—*ours is a political marriage.*

By the time she reached the armoury she had regained her composure. Two boys were sitting on three-legged stools in a stripe of light from a window, fletching arrows. A scatter of unfletched arrow-shafts lay on the table before them. Isobel blinked hard, the stink of glue was eye-watering.

The boys sprang to their feet. 'Countess Isobel! May we be of assistance?'

'It's all right, Renan,' Sir Gawain said. 'Please continue. I am looking after the Countess this morning.'

The boys sat and bent over their work.

The armoury was immaculate. The curved walls were whitewashed and hung with shields; a trestle held an assortment of swords and daggers of all sizes; several bows hung on a rack; and a collection of spears was stacked in a stand—tips gleaming razor-sharp. It would seem that the herb garden was not the only well-run part of the castle.

'How very telling,' Isobel murmured.

'My lady?'

'The armoury and guard-room betray where my husband's heart lies.' She lifted her chin. 'I cannot help but regret that he did not find someone reliable to take charge in the domestic sphere.'

Sir Gawain looked distinctly uncomfortable. 'Yes, my lady.'

Isobel watched the boys at their fletching, it was clear they had been well schooled. She sighed. She should feel relieved to have learned that in military matters her husband was in full command. But she didn't. She felt sick to the bone.

She looked brightly at Sir Gawain. 'Thank you for bringing me here. I shall go up the tower next.'

Sir Gawain's smile froze. 'The rooms above are disused, I wouldn't recommend it. It will be dusty. Dirty. Come, my lady.' He made a shooing gesture, urging her towards the stairwell. 'I will show you the kitchens.'

'I saw the kitchens yesterday.'

'Have you seen the log store, my lady? The undercroft?'

Sir Gawain was most anxious to dissuade her from climbing the tower. Isobel looked thoughtfully at him. What was he trying to hide? Her interest quickened. 'The *log store*? Really, sir, can't you do better than that?'

'My lady?'

Isobel gave him a straight look. 'Count Lucien has already told me the log store is empty. Since he has himself ordered supplies, I have no need to see it.'

'My lady...'

The desperation in Sir Gawain's expression would be laughable, if it were not so worrying. There was something on a higher floor that he was adamant she must not see. Evidence of Lucien's mistress? A bedchamber, perhaps? The more Lucien's knight tried to prevent her from climbing those stairs, the more anxious she was to go up.

'My lady, no one's been above the armoury in an age. It will be filthy up there. Unswept. You risk soiling that lovely gown—'

'Sir, I care not about my gown.' Giving him a sweet smile, Isobel picked up her skirts and stepped into the shady chill of the stairwell. 'I expect there will be a good view of my lord's lands from the top. Elise, you may wait below if you wish.'

'I shall come with you,' Elise said.

As Isobel and Elise began to climb, Sir Gawain's

voice wound up after them. 'The best view is from the *western* tower! My lady, Count Lucien will be most concerned to hear you have been risking yourself in such a way. I am not sure the upper floors are sound. Countess, this is most ill advised...'

The round chamber directly above the armoury appeared to be, as Sir Gawain had suggested, a storage room. Spare trestles were stacked against the wall, next to several packing crates. They were festooned with spiders' webs. A faded blue banner was propped next to them. Moths had eaten it down to the backing cloth—Lucien's raven looked as though it were in moult. There were two broken stools. A cracked clay pot. The rusted head of an axe lay in one corner, alongside a number of broken arrow shafts that should have gone for kindling months ago.

'It is as Sir Gawain said...' Elise murmured, lip curling as she fingered the banner and sent up a cloud of dust '...a storage room. Shall we go on?'

Isobel murmured assent, and followed Elise up another turn. She was relieved that Sir Gawain had not come with them. The room they had left might only be a storage room but she was certain there were secrets at the top.

The stairs came to an abrupt halt at a bolted iron

door leading on to the parapet. A wooden door next to it opened on another round chamber. It was not a bedchamber, it was a workroom. Of sorts.

'Blessed Mary, what is this place?' There was a table opposite the door and in the centre stood a stoppered glass jar of some rarity. Isobel's attention was caught, not by the jar, but by the contents. 'Is that a dead—?' She broke off abruptly.

Elise stood as though turned to stone in the middle of the chamber, hand over her mouth. The colour had leached from her face. Never had Isobel see anyone look more horrified. It was not hard to see why. Aside from the glass jar with its gruesome contents, there was a dead bird on the table, and any number of tiny bones. A scattering of shrivelled leaves had gone blue with dust. There were bunches of withered plants, dried roots...

Isobel drew Elise's hand away from her mouth. 'You need not stay,' she said softly. 'If you prefer, you can wait for me in the bailey.'

Elise's eyes were glassy with tears. 'It looks like a witch's lair.'

'I don't think there's anything here that can hurt you, Elise.'

'Is there not?' Elise asked, in a high, tight voice.

'It does look rather...unpleasant,' Isobel said, soothingly. 'Although I am sure there will be a perfectly innocent explanation. No witch has been here. Perhaps Solène uses this chamber to dry her herbs, perhaps—'

'This was not Solène's chamber.'

Isobel blinked, Elise sounded so definite. 'How can you know?'

Shaking her head, eyes brimming with tears, Elise backed out of the chamber. 'I…I am sorry, my lady. I cannot stay.'

Isobel nodded and Elise fled. Turning back to the trestle, Isobel looked blindly at the grisly display and gritted her teeth. Determination pinned her in place when, in truth, it would have been easier to go after Elise; she did seem upset. *I have to find out what this chamber was used for and, more importantly, who has been using it. Lucien's mistress? Solène?* There would be time to reassure Elise later. When Isobel heard what she had been waiting for—the bang of the door at the base of the tower—she lifted her head.

The room was lit by a lancet on the south wall, and the light was much dimmed by a curtain of cobwebs. Isobel wiped the embrasure clear of the worst of the cobwebs and dust, and brushed off her hands.

The window was unglazed. Outside, the wind was rushing past the tower, a waterfall of cold poured in on her. There was no fireplace. Come midwinter everything would freeze solid. Ignoring the chill, Isobel looked out of the window.

Sir Gawain had lied about the view. From the top of the east tower, one could see everything. Down there was the bailey and the stables. Down there was the gatehouse and curtain wall, and beyond that the fields and vineyards. The forest was a charcoal smudge, darkening the horizon. Rooks dotted the sky. Isobel could see the stone cross mounted on the roof of the village church. Riders were approaching—a knight and his squire. The knight's destrier was black and a blue shield was strapped on his left. He had looped his helmet over the pommel of his saddle.

Lucien! She had not expected him back from Troyes so soon. Wanting to observe him without being seen herself, she kept very still. From her high vantage point, his features were indistinguishable—he was simply a dark-haired knight riding through the arch with his squire at his side. Isobel could hear the faint clop of hoofs and a guard greeting his returning lord.

Lucien was trotting into the bailey when a woman called out. *'Count Lucien! My lord!'*

Isobel watched him twist in the saddle to look back. She couldn't breathe. She caught a hint of movement outside her line of sight beyond the gatehouse—something moss green in colour and…

The woman spoke again. Her words were snatched by the wind. Isobel pinned her gaze on Lucien. Earlier, a woman in a moss-green cloak had been speaking to the sentries. Had she been waiting for Lucien? Her heart sank. *Was this his mistress?*

Dismounting, Lucien strode back to the gatehouse, leaving Joris to lead Demon into the stable. By craning her neck and pressing her cheek against the cold stone embrasure, Isobel kept her husband in sight. He stood under the arch next to a guard, taller than he by a head. There was a tantalising flash of green, and an exchange of words that Isobel had no chance of hearing. Lucien made a dismissive gesture, and turned on his heel.

Isobel released her breath. What was that about?

She watched as Sir Gawain appeared in the bailey, and Lucien altered course to meet him. Her pulse jumped. More words were exchanged and they too were whipped away, but Isobel did not need to hear them to know what Sir Gawain had said.

He had told Lucien that his lady had gone into the east tower. When Sir Gawain pointed up, she ducked out of sight. When she next looked, the bailey was empty save for a flurry of leaves skittering across the stones by the water troughs. Her nails dug into her palms. Her investigation of this chamber was going to have to wait, for if she was not mistaken, her husband was about to join her.

A couple of heartbeats later, quick footsteps mounted the stairs a few turns below.

Ignoring the chainmail weighing him down, Lucien forged up the spiralling stairs. He was hoping against hope that Gawain was mistaken. Gawain had to be mistaken. He did not want to find Isobel in Morwenna's room because it was too soon to confess past sins, far too soon. Lucien wanted his new wife's regard, but he did not flatter himself that she loved him. *The bond between us is, as yet, ephemeral. Yes, we are married, but she is not ready to hear about Morwenna.*

That morning, Lucien had instructed Gawain to keep Isobel away from Morwenna's workroom. Lulled by the carnal attraction between them, he had thought that Isobel would heed Gawain's advice. More fool he. Isobel only did as she was told when it suited her; she was a wilful woman. One reason he had changed his mind about bringing her to Ravenshold was because she had flouted his authority over the All Hallows Tourney. He had thought he could keep an eye on her at Ravenshold. He had thought…

He pounded up another twist of stairs, and cursed himself for being a sentimental fool. He should not have given her the run of Ravenshold until Morwenna's workroom had been cleared. He would be the first to admit he was no expert on women, but he was clear on one point. Isobel did not yet fully trust him, she did not love him. And he wanted her love. Lucien might struggle to understand what love was, but he wanted his new wife to love him. He wanted it more than he had wanted the champion's prize at the last tourney, which was passing strange, since he was not certain that he himself was capable of love.

Morwenna had made certain of that. Never again would he look at a woman and know that she was the sum of his desires. Never again would he…

Hell, what did it matter? In the deepest recesses of his soul, despite the wailings of the troubadours, Lucien had long suspected that love did not exist. He could not think why he should crave Isobel's love. Love was likely a delusion brought on by an excess of desire. Of lust. Love was longing for the unattainable. There was little to be gained by him desiring Isobel's.

Far better to win her affection. That was the real prize. If he had Isobel's affection, he would have the upper hand. He would have control. That was what counted with women, they needed to know who had the upper hand. If Isobel felt affection for him, she would be more likely to give him children. Children with green eyes and…

Chest heaving, Lucien reached the top. Isobel was standing in front of Morwenna's workbench. The way she was looking at him sent icy sweat trickling down his neck.

'Is that your mistress?'

'What?' Lucien's mind was still populated with green-eyed children, and her question threw him. 'What are you talking about?'

'The woman by the gatehouse, is she your *belle amie*?'

'Isobel, how many times must I tell you? I have no *belle amie*.'

'You, my lord, are a liar.' Isobel spread her arms to encompass the chamber. 'Whose workroom is this? Why was Sir Gawain so keen to prevent me coming in here?' A slim finger poked disdainfully at an empty eggshell. 'To whom do these squalid objects belong?'

The time for prevarication was over. Lucien looked her straight in the eye. 'I asked Gawain to steer you clear of here because I didn't think you were ready for the truth.'

'The truth? What truth?'

With a sigh, Lucien picked a purple bead out of

the mess on the table and stared sadly at it. It was glass, one side of it was chipped. He remembered Morwenna's excitement when she had found it. Her eyes had taken fire as she had told him that it was ancient, a relic of the era when Troyes had been occupied by the Romans. 'I hoped to have more time with you, Isobel, before I explained.'

'Where is the woman to whom these things belong? Have you sent her away?'

Taking her arm, Lucien took her to the window. 'See the church?'

She sent him a puzzled look. 'I can see the cross on the church roof.'

Lucien took a huge breath before he spoke again. 'She lies in the graveyard.'

'I…I don't understand.'

'The woman who used to work in here is dead. This was my wife Morwenna's chamber. She lies in the churchyard yonder.'

Isobel went white. The rooks cawed outside. 'You were married before? To a woman called Morwenna?'

'Yes.'

She groped for a stool and sank down. Swallowed. 'So there never was a mistress.'

'No.'

'Just a wife. A *wife*.'

'Isobel—'

'When...when did she die, this Morwenna?'

Holding her gaze, Lucien put his hand on her shoulder. She shrugged it off.

'When?'

'At summer's end.'

'This summer just past?'

'Yes.'

'That would be about the time my mother died,' she said softly.

She was staring at the wall, her face a mask. Again, he reached for her shoulder, again she shook him off. 'Isobel?'

'I am your *second* wife.'

He nodded; anxiety sat chill in his guts. *It is too soon. She is not ready to hear this.* Briefly, he debated with himself whether there was anything to be gained by fending off further questions. *No. She has been deceived for too long.* It was a pity she had stumbled across this chamber so soon after her arrival, but since she had, he would confess all.

'When did you marry her?'

He pinched the bridge of his nose. 'Iso—'

She jumped to her feet, hands clenched at her sides. *'When?'*

'I was fifteen.'

Her mouth fell open. Jerking her gaze away, she

glowered at the cluttered table. 'My lord, you were fifteen at our betrothal ceremony.'

He reached for her chin and waited for those green eyes to meet his. 'My first marriage was a mistake, Isobel. A youthful folly. I hoped…I thought to get an annulment.'

'Did your father know?'

Lucien took her hand and led her firmly away from the table. 'I told him, yes. He disapproved most heartily and pushed for an annulment. At first, I did not agree.' She opened her mouth, but he pressed on. 'Hear me out, Isobel, I am tired of living this lie. When I married Morwenna, I fancied myself in love with her. She was a few years older than me—and very beautiful. I should not have married her, I know. I went against my father's wishes to do so.' He shrugged. 'What can I say? I was young and Morwenna was an enchantress.'

'You fell in love.'

'I *thought* I fell in love. In truth, I was in love with a pretty shell. I didn't know her. It didn't take long to discover what a schemer she was. Morwenna married me for the lands that I would inherit on my father's death.'

Isobel made an impatient sound. 'In itself that is no sin. You are the Comte d'Aveyron, I was to marry you for the same reason. Just as you have married me for Turenne. Our marriage is dynastic.'

Lucien looked down at the hand he had enfolded in his. It was so small. He squeezed it and whilst she did not return the gesture, he took it as a good sign that she had not wrenched it away from him. 'You don't understand. Before our wedding, Morwenna told me she loved me. When she told me she was pregnant, I believed her. I married her because she said she was carrying my child.'

Green eyes looked steadily into his. 'And she wasn't?'

He grimaced, shaking his head. 'She thought to force my hand. Though if the truth be known, I was so bedazzled, I would have married her anyway.'

'Fifteen.' Her voice was strangled. 'And you allowed our betrothal to take place.'

'For that I can only say I am deeply sorry.'

'Why? Why betroth yourself to me when you were already married?'

Lucien shoved his hand through his hair. 'That was my father's doing. He almost had an apoplexy when he heard how I had been trapped into marriage. Negotiations for my betrothal to you were well in hand, and Father decided I could be extricated from my marriage to Morwenna without anyone knowing about it.' Lucien gave a bitter laugh. 'He thought it would be simple.'

'Your father was pressing for an annulment at the time of our betrothal?'

Lucien nodded. 'Most vigorously. He insisted our betrothal went ahead—he was confident it would take but a couple of months to be granted an annulment. By the time you and I were betrothed, I was desperate for him to be right. The scales had fallen from my eyes and I saw Morwenna clearly. In marrying her, I had made a grievous error of judgement.' Gently, he touched her cheek. 'I wanted nothing more than to end the marriage, but as the years went by, I realised an annulment was not going to be possible.'

'Where was honour in this?' she asked, voice sharp. 'Honour should have dictated you confessed about your marriage. Honour would insist that you waited before becoming betrothed to me.'

'I won't deny it, you are in the right. My only defence—and it is no excuse—is that Father convinced me an annulment could be swiftly achieved. He was loath to risk the alliance between d'Aveyron and Turenne.'

Isobel was listening, but Lucien sensed that she was poised for flight and might bolt at any moment. He tightened his hold and watched as she glanced down at their joined hands. Her mouth was set in a bitter line. It was not the mouth of the woman he had been wooing over the last few days; it was the mouth of a slighted woman, a woman who might never forgive him.

'Release me, my lord.'

Lucien's breath caught. For a sickening moment, he thought she was saying she wanted their marriage annulled.

She moved her hand. 'Count Lucien, I can no longer feel my fingers.'

Count Lucien. His hand fell away from hers.

'Thank you. My lord, I accept you were young when we were betrothed. We both were. Child that I was, I believed you to be the soul of honour. And now I find…' She broke off, shaking her head. 'My lord, the deception you practised upon me is so far from honourable as to be unspeakable. You say you did not know Morwenna when you married her. I say I did not know you when we were betrothed. I am no wiser today. What sort of a man are you? An honourable knight?' Her eyes held nothing but scorn. 'A champion who is the pattern of chivalry?'

'Isobel, I deeply regret—'

'When were you going to tell me? Were you ever going to tell me?'

'I was waiting for the right moment. I hoped to

earn your regard first. I feared that if you learned too soon into our marriage, you would hate me.'

'My lord, the right moment to tell me was nine years ago.'

'Forgive me.'

'I am not sure that I can.' Her voice was calm. Distant. She went to the door, her movements as unhurried and cool as her voice. Lucien would have felt better if she railed and shouted at him; this *sang-froid* seemed unnatural. Ominous.

'Isobel, wait, there is more. I would have you know it all before I am condemned.'

She paused on the threshold. Her chest heaved. 'I don't want to hear it, I can't.' She gave him a brief curtsy. 'Doubtless, I shall see you at the evening meal. Until then, my lord, I should be grateful if you would grant me space to breathe.'

Lucien's deception had cut Isobel to the quick, she had run to the bedchamber in the west tower before remembering that her husband would be well within his rights to follow her.

Elise was sitting disconsolately on the bed—her eyelids were swollen and her eyes red. She leaped to her feet and hastily smoothed the blankets. 'My lady, I must apologise. I should not have rushed off like that, it is just...' With a sniff, Elise rubbed her nose with the back of her hand.

Elise looked so woebegone that Isobel gave her a quick hug. 'What was it about the workroom in the east tower that so upset you? I grant you, it's not particularly pleasant, but there is nothing there that can harm you.' She couldn't bring herself to tell Elise that the workroom had been used by Lucien's first wife; she had some pride.

His first wife. Lord, what a revelation! At least Lucien had had the grace to look ashamed when he had told her.

Elise gulped. 'It...I...'

'You need not fear. The person who used that chamber is no longer at Ravenshold.'

'I knew that as soon as I saw it,' came the surprising reply. 'I am sorry to make such a fuss—I don't know what came over me.'

'I knew that as soon as I saw it.' What does that mean? Thoughtfully, Isobel studied her. When they had gone up on the battlements, Elise had warned her to take care. What else had she said? Something about Lucien...

'Elise, I can see you know more than you have told me. What did you mean when you told me that my lord was not what he seemed?'

Did Elise know that Lucien had been married before? If so, how? The secret of his first marriage had apparently been better guarded than silver in the King's treasury…though given how long Morwenna had lived at Ravenshold, a number of people must have known about it. Who were they? Sir Gawain had tried to prevent her from climbing to the top of the east tower, so he must know. Did Sir Raoul know? How many others?

'The women in Troyes spoke of a mistress,' Isobel murmured, thinking aloud. 'They knew he kept someone here, only they did not realise it was his—' She broke off, Elise's eyes were particularly sharp. Watchful. Isobel needed to think before she aired the matter of her husband's first marriage with a young woman she had met only a few days ago. 'Elise, I need time for reflection.'

Elise edged to the door. 'I shall leave you in peace.'

'My thanks, but you may stay if you are in need of company.'

'I am fine, thank you, my lady. I would welcome the chance to speak to Solène.'

'About the herb garden? That is a good idea.' Isobel smiled, but it was a false smile, there was a burning sensation at the back of her eyes. 'Solène will welcome your company. You're quite an expert, after all.'

When Elise had gone, Isobel moved to the window embrasure. The shutter was pinned back, but the bedchamber was gloomy and shadowed—a dark mass of cloud was filling the sky. *Lucien was married. All those years I waited for him to come for me and he was married.* It was hard to know whether to laugh or cry. *He belittled me.* And yet—the shock must have disordered her mind—she felt no surprise.

This could explain much...Lucien's tardiness at claiming me when most of the other girls had left the convent to be married...and, possibly, his obsession with tournaments.

It struck her that Lucien had not mentioned Morwenna's family. Who was she? Had she brought him lands? Prestige?

Her stomach was churning. She forced herself to think logically, to tease what she had learned into some kind of order. *Lucien was young when he married Morwenna. Fifteen. He was little more than a boy.* Lucien claimed to have soon become disillusioned as to his wife's character; he claimed to have wanted an annulment. Isobel shook her head. What a tangle...

Lucien loved Morwenna when he married her. Does he still love her? For her, that was a key question. It ought not to be. *Ours is a political marriage. Love is irrelevant, however much I might wish otherwise.*

Taking a deep breath, Isobel stared at a faded wall-hanging. There was much left to sort. The lack of an annulment appeared to confirm Lucien's continuing love for Morwenna. However, she was coming to know him; he had looked sincere when he had said that his first marriage had been a youthful folly.

Isobel had hardly known the previous Comte d'Aveyron, Lucien's father. She had met him but once, at the betrothal. A heavy-set man with a stiff gait and a bark for a voice, Lucien's father had made her eleven-year-old self shake in her shoes. And if Lucien could be believed, his father had decreed that the marriage to Morwenna must be annulled. This had not happened. Why? If Lucien's father had insisted on an annulment, it would have been hard, if not impossible, for his fifteen-year-old son to gainsay him.

Lucien must have loved her. Despite his protestations to the contrary, the lack of an annulment pointed strongly that way. Though if that were the case, why devote so much of his life to tourneying? Why visit Ravenshold so rarely?

Here was mystery. Mystery upon mystery. She clenched her fists. She should not have rushed out of that horrible chamber, she should have stayed to learn more. If she had not been so upset, she would have done. *I care too much. I really do care for him—that is why I am upset.*

It was an unwelcome thought. And impossible. She should not care about a man who had deceived her so shamefully. Picking up her skirts, she left the bedchamber and went in search of him.

Chapter Fifteen

Lucien wasn't in the hall or the bailey. No matter. Isobel made a beeline for the east tower, and hurried up the circling stairs. She half-expected someone to stop her, but no one did. Up she went, up past the guardhouse and armoury, up past the storeroom and into Morwenna's workroom. Lucien wasn't there either. She felt herself relax. In truth, it would be easier looking for answers without him breathing over her shoulder.

Who was Morwenna? Why the great mystery surrounding their marriage? Once Lucien had dropped the idea of an annulment, why the continuing secrecy?

A slash of sun lay bright as a sword across the dusty table. The glass bead winked in the light. When Lucien had looked at that bead, his face had been lined with pain and regret.

'Morwenna's workroom,' Isobel murmured, running her gaze over the pestle and mortar; over a curl of yellowing parchment and scrap of red linen; over the dried herbs and tiny bones...

It was such a grisly collection. She poked at a tiny skull—a vole's?—and shuddered. What use could Morwenna possibly have had for the skull of a vole?

This chamber belonged to Lucien's wife. His wife. It was impossible to remain dispassionate. Elise was right—it might be taken for a witch's lair. It would take time to sort through everything; she must be methodical. Calm. Taking a deep breath, Isobel pushed back her sleeves and began.

It didn't take as long as she had imagined. Half an hour and she had combed through the entire collection. Her fingertips were grey with dust, her nose itched, and she had found nothing to throw light on Morwenna and Lucien's marriage. Rubbing her nose to hold in a sneeze, she stepped back from the table. It was time to seek out her husband. Lucien must be made to leave the past behind. Whatever he felt for Morwenna, it mattered little. *Morwenna is dead. There will be no ghosts in our marriage—Lucien has married me, and I intend to keep him.*

Their future might be loveless, but that would not affect her ability to manage his household. She had been well taught. Difficulties might arise with her other duties. She must give him sons. Doubt was a sour taste in her mouth, almost as bitter as the herbs she had taken for so brief a time. Only God knew whether she was capable of giving him a son. Only God knew whether she would survive. *I must put my trust in God.*

Today, she would begin her management of Lucien's household by having this chamber cleared. Almost everything could go straight on a fire. The plaster must be renewed—large sections had come away from the wall. Then the chamber could be whitewashed, and then...

Her gaze sharpened. At about waist height, the plaster had fallen away to reveal the wall behind. A small stone protruded. It looked loose, out of place...

The skin prickled on the back of her neck and before she knew it, she had pushed her fingers into the crack and was working at the stone. Pulling, twisting. A fingernail snagged but she kept going until, grating slightly, the stone shifted and thudded to the floor. What remained was a small shelf, rather like a church aumbry. Heart thudding, she peered in. The sharp shine of blue enamel winked out at her. The softer shine of gold. A Limoges reliquary! And she recognised it.

Fingers trembling, she lifted it out. *The stolen*

reliquary! Here? How is this possible? Does Lucien know?

Even as that last question formed, she dismissed it. Lucien had kept her in the dark about Morwenna, but he would have no dealings with thieves. Besides, he had been with her when the relic was taken.

The reliquary glittered, the enamel was jewel-bright. Sapphire, ruby, emerald...

Who put it here? Someone in Ravenshold was in collusion with the thief. Who?

It could not have been Morwenna; she had died before the theft took place.

Isobel put the reliquary on the trestle. Was there no end to the mysteries? Saints, when she had ridden into Ravenshold, she had ridden into a maze.

At the bottom of the stairs, a door slammed. Quick footsteps, Lucien's, were hurrying up the stairs. Good. She flicked the scrap of red linen over the reliquary. Lucien had said he had more to tell her earlier, and she had refused to hear him. This time she would listen. She would ask her questions. She needed to hear about Morwenna.

Then she would show him the reliquary.

Lucien halted in the doorway. He had removed his chainmail and wore a blue tunic over a grey shirt. His hair was damp at the ends—he had washed away the dirt of the road before presenting himself to her again.

Hand on his sword-hilt, he gave her a crooked smile. A charming smile. A smile that had doubtless melted the hearts of a dozen maidens on the tourney circuit. It certainly went some way to melting hers. Lucien was far too attractive for Isobel's peace of mind, it was hard to remain aloof. He was blessed with both strength and height—far better formed than his father. His every feature somehow contrived to give him the advantage, even that scar. It wasn't fair.

Next to him, she must look a mess. Her hands were dirty, and there was dust on the hem of her gown. It was likely she had cobwebs in her hair and veil. She lifted her chin. 'My lord?' When he bowed, the formality of it tugged at her heartstrings.

'My Lady, you will hear me out?'

Steeling herself against him as he came towards her, she nodded. She was not going to notice the width of the broad shoulders stretching the blue cloth of his tunic. She was not going to notice that the colour of his tunic matched his eyes.

'Morwenna was beautiful,' he said, going straight to the heart of things. 'She was beautiful, she was older than I and, although I did not realise when I met her, experienced with men. Morwenna had power, the power of a seductress. Once she saw she fascinated me, she did not hesitate to use it.'

'She seduced you.'

'It was more than that—I imagined myself in love with her.'

Isobel held her breath. 'And now?'

He made a swift, negative gesture. 'What I felt for Morwenna has long gone. Her lies about carrying my child saw to that.'

Isobel let what he had said sink deep into her mind. His demeanour, his expression, his tone of voice—all spoke of sincerity. *He is so convincing, I ache to believe him. And that is my weakness, I want to believe him.*

She stood very straight. 'My lord, earlier you said that both you and your father wanted your first marriage to be annulled. Why was it allowed to stand?'

Lucien stared bleakly at the littered table. 'It was allowed to stand because it became clear that Morwenna was not capable of living on her own.'

Isobel's chest squeezed. This was the source of his pain. His regret. She touched his sleeve. 'Tell me more. Could she not have returned to her family?'

The dark head lifted. 'Morwenna had no family, or none that I could find. Her lack of status was at the root of my father's objections.' He inhaled deeply.

'As I understand it, her father was a troubadour. She was illegitimate.'

'Her father was a troubadour?' Isobel felt her jaw drop, and quickly wiped the shock from her face. It was one thing for Lucien to flout his father's wishes by marrying without his permission, but quite another for him to have married the illegitimate daughter of a trouvère. He must have been well and truly bespelled. No wonder his father had been so displeased. Lucien had married far, far below him.

'Imagine, the heir to the Comte d'Aveyron marrying the illegitimate daughter of a troubadour,' he said, mouth twisting. 'My father damn near disowned me. He would have done if he had had a second son.' He glanced at her, face softening. 'As you know, he planned for me to marry a different woman altogether. A noblewoman from a proud and ancient family.' A strong hand came up and gently straightened her veil. 'Isobel, he wanted to see us wed, and I regret very much that he did not live to see that day. Believe me when I say I also regret that you and I were not able to marry sooner.'

Isobel hesitated. The more Lucien told her about his first marriage, the more questions sprang into being. Morwenna's lack of family on its own was not enough to explain why the marriage had not been annulled. Women whose husbands set them aside had choices, limited ones to be sure, but they still had choices. Morwenna could have entered a convent; Lucien could have given her a small grant of land; he could have—

'Isobel?'

She grimaced. 'My mind is in a tangle; it is hard to know what to think. But Morwenna's lack of family in itself does not explain why she was not…' *how had he put it?* '…capable of living on her own.'

Lucien fingered the scar on his temple, and looked bleakly at the cluttered table. 'It was all this…this witchery.'

Isobel's blood went cold. 'Witchery?'

'Not witchery, of course, I don't mean that literally. But you can see for yourself how she was. Her interest in herbs bordered on the obsessive. Morwenna was for ever making ointments and potions and elixirs. You couldn't get her out of here. It was unnatural. When my father met her, he disliked her on sight. Frankly, he thought her mad.'

He was fingering the scar on the side of his temple again, his gaze focused on a grim landscape in his past.

'Your father died not long after our betrothal,' Isobel said softly. There was a lump in her throat as she came to a dreadful realisation. *Lucien blames himself for his father's death.*

'My father died shortly after I told him that I had changed my mind about seeking an annulment.'

Reaching out to cup her face with his palms, blue eyes looked deeply into hers. 'Isobel, I wanted nothing more than to escape Morwenna. I couldn't. She was incapable of living on her own. Excited. Dabbling one minute—suicidal the next. I had married her, and I had a responsibility to her. She had never known security, so I brought her to Ravenshold, hoping that she would come to her senses if she spent some time in a safe place.' His hands fell away, his expression was tortured.

'You brought her here because Ravenshold is far from d'Aveyron,' Isobel said.

'Exactly. I took pains not to broadcast news of my marriage, and only a handful of trusted friends and retainers know of it. My father had fought for the alliance with your family and after his death I was determined that some day, somehow, I would honour our betrothal agreement. I kept waiting for Morwenna to come to her senses, at least enough so that I could divorce her and give her a settlement.' He touched the scar on his temple. 'After the stoning, there was no hope of that.'

Isobel's eyes widened. 'The *stoning*?'

'The villagers feared her. Rumours spread that I kept a witch as a mistress. One day Morwenna left

Ravenshold to collect wild herbs and a mob gathered. They started by throwing taunts. Stones soon followed. I intervened.'

'So that is how you got that scar. I had assumed it was a battle-scar.'

His mouth thinned. 'It is a battle-scar—I got it dragging Morwenna back into the bailey.'

'You saved her. And kept her here.' She gestured about the chamber, at the trestle table, at the cobweb-hung lancet.

His eyebrows snapped together. 'Morwenna was not imprisoned! She had the run of Ravenshold. Although after the stoning, she was reluctant to venture past the gates.'

'No one can blame her for that.'

Silence stretched between them. Wind whistled past the cobwebs, lifting a feather from the table, wafting it from side to side as it fell to the floor.

Lucien did his best for Morwenna. He says he no longer loved her—there is no way I may discover whether that is the truth or not. In a sense, it is irrelevant. What matters is that Lucien fulfilled his duties as her husband. He behaved honourably towards her. It would have been impossible for him to honour his duty to Morwenna and to me. Impossible.

If only I had known...all those years I resented his neglect.

All those lost years...

He searched her face. 'I deceived you. You cannot forgive me.'

'I didn't say that.' When he shifted closer, she held up her hand to keep him at bay. 'Although I confess it is hard. I can see you did your best for Morwenna. You treated her with honour, by seeing she was safe. No convent would have taken her in with whispers of witchcraft hanging about her.'

'Morwenna was not fit to look after herself.'

'So she remained here, and one of your knights acted as her guardian.'

'Exactly. Sir Arthur Ferrer—you have yet to meet him—was invaluable. As was Solène. They kept me informed as to Morwenna's well-being. It was painful to visit, and latterly, when my presence began to distress her, I remained away. As a courtesy I gave her the run of Ravenshold. As long as she did herself no harm, I told Arthur to allow her complete authority within the castle.'

'And Morwenna let it fall into ruin.'

'As you see.' He smiled sadly. 'It was a blessing I put the lands in Arthur's charge, they are in good order.'

Isobel was beginning to see daylight. Morwenna had not shown any interest in the castle's upkeep, and Lucien had stayed away. The castle's dereliction was not due to Lucien's negligence or his incompetence as an overlord. *It looks as though I have misjudged him.*

'Lucien, forgive me if this is painful, but how did she die?'

A pulse beat in his cheek, just below the scar. 'She drowned in the moat.'

'She drowned! Lucien, I am so sorry.' Impulsively, she squeezed his arm. The moat was *outside* the bailey walls. So… 'Morwenna must have found a reason to leave the castle.'

'You are astute. I have been wondering about that too. After the attack on her, she rarely set foot past the gatehouse.' His chest heaved. 'Yet the day she died, something made her go outside. Solène has suggested she went to gather herbs. She used to do that often before the villagers turned against her.'

'Did it happen in daylight? Surely someone saw something? A guard? A villager?'

'We can find no witnesses, no one will admit to seeing a thing. Sir Arthur made enquiries. He left no stone unturned and he found nothing. Sir Gawain and I have done no better. Personally, I am inclined to believe Solène has the right of it. Morwenna went out to gather herbs. I suspect we shall never know the full truth.'

Isobel glanced thoughtfully at the reliquary concealed beneath the red cloth. It made no sense to find it in Morwenna's workroom, the theft had happened *after* her death. Thank the Lord, there could be no possible link between Morwenna and the thief. Lucien had had enough to concern him without the added worry that his dead wife might have been colluding with thieves.

Although someone in Ravenshold had to be involved. Who? Sir Raoul was out of the question. As was Sir Gawain. And Solène had struck her as an honest woman…

'Where is Sir Arthur?'

'Arthur's in Troyes. His tenure here has finished—he's enlisted as one of Count Henry's Guardians.'

'Do you trust him?'

'I would put my life in his hands and rest easy.'

Helplessly, Isobel looked at Lucien. She had not been at Ravenshold long enough to know who else might be involved. And the relic ought to be returned to Abbess Ursula as soon as possible. She must set aside her reservations, her anger, and her hurt pride. She and Lucien were married. If they did not learn to work together, there was no hope for them.

This is the time to tell him about the reliquary.

Isobel looked like a queen, Lucien thought. Beautiful and unattainable. She was standing in a shaft of sunlight, though how she looked so queenly was a mystery given she was wearing the most dusty, unqueenly gown in Champagne. The gown revealed more curves than it concealed—a waist that he could span with two hands; the roundness of her hips; the alluring press of soft breasts against the bodice. Tendrils of hair curled in some disorder about her forehead—fine filaments of pure gold. A fitting crown for a woman who had the bearing of a queen. A very desirable queen.

Her mouth was turned down at the corners. There was a wariness about her that he had not seen before; it had been apparent the moment he'd walked in. It was hardly surprising—learning about Morwenna had opened a gulf between them. Lucien had anticipated just such an outcome. What he had not anticipated was how much it would disturb him. He did not want to be distanced from Isobel.

Isobel had control, he would give her that. Learning about Morwenna must have knocked her back. Yet she had not shouted and screamed, she had simply retreated. He smiled to himself. Her training was showing, retreat was a nun's solution. He looked at her mouth again, wondering when he would win another smile. Isobel might have been trained by nuns, but she was no nun herself.

She had returned to hear him out. In similar circumstances, Morwenna would have raged and stormed, there would have been floods of tears and the rending of clothes. The two women could not be more different.

Lucien found himself watching her mouth, hoping to see it relax. He ached to kiss her. He wanted to carry her off to his bed and make love to her. If Isobel gave him leave, if she let their bodies speak to each other, he was certain they could bridge that gulf.

Trust. Isobel no longer trusts me, I have to teach her to trust me. This was of overriding importance. Lucien couldn't quite account for how important it was, save to say that it was simply unacceptable for there to be distance between them. The quickest way to regain that sense of closeness was surely to possess her. Utterly. Thoroughly. *I want her.*

The chill in her eyes told him there was slim chance of that happening until he had made amends. Despite the polite facade, Isobel had not buried her anger. She was shocked, perhaps hurt. What else was going through her head? He had no idea. What had she been doing when he came in? Trying to find out about Morwenna? It was only natural, he supposed. Women were inquisitive.

She was biting her lip and he wished she wouldn't. Particularly when he was trying to do the right thing and stop thinking about kissing her. About more than kissing her—

'Lucien, there's something you must see.'

'Hmm?'

Her brow furrowed and she blushed so prettily he felt a secret throb of desire. 'Lucien, you are not paying attention. This is important.'

Lucien hid a smile, she looked so earnest. He might not know his wife's thoughts, but apparently she found it easy to divine the carnal direction of his. Heartened by the blush—it must mean her heart was not set completely against him—he moved closer, but the moment he was inhaling that tantalising hint of honeysuckle and roses, an imperious hand was raised to hold him off. None the less, he would swear the sparkle was back in her eyes. She looked less guarded. Something inside him relaxed. Thank God, the gulf was not impassable...

He looked down at her. 'You have something to show me, little dove?'

Her flush deepened, and she made a 'tsking' sound. 'Lucien, please.' But he could see how her eyes had darkened. Triumphant—*she still desires me!*—he reached for her even as she twisted away. His arms closed on empty air.

'Lucien, look.'

There was a faded red cloth on the table. She

whisked it aside and he found himself staring at a gilt casket, an enamelled gilt casket of great rarity. One glance and he knew its provenance. *Limoges reliquary.* Blue enamel gleamed; gold glittered; long-robed saints peered out through a border of roses.

'What the devil?' Lucien picked it up. 'This is the reliquary that was snatched from the Abbey.' He took the time to study it. The border of roses formed a trellis behind which the saints marched along, haloes agleam. Each figure and rose was enamelled with breathtaking artistry. Here was the blue of lapis lazuli; this red reminded him of poppies; this yellow was the colour of Isobel's hair when touched by sunlight...

Their eyes met.

'What the blazes is this doing at Ravenshold?'

Isobel spread her hands. 'I was hoping you might offer a suggestion...'

'Where did you find it? It wasn't on the table earlier.'

She waved at a cavity in the wall where the plaster had fallen away. 'It was in there. This stone...' she nudged a chunk of fallen masonry with her shoe '...was wedged in front to hide it.'

He gave her a penetrating look. 'It can't have been

Morwenna, if that is what you are implying. Morwenna—'

'—died before the reliquary was taken.' Cool fingers briefly touched his. 'Lucien, I realise Morwenna wasn't involved. But someone was. It didn't get there by itself.'

Lucien shook his head. 'If I hadn't seen it here I would never have believed it. No one at Ravenshold would—' He broke off, thinking. Remembering. 'Geoffrey,' he said, and even to his own ears, his voice was hollow. 'It could have been Geoffrey.'

Lucien set the reliquary back on the trestle and rubbed his forehead. 'I was beginning to suspect he might be involved. Earlier, when Joris and I came back from Troyes, a woman hailed me by the gatehouse.'

'The girl in the dark-green cloak?'

'That's the one.'

Isobel nodded. 'I saw her from the walkway and wondered who she was.'

Lucien felt empty. Geoffrey had been involved with theft. For God's sake why? In a flash, his brain supplied him with the answer. *For money. Geoffrey needed money to buy medicines for his mother.*

It was an unpleasant realisation, but the more he thought about it, the more it made sense. Geoffrey had had access to the tower room; and he had likely died in a thieves' quarrel. *Lord, the shame of it. That one of my household knights should stoop to treat with a thief!*

Lucien blamed himself. If he had shown more interest in Ravenshold, Geoffrey could have applied to him for help. If he had been a better lord he would have given it without being asked. *I knew the lad's mother was ill, but whenever I left Ravenshold, I couldn't get away fast enough.*

'*Mon Dieu*, Isobel.' Reaching for her, he slid an arm about her waist. Her body felt stiff against his, she was still upset, but she did not rebuff him.

'Lucien, the girl at the gate—who is she?'

'Her name is Clare. She's the girl I suspect was Geoffrey's sweetheart.'

'What did she want?'

'She wants me to protect Geoffrey's name. She reminded me that he was a good man. As if I needed telling. What she was saying made no sense earlier. It does now.' He glanced at the reliquary. 'Good man or not, Geoffrey was embroiled with thieves. And it got him killed.'

Isobel looked earnestly up at him. 'Why? Why should a knight stoop so low?'

'Geoffrey had no land; his mother's ailing and he is—was—a loving son. My guess is that Geoffrey needed money for her.'

'It would help to know more.'

'It would indeed. Clare asked me to protect Geoffrey's reputation for his mother's sake. I shall need to speak to her again. As well as Count Henry.'

'Oh?'

'Troyes has suffered a spate of thefts recently, the theft of the relic is but one of them.'

She looked pensive. 'There's a gang of outlaws in the area?'

'It would seem so. There has to be a ringleader and Count Henry wants him caught. Henry won't allow anything to tarnish the reputation of his fairs. It's a matter of revenues.'

'If traffic to the Winter Fair is diminished, so are Count Henry's revenues.'

'Exactly. The fellow who took this...' Lucien jerked his head at the reliquary '...could be the man Count Henry is looking for.'

'He's a cold-blooded murderer.'

'He will be caught. Whatever Geoffrey did, I doubt he deserved to die.' The reliquary gleamed up at him from the table. 'Tomorrow, I shall inform the Abbess that the relic has been found. Before she gets it back, she will have to convince me that adequate arrangements have been made to keep it safe. After that I shall speak to Clare. She's still living with Geoffrey's mother.'

Isobel curled her fingers into his sleeve. 'Lucien, do be careful what you say, Geoffrey's mother—'

'I shall be tactful.'

She frowned at the reliquary. 'If you are right and Geoffrey brought the relic here, why was he killed?'

'At the moment, all we have to go on are assumptions. Everyone knew the relic was coming to Troyes, it could have been stolen to order. If Geoffrey was in collusion with the thief, we might assume that his role was to make contact with the buyer.'

Her eyes held his. 'And the tournament was the ideal place for Geoffrey to arrange to meet them.'

'It seems plausible.' Lucien shook his head. 'Although none of this answers the question of why my knight was killed.'

'He got greedy? He wanted too large a share of the proceeds?'

Lucien nodded, that was his assessment too. He frowned at the wall cavity. 'Do you reckon the killer knew where Geoffrey put it?'

'I have no idea.' She looked earnestly up at him. 'If he does, he is certainly bold enough to try to get it back. Will you be increasing the guard?'

Lucien grunted. Isobel's nose was aristocratic, straight and slim. He had never given noses much thought before now, but he rather liked hers. At this moment it was well within kissing distance. 'The guard? Yes, I shall double the guard on the gatehouse and increase the night watch. The men will be given orders to detain anyone—save you, little dove—who attempts to come up here.' Leaning forwards, he dropped a light kiss on her nose. He was relieved when she did not push him away. He picked up the Limoges casket. 'In the meantime, this is going straight in my strongbox.'

Chapter Sixteen

Over the next few weeks, Isobel saw little of her husband. A pattern evolved, and it was as though she had married a lord of the night. He rode out of Ravenshold each dawn, and it was rare that he returned before sunset.

Isobel understood what he was doing. In the town, St Rémi's Fair—the Winter Fair—was in full swing and Count Henry's Guardian Knights needed his assistance. Lucien was helping with investigations into Sir Geoffrey's death. It had become something of a personal quest for him, and it could scarcely be a more awkward, embarrassing quest. Lucien was appalled and shamed that one of his household knights had been involved with outlaws. He wanted to atone by running the thief to earth. He also wanted justice for Geoffrey.

One morning towards Christmas, they woke when it was still dark. The fire had burned out, and the air was chill. They held each other, cuddling sleepily for warmth until their bodies awoke. They made love. Afterwards, Isobel was lying in Lucien's arms, when a clatter from outside told them the servants were up.

Lucien's chest lifted in a sigh. 'Time to go,' he murmured. 'More knights are being recruited and I have offered to train them. I'm taking them on patrol.'

'Must you?' Isobel was physically satisfied, and yet…she always had a sense that something was missing—that however physically close they became, she would never truly touch him. Lucien's heart was closed.

December was slipping by and the bond between them was no stronger. If Lucien was the lover she had dreamed of, he was also a stranger. A knight who rode out on patrol every morning and joined her in their bed each night. There was passion a-plenty, but…

I want Lucien's love. He beds me purely to get me with child—the enjoyment we give each other is incidental to his desire for an heir. If something doesn't change—and soon—we are in danger of losing each other for ever. The distance between us will become a habit.

She pressed a kiss to his broad, muscled chest. 'Can't Sir Arthur take the new men on patrol?'

'Isobel, I thought you understood.'

'I do, Lucien, only too well.'

Blue eyes frowned into hers. 'And what might that mean?'

'You are not responsible for Sir Geoffrey's flaws.'

The pulse near his scar throbbed. 'I want the man who killed him.'

'Has there been a sighting?'

'Only rumours. Each day a new one springs up, but…' He rubbed his face and sighed. 'Incidentally, did I tell you that Abbess Ursula wheedled two Guardian Knights out of Count Henry?'

'She did?'

'They've been standing vigil over the reliquary. In my opinion they've been wasting their time. I told the Abbess that when the man strikes again, he will pick a different target. When the fair comes to an end and the Guardians have seen it safely back to St Foye's, they will be reassigned in town.'

'I am glad the relic's going back to Conques.'

Idly, Lucien caressed her waist, his hand slid up to cover a breast before lifting away. 'I thought you would be.' He glanced at the door. 'Where's Joris? It's time I left.'

'Don't go, Lucien. Stay with me. The castle—we

need to make plans…' She brought his head back to hers, even though it was clear that in his mind he was already patrolling the highways of Champagne.

'Don't you want that outlaw caught?' he asked, pressing a cursory kiss to her cheek. He tossed back the bedcovers. 'I'm sure he tried to kill you. I am leading the patrols for you, Isobel.'

After Lucien had scooped up his things and gone in search of Joris, Isobel stared after him. *He is doing it for me? That is surely an excuse. Sir Geoffrey's involvement has pricked his conscience—he feels honour-bound to put things right.* And despite the wrongs done by his knight, he wanted the killer brought to justice.

It came to her that Lucien enjoyed the company of men and was at ease with them in a way he was not at ease with women. Thoughtfully, she twisted a strand of hair about her finger. *He is very male.* Lucien enjoyed riding out on patrol. There was an unruly element in his nature, one that she did not think would ever be tamed. Part of her would not want to tame it. If only he relished her company a little more. The only time they were close, truly close, was when they were physically joined.

We cannot go on like this. I will not go on like this. Mentally, she felt numb. Her marriage was turning out to be a disaster. Here, there was much for her to do and she had made progress. She sat up, straightening the blue coverlet over her knees. She and Elise had worked on it together and when he had seen it, Lucien had given her a slow smile. He approved. Just as he had approved of the new standard they had worked for the hall. Slowly, his neglected castle was being brought back to life. But his approval in the domestic sphere was not enough. There was one vital area in which she was failing him.

I am not with child. Am I to fail him in this, my main duty? The thought made her sick at heart. Providing an heir was her first duty, but it had somehow become more than mere duty. She wanted to please him. It seemed that her fear of childbirth had been eclipsed by a growing affection for her husband.

It had turned her world upside-down to learn that during her nine years of waiting, Lucien had been married, but as the days had slipped by she had come to accept, even understand it. A strong point in Lucien's favour had been his explanation as to why he had allowed his marriage to Morwenna to stand. He had kept Isobel in the dark because a moment of youthful folly had saddled him with an ailing wife. A wife tortured by inner demons. He had not acted out of malice, or avarice, or fecklessness. He was not callously cruel. In similar circumstances, most men would have had no compunction in throwing

Morwenna to the wolves. Most men would have abandoned her.

Not Lucien.

Even though his marriage had not been a true marriage in any sense of the word, he had given Morwenna the run of Ravenshold. The carefree champion of the tourney field had been far from carefree. The paradox was that although Lucien had behaved dishonourably in deceiving Isobel, he had done so for honourable motives.

He had honoured his obligations to Morwenna, even though it had gone against his interests to do so. That deserved respect. And that was at the root of the paradox. The knight who sneered at the *chansons*, the knight who declared that love was little more than a cold-blooded decision was, she suspected, more chivalrous than any other.

Her eyes strayed to the jewel casket where the herbs she had bought from the apothecary lay. She doubted she would use them again. Somewhere on the journey from Turenne to Ravenshold, the thought of childbirth had lost its power to terrify. More terrifying by far was the fear that her husband would never open his heart to her.

In the Great Hall, Elise and a couple of serving girls had finished hanging holly balls for the Christmas feast, five days' hence. Sprays of bay and ivy had been tied up with red ribbons and nailed to the beams. Beeswax candles burned on tables and wall sconces.

As the girls clambered down from their ladders, Isobel surveyed the hall. In the main, she was pleased—it no longer smelled like a midden. Lucien's hall—and the rest of Ravenshold—had been transformed. Dirty rushes had been burned and the floors thoroughly scoured. Cellars had been cleared out and swept clean. Stores had been checked and restocked. There was plenty left to do but, come the Christmas feast, they would not be eating in a midden.

'Lucie, Emily, thank you, that looks lovely. You may remove the ladders.'

As the girls clattered out, Isobel resumed her review. A fresh coat of limewash hid the soot of decades. And thanks to a cartload of wood that had been properly stored, the fire had stopped hissing like a sackful of snakes. Gouts of black smoke no longer belched from the fireplace. Solène had supplied rushes and herbs for the floor and at each footfall, the scents of thyme and lavender were released into the air.

'Elise, please stay,' Isobel said, bending to pull cloths out of a coffer. The linen was yellow and creased—spotted with candle wax, gravy and spilled wine. She'd been so busy elsewhere, the table linen had had to wait. 'This really lets us down. See how badly laundered these are. And so frayed! This is beyond even your darning skills.'

'They do look old,' Elise agreed.

'There's a day or two left of the Winter Fair. When my lord returns I shall ask him if he will take me into Troyes to buy linen.'

'It will be too late for this year, my lady. We'll never get the cloths hemmed by the Christmas revels.'

'I shall see what might be done in the laundry. However, buying linen is in part an excuse. I'd like to see the Winter Fair before it closes.' *If Lucien agrees, it will give us time together. Time away from the bedchamber, time when we might talk without the intrusion of our baser desires...*

The door from the bailey opened and the candle flames swayed. Lucien strode in. The man at his side looked vaguely familiar.

'There's the Countess, by the coffer,' Lucien said.

Isobel let the threadbare cloth drop on to the table as they approached. Recognising Lucien's companion as one of her father's equerries, a pang of foreboding shot through her. The equerry bowed, tugged straight his tunic, and produced a beribboned scroll.

As he passed it to her, the ribbons trembled. *He is shaking. He will not meet my eyes.*

'Your name is Edouard, is it not?'

'Yes, my lady.'

'This is from my father?'

Edouard's throat worked.

'My apologies,' Isobel said, moving to the sideboard. Setting down the scroll, she poured some ale. 'You have ridden far. Please take this. Then you may give us your news.'

'Thank you, my lady.' Edouard took the cup and drained it.

'More?'

'No, thank you, my lady.'

Edouard took a deep breath. His eyes, as they met hers, were stricken. Whatever his message was, he was reluctant to deliver it. Icy fingers ran down her spine. *My father!*

'My lady, I regret to tell you that Viscount Gautier has died.'

At a stroke, Isobel was looking at everything from a great distance. *Father is dead.* She heard Lucien's sharp, indrawn breath; she heard his footsteps as he came to her side; she felt the warmth of his body. And she might have been in another world.

'Viscount Gautier has died?' Lucien's voice shattered the silence. 'When?'

'The Viscount died a week since, *mon seigneur.*'

'How did it happen?' Isobel asked, forcing words past her teeth. It seemed so unreal. *Father is dead.*

'It was a peaceful death, my lady. Lady Angelina found him; he had died in his sleep.'

Gripped by a sense of unreality, Isobel nodded as though she was taking in Edouard's message. *Father is dead.* The words made sense, she understood them, but they seemed meaningless. Worthless. It couldn't be true. Blindly, she reached for the jug of ale. 'Please, you must still be thirsty.'

'Thank you, my lady.' Edouard jerked his head at the parchment on the side-table. 'Lady Angelina has other news—it will be in the letter.'

'The letter. Oh, yes. My thanks.' Isobel picked up the letter and moved into a fall of light beneath a wall-sconce. Fingers on the seal, she added, 'If you are hungry and cannot wait for supper, Elise will show you to the kitchens. Sir Gawain is the man to find about bedding and a space for the night.'

'Thank you, my lady. Please accept my condolences.'

Isobel cracked the seal on her stepmother's letter. Her father's health had been poor of late, his death should not be a shock. Yet shock it was. Much of her life had been lived away from Turenne, away from her father. In the back of her mind she had cherished the hope that one day she would get to know her father better. *That will not happen.* She felt Lucien's gaze burning into her as she bent over her stepmother's letter and began to read.

My dear Isobel,
I greet you warmly, and send you God's bless-ing. It is with much grief that I write to tell you this ill news. Your father the Viscount has gone to God. I know you will share my sorrow. It will relieve your mind to hear that he did not suffer. One day he was with us, and the next day God had taken him. I beg that you pray for your fa-ther's soul. May he rest in peace.

Of my other news, you know already. And al-though I am grieved to lose your father after so short a time, you will be pleased to hear that I remain in good health. Daily I thank the Lord that your father knew about our baby. A child who will, I trust, act in some measure as a balm to the wound of your father's death...

The baby Angelina carried was indeed balm for the pain of her father's death. And since the child was expected in January, her stepmother had passed the time when miscarriage was most likely. Her eyes prickled.

Lucien took her hand. 'Isobel? Do you need to sit down? You look very pale.'

Father is dead. She stiffened her spine. Lucien would have to learn about Angelina's baby soon, such news couldn't be kept from him for ever, but after learning about her father, she didn't have the strength. *I will tell Lucien about the child, later.* In the meantime, she would teach him to open his heart to her.

I must because I love him. What I feel for him is far more than affection. Why did I not see this before? I love Lucien.

Grief for her father was a dull pain that pervaded every fibre of her being. She was full of regret. Because of her sex she had never had a chance to know her father. But love for Lucien overrode all that, even the hope that soon, Isobel of Turenne would have someone else to love.

I love Lucien. The baby will be born in January... I have until then to win him...

'Isobel?'

Could Lucien read? Many noblemen could not. Had he seen what Angelina had written about the baby? Blinking away a blur of tears, Isobel rolled up the scroll and looked up at him. His gaze was enquiring. She did not think he had read the letter.

'My lord, if you will excuse me, I should like to go to the chapel.'

'You wish to pray for your father. Allow me to accompany you.'

'That is kind, my lord, but I would prefer to pray on my own.'

Lucien kept pace with her until she reached the foot of the tower stair. 'Isobel, a moment.'

'My lord?'

'You realise this will alter our plans for Christmas?'

The chilly fingers inched along Isobel's back. She knew what he was about to say, and she had no wish to hear it. 'Will it?'

He made an impatient movement. 'Of course. We must visit Turenne to lay claim to your lands.'

No! If we go to Turenne, you will see that my stepmother is pregnant. You will realise that I may be disinherited...

That moment must be delayed as long as possible. Lucien had remained married to Morwenna because she had been unable to take care of herself. Isobel's circumstances were entirely different—Lucien would be able to annul his marriage to her with a clear conscience. No matter that the marriage agreement had been drawn up between her father and his, if he wanted to divorce her, he could. Powerful men usually got their way.

My marriage is a house built on sand. She did not mind about her inheritance for herself, but Lucien surely would. The only way to make sure of him was to give him his heir. She was vaguely aware of Lucien's voice washing over her.

'Isobel, I shall send Joris to Count Henry with a message. Someone else can train up the Guardian Knights; someone else can organise the Twelfth Night Joust.'

It was ironic that what she had feared most when she married him—giving birth—had become what she most longed for. If she gave Lucien a son, her marriage would be safe, whether or not she was an heiress. She could not rely on love, if she waited until she had won his love, she might be waiting until doomsday. For Lucien love was not just a feeling—Morwenna had taught him that. Morwenna had taught him that love was a decision. *Lucien does have feelings for me. When his desire is strong so are his feelings—but he mistrusts them.*

He had never said out loud that he felt anything for her other than desire. At the very least, Isobel had been hoping for affection from him, but even that would not be enough to banish the possibility of her being set aside as unsuitable.

Lucien mistrusts emotions. When listening to Bernez at their wedding feast, he had muttered something about the transitory nature of feelings. He had said that if love exists—*if* love exists—it was not a feeling, it was a decision. A decision. How cold that sounded. How mercenary. How convenient.

Lucien understood lust, and he understood marriage alliances made to benefit both parties. *The only way I can secure him is to give him his heir. It is too soon to go to Turenne. I have to conceive before he sees Angelina.*

Stepping up to him, she placed her hand on his arm. Surprise flared in his eyes, she was not in the habit of making public gestures of affection and he was uncertain how to respond. His gaze dropped briefly to her lips. He cleared his throat and a strong arm wound about her waist.

'My lord, your tenants will be sorely disappointed if we leave Ravenshold before Christmas.'

'They will?'

He opened his mouth to say more, but Isobel intervened. 'I need time, my lord,' she said quietly. 'Time to absorb this loss. Surely we can discuss our plans in the morning?'

Lucien's fingers moved in a small caress. 'As you wish.'

Isobel did need time, and not just to grieve for her father. She needed time to prove to her husband that love was more than a decision made for cold-blooded political purposes, love was a feeling too. It was glorious, enchanting, overpowering—it would never die. She loved him.

She loved him in the cool, calculating way she had always tried to love him—as the man chosen for her by her father. But that was not the only way in which she loved him. She loved him in the po-etic way too, in the pretty, mind-muddling way of the poets. Such love was *not* ephemeral. It was not untrustworthy.

It would be her quest to teach Lucien about love in all its guises. Finding out about Morwenna ex-plained so much. Morwenna had all but ruined him. Isobel's task would have been hard enough without Angelina being pregnant.

Father's child will be born soon. She felt bad about misleading Lucien, but it would not be for long. She would not fail.

Lucien's mouth softened as he looked at her. He raised her hand to his lips—a courtly gesture that squeezed her heart. 'If you wish to celebrate

Christmas here, I expect we could delay our visit to Turenne. I take it your father has a good steward?'

'The best.' *He is concerned for my lands. The wastrel I at one time imagined I had married would not have been concerned. He is a diligent, responsible man.*

'Very well. We shall wait before planning our journey.'

'Thank you, my lord.' Picking up her skirts she started up the spiralling stairs. She had not actually lied about Angelina being with child, but she felt quite sick. And it was painfully clear that Lucien's main concern was to secure her lands.

In the Great Hall later that evening, Lucien found himself sitting in his high-backed chair, breaking bread with Sir Raoul and Sir Gawain. 'Where is my wife?'

'The Countess is in the chapel, I believe,' Gawain said.

Lucien tossed down his bread. 'She can't *still* be in the chapel?'

Gawain leaned across the table to spear a slice of pork from the platter and grunted. 'Father Thomas is holding some sort of vigil for Viscount Gautier.'

'I should imagine Lady Isobel feels badly that she

missed her father's funeral,' Raoul said. 'The rites will do her good.'

Lucien looked at the empty space beside him and pushed back his chair. 'Did she eat at noon-tide?'

'I couldn't say.' Raoul shrugged. 'I was with you all afternoon.'

'Hell.' Stomach cramping with concern, Lucien shoved back his chair. 'Girande?'

'Count Lucien?'

'Put bread, meat and wine for two on a tray and take it to my bedchamber, will you?'

'At once, my lord.'

The chapel in Ravenshold was in the west tower, on the floor below their bedchamber. As Lucien rounded the last turn in the stairs, the priest's chanting floated out to meet him. Isobel was standing in front of Father Thomas, blue gown bright against the dark priestly robes. Her palms were clasped at her breast, her head was bent. She looked pale, and her skin had a translucent quality Lucien had not seen before, like white marble. She looked like a statue of the Madonna. A Madonna who was swaying on her feet. Her eyes were shadowed—she had been crying.

She has been here too long.

'Isobel?' Lucien spoke softly. The candles on the

altar were reflected in her eyes, eyes which held a world of sorrow.

'My lord?'

Pain shaped her posture—she was holding herself with a kind of dogged stiffness. Lucien had not seen that in her before either. He had no remedy against grief like this. A wave of regret washed over him, rarely had he felt so useless.

'Is your ceremony almost finished?' he asked.

She shook her head. In the fitful light of the candles her lips were bloodless. 'Father Thomas has promised to keep vigil with me all night.'

'All night?' Covering her clasped hands, he peeled them apart and interlaced his fingers with hers. She was ice-cold. 'Isobel, you will make yourself ill.'

'The loss of one night's sleep cannot do much harm.'

Father Thomas was ignoring them—his chanting flowed on unabated. It was one of the psalms. *'Put not your trust in princes, nor in any child of man: for there is no help in them.'* The verses of the psalm were uttered so softly there was no echo; the words simply fell into the mournful quiet and vanished, like stones dropped into a well.

'Isobel, you must eat,' Lucien said.

She bit her lip. 'I broke my fast this morning.'

'*...then all his thoughts should perish,*' intoned the priest.

'Have you eaten since then?'

She stared at the cross on the altar, lips moving as she joined in the psalm. *'Blessed is he—'*

Lucien shifted. 'Isobel? Did you eat at noon?'

'Truly, my lord, I am sure—'

'You need to eat. You have been here long enough.' He raised his voice. 'Father Thomas?'

'*Who made heaven and...*my lord?'

'The Countess needs to retire. Is the vigil almost over?'

'My lord, we have run through the office several times already. I can finish this round on my own, if you wish.'

'Thank you, Father. That would be kind.'

Lucien placed Isobel's cold fingers on his arm. 'Come, Isobel, you must eat. And then you must rest.'

Chapter Seventeen

On the morning of the shortest day—it was the Winter solstice—Isobel woke alone under the blue coverlet. Wanting to make the most of what little light there was, Lucien had gone out on patrol.

Grief hung over her, like a pall. It was hard to accept that her gruff, bluff father was dead, and that his harsh voice would never again call her name. She must accept it.

She tugged the coverlet more firmly about her. Guilt was an uncomfortable bedfellow. She was deceiving Lucien, she should tell him that Father's widow was with child. Lucien had neglected her for years—he was himself no stranger to deception and she had harboured some resentment against him. No longer. Her innards felt as though they were in knots because she had not told him about Angelina. Why? She was merely paying him back in his own coin, she shouldn't feel this bad.

When Isobel had arrived in Champagne, she had not expected the Comte d'Aveyron to be so personable. And she wasn't simply thinking about his appearance; although who wouldn't want to be married to a strong, long-limbed knight with thick glossy hair, a chiselled bone structure, and intelligent blue eyes? She had expected scars, and the one on Lucien's face was prominent, but without it—well, he would simply be too beautiful. That scar showed his human side, Lucien had won it protecting Morwenna.

It was a side that Isobel had not thought to look for whilst nursing her anger at the endless delays forced upon her. Nine years! Since arriving in Troyes, Lucien's unexpected thoughtfulness had, she supposed, disarmed her. Thoughtfulness which had begun with him ensuring her removal to Count Henry's palace when he had realised how she disliked lodging at the Abbey. He had chastised her for her disobedience over the tourney, but that hadn't stopped him giving her that brooch. Of course, he had given her the brooch to keep her sweet. He wanted her for her lands. Nevertheless...

Last night he had removed her from the chapel and had insisted that she ate.

Lucien looks after me because I am valuable to him. I bring him Turenne. Lucien might have a human side, but she must never forget there was determination as well as intelligence in those blue eyes. His gaze was that of a man who had fought— and won—many battles. A champion. It was hard to remember that in a sense, she was just another trophy. He did not love her.

The noise of hoofbeats filtered through the lancet, and a rook cawed. Someone tapped on the door.

'Come in.'

Elise stepped in with a jug of steaming water. 'Good morning, my lady. May I attend you?'

'Of course. Where's Girande?'

'She's feeling queasy again, my lady.'

'I am sorry to hear it.' Isobel padded across to the ewer, while Elise straightened the bed.

'My lady, I was sorry to hear of your father's death. Please accept my sympathies.'

Isobel's eyes prickled. 'Thank you, Elise.' She reached for a washcloth.

'Which gown will you wear today?'

'The grey with the gold-and-red edging,' Isobel said quietly. Gold and red were her father's colours. And Lucien's too, if Angelina was carrying a daughter. But if Angelina was carrying a son...

Saints preserve me, I shall not lose him.

'My lady?'

Isobel started. Elise had been speaking and she

had not noticed. 'My apologies, Elise, I missed what you said.'

'You know, don't you?' Elise said, holding out a drying cloth.

'Know what?'

'About Morwenna, Count Lucien's first wife.'

Every muscle in Isobel's body went taut as a bowstring. 'You know about Morwenna?' *Surely the marriage was kept secret?*

Chewing her lip, Elise took the drying cloth from her. 'I have known about it for some time, my lady. There were…rumours, you understand.'

'Yet you said nothing to me.' A chill of realisation shot through her. *Elise knew about Morwenna when she introduced herself to me at the Abbey!*

Unhappily, Elise twisted the cloth. 'I could not. I dare not. My lady, I lied about Girande being sick this morning. I asked her if I could tend to you because I wanted to warn you. I have come to like you…to respect you.'

Isobel's heart turned to lead.

'My lady, take care with Count Lucien, do not anger him. I fear for you.'

Isobel stared. 'You think Count Lucien would harm me?'

'My lady, Morwenna was kept prisoner.' Elise

spoke in a rush, her face was red. 'She was not allowed out, she—'

'You are mistaken. Elise, you have it all wrong.'

Elise's eyes were glassy with tears. 'My lady, please take care, you are in grave danger—'

'Nonsense!' It went completely against the grain to believe that Lucien would harm her. Last night he had winkled her out of the chapel, he had fed her and watered her and put her to bed. He had held her in his arms, allowing her to grieve while he had stroked her hair. He had made no demands. If he were any other man she might call his behaviour loving. Lucien? Hurt her? No.

To be sure, he would hurt her if he were to annul their marriage, but Elise was not referring to that kind of hurt. *I trust him.* Lucien had locked Morwenna up for her own good. That was the truth. Grief might have tangled her thoughts, but none the less, she was clear on one point. Lucien would never hurt her. Not physically.

'My lord would never knowingly hurt a woman.'

A tear glistened on Elise's cheek. 'I wish I could believe it.'

'Elise!'

Isobel drew breath to say more, but Elise rushed on. 'My lady, Count Lucien denied Morwenna her freedom. He neglected her for years. And then, when his spy told him that you had grown into a beauty, he had her murdered. My lady, you must take care, he—'

'Elise, that's enough! This talk of spies and murder is madness. My lord…you simply do not understand.' Isobel had no intention of revealing to Elise what Lucien had told her in confidence. She fixed her with a look. 'I thank you for your interest, but you overreach yourself when you speak to me in this manner.'

Elise made a gulping sound, dropped the linen cloth, and stumbled from the bedchamber. The door banged, and the latch clicked into place.

Lucien—a murderer? The idea was preposterous.

Absently, Isobel bent to retrieve the cloth. Elise had let what she had seen in the east tower eat away at her. *That tower must be cleared. Today.*

She dragged the grey gown over her head, almost thankful for Elise's extraordinary outburst. Somehow, it had distracted her. It was unthinkable that Lucien would harm a woman. By coming here this morning, and by speaking her mind, Elise had clarified Isobel's thoughts.

Lucien was a good man. He could scarcely be more different from the carefree tourney champion she had envisaged. And that was something for which she could only be grateful. The real Lucien was worth fighting for.

Secondly, the sooner that festering chamber at the top of the east tower was cleared, the better for everyone.

It happened towards the end of Christmastide, when Twelfth Night was almost upon them. Lucien had been patrolling the roads around Troyes every day, to no avail. His quarry seemed to have gone to earth.

Finally, his luck turned. He had just trotted through the Madeleine Gate at the head of his *conroi* when something in the moat caught his eye. The moat encircling Troyes was a dry one—a deep dip in front of the city walls—and the townsfolk were in the habit of using it as a midden. Refuse of all sorts was flung into it—rotting vegetable peelings, cooked animal bones. And worse.

Reining in, Lucien found himself staring at a bundle of brown rags and what looked like a tangle of greasy brown hair. He felt himself go still. Somewhere a cock was crowing.

'Joris, search the moat.'

'Not the moat, my lord.' Joris pulled a face. 'I did that yesterday.'

'The moat, Joris. I have a feeling you were less than thorough. Sergeant, you go with him.'

'Yes, *mon seigneur*,' the sergeant said, dismounting smartly.

Joris sent him a pleading look. 'It stinks down there.'

'Thank God it's not summer then, it's worse in summer. Start over there.' Lucien pointed towards the pile of brown rags. 'You are my squire, I assume it is your ambition to become a knight?'

'Yes, my lord.'

'However distasteful the task, a knight cannot afford to be less than thorough. Get off that horse and into the ditch.'

'Yes, my lord.'

Nose wrinkling, Joris obeyed. Lucien watched him slither into the moat. He didn't have long to wait. When Joris next looked towards him, his face was white as bone.

'My lord! Count Lucien! There's a b-body. It… he…' the young voice cracked '…he's been murdered.'

Lucien had known who it was even before he had seen the face. It was the man who he had been hunting for nigh on two months. The man who had taken the relic and murdered Geoffrey; the man who he feared might come after Isobel. The body was battered; there had clearly been a fight. The thief's face and knuckles were bruised, and there were marks about his neck. He'd been strangled. Lucien felt only relief. *Geoffrey's murderer is no longer loose in Champagne. Isobel is safe.*

Because of the body, Lucien left Troyes that evening later than planned.

Count Henry had to be informed of what they had found. Lucien had spoken to him, and suggested that the moat should be cleared weekly. He had also suggested that his former steward, Sir Arthur, should be promoted to captain of the Guardians.

That done, Lucien had sought out Geoffrey's family. He had been planning to visit them in any case. The year had turned, and Lucien had wanted to reassure himself that Geoffrey's mother and sister were surviving. It had been good to tell Nicola that whilst her son's murderer had not faced Count Henry's justice, justice of sorts had been done. He had given her more money, telling her that Geoffrey had earned it by his service at Ravenshold, and that he had only now discovered that more was due. He wanted to help. It was obvious Nicola struggled to put food on the table.

Lucien had been hoping to gain the trust of the girl, Clare. He was certain she knew about Geoffrey's involvement with the dead man. Unfortunately, Clare was loyal to a fault, and would say not a word.

'The mist is thickening, my lord.' Joris's saddle creaked as he leaned on the cantle to peer over his shoulder. 'We might miss our way.'

They were heading back to Ravenshold. Strips of fog were weaving in and out of the trees, like wraiths in the gathering dark. Ghostly grey pools lay in the hollows.

'Never fear, we shan't lose the road,' Lucien said. Joris was nervy, and understandably so. It wasn't every day the boy found a body in a ditch.

'Night falls too soon around the turn of the year,' Joris added, shrinking into his hood.

Lucien grunted, he was thinking about the dead man. 'He might have met his end in a tavern brawl,' he muttered. 'It's a pity Clare was not more forthcoming about Geoffrey's involvement.'

'Yes, my lord.'

Lucien swore under his breath. Whatever Geoffrey had done, it could not have warranted his death.

Joris's teeth were chattering, and his face had taken a blue tinge. The dark was closing in on them. 'We'll be home soon, Joris.'

Tonight, Lucien would tell Isobel that his stint

with the Guardian Knights was over. Count Henry had more than enough men, and with Sir Arthur as their captain, the roads and highways of Champagne would be secure. Hopefully, Isobel would be able to put the entire business out of her mind.

Isobel is waiting for me at Ravenshold. Grinning to himself, unable to believe the way his heart lifted when he thought of her, Lucien heeled Demon into a trot. Joris shot him an enquiring look.

'Don't dawdle,' Lucien said. 'You were right about the mist, it is thickening.'

Lucien emerged from the stables into a courtyard so murky it might have been midnight. Above the circle of spluttering torches, there were no stars. The mist was crawling over the curtain walls. The cookhouse was shrouded in grey, and he could barely see the hall. As was his habit, he counted the lights up on the walkway. They glowed weakly tonight, two to the left of the gatehouse, two to the right, and...

A flash of scarlet caught his attention. A woman was on the walkway, and the scarlet—a cloak, he thought—was an extra flare of brightness in the mist and the dark. A red banner in the night.

A *scarlet* cloak? Lucien's heart cramped. Morwenna had owned a cloak in just such a scarlet, it had been lined with squirrel. A light on the curtain wall wavered, dimmed by a finger of mist creeping in from the road. Clenching his jaw, Lucien found himself striding towards the steps. He began to climb.

It was quiet as death on the ramparts. He had stepped into another world. Somewhere out there lay the village. Lord, the mist was so thick, Lucien could scarcely see his own bailey. The silence was unearthly.

Pale light streamed from the stables and gatehouse. A candle shone briefly at the top of the west tower—Isobel or her maid must be in the bedchamber. Then the mist rolled around the tower and the light was gone. For the space of a heartbeat, Lucien was alone. There was mist. There was dark. And bone-numbing cold.

The sound when it came had hairs rising on the back of his neck. Singing. *Singing?* The woman was close. The walkway glistened with damp. Lucien lifted a torch from its bracket and followed the sound as a hound follows a scent. It was a love-song. Lucien wasn't one for love-songs, but this one he knew. Morwenna had loved it. She had sung it for him a number of times in the days of their courtship. The voice on the walkway was an eerie echo of Morwenna's. The woman was not in sight, but the similarity in sound chilled him to his core. That cloak, that voice, that song…

Morwenna! *Mon Dieu*, what witchery was this? Morwenna was dead, it could not be her. A cold dread had him in its grip. Lucien was reluctant to move forwards, reluctant to come face to face with… who? *Who is it?* Heat from the torch warmed his hand and face. And there it was again. Singing—soft and clear, each note sung true. It was a song from the south, and it was being sung exactly as Morwenna had sung it, with the same phrases, the same cadences, even the same plangency. It couldn't be Morwenna, Morwenna had been laid to her rest. But that voice—that song—he was listening to her ghost.

The mist was writhing about the ramparts like a living thing. Gripping the torch, Lucien forced himself through it. The woman must be beyond the next turn in the walls. It was not Morwenna; this was no wraith from his past. There had to be a rational explanation. Notwithstanding, ice filled his veins. He dreaded taking that step round the corner, dreaded what he would find. *God help me. It is not Morwenna.*

Thoughts do not follow time's rules. Dozens can pass through a man's head while he braces himself. And there on the walkway, with the love-song from his past bleeding gently into the fog-bound night,

Lucien's thoughts all but unmanned him. *It is not Morwenna. It is not.* That was the truth, it had to be, because if it was Morwenna singing…

His marriage to Isobel was invalid. His chest seized up. His heart was in his mouth, as hard and cold as the stones in the parapet wall. Morwenna was dead. *Has there been a hideous mistake?*

His marriage to Isobel was the truest thing he had ever known. It was not a lie. Grasping the torch so tightly his knuckles gleamed white, Lucien stepped round the corner.

'Who is there?'

The woman stood by a sentry post, cloak gleaming bright as blood through the mist. Her face was white, a blur.

The song cut off. 'My lord?'

'Who is that?'

The torch flared, tendrils of smoke were swallowed by the January night. The cloak flickered— a dying ember in the dark—and was gone.

Lucien flung himself after her. He was fast, but the woman had wings. By the time he reached the next bend in the walkway, she was gone. She was not in the bailey—no one could have got down those steps so quickly. He leaned through a crenel, straining his eyes for the road below. Nothing. Only darkness and mist. No swirling red cloak. *No Morwenna.*

Briefly, he shut his eyes. He was not a superstitious man. Father Thomas had told him Morwenna was dead. She was dead. So why in God's name did he feel this doubt? Why was dread gnawing at his innards? His heart was pounding so loudly he could hear it. Why?

Isobel is my soul-mate. Isobel is my wife.

Across the bailey, lights winked through the windows of the hall and keep. Isobel would be wondering where he was. He must join her.

As Lucien reached the head of the steps, he frowned. The dread had not left him. He couldn't understand how he felt, but he wanted to try. *Isobel is mine.* Even the possibility that Morwenna might still be alive and his marriage to Isobel might be invalid was not to be borne. His lips twisted. *Who would have thought it? Such a ridiculous notion, and it all but unmans me!*

Isobel is mine. The thought of losing her was extraordinarily painful, far too painful to contemplate. Lucien increased his pace as he crossed the bailey and went into the keep to find her.

He caught up with her as she was leaving the cookhouse.

'There you are.' Taking Isobel's hand, he pulled her close. He only intended to give her a light kiss;

he hadn't bargained for the sense of rightness that flooded through him the instant their lips touched. The smell of her—of Isobel, warm and womanly—brought every sense to life. He pulled her close, deepening the kiss. *Mine.*

A serving girl edged past them. Dimly, Lucien heard her smothered giggle. He ignored the giggle and the kiss went on. When he touched his tongue to Isobel's, his loins tightened. He fought with the impulse to stroke her breasts.

'My lord!' She broke free, smiling. Blushing like a rose. 'Anyone might see us.'

With difficulty he eased back. He had forgotten himself. There was only Isobel. His mind was filled with desire—its hot, fiery pulse was fierce in his veins.

She cleared her throat. 'I have been checking on the dough for tomorrow's baking. We shall be eating soon, are you hungry?'

'Mmm.' He shifted closer. 'But not for food.'

The serving girl emerged from the cookhouse with a batch of loaves for supper. Lucien heard another giggle and Isobel's blush deepened to scarlet.

Tightening his hold on Isobel, Lucien steered her towards the twisting stairs that led to their bedchamber. He would tell her about finding Geoffrey's killer later. First, he must communicate with her in an altogether different way…

'Come along, little dove, we can send for food later.'

Lying on the bed afterwards, Lucien wove a tress of golden hair round his fingers and wondered why his heart ached. Isobel was dozing, a smile on her lips. Once he had convinced her that his most urgent need was not for food, her response had been as satisfactory as a man could wish.

I have lost all honour.

He felt he ought to have told Isobel what he had seen—what he *imagined* he had seen—up on the battlements. He should have told her before they had made love. Which was quite ridiculous, because his fear that he had seen Morwenna was completely unfounded. Just as his fear that his marriage to Isobel might be bigamous. He was being illogical. Neither Arthur nor Father Thomas would lie to him. It was ridiculous the way the woman on the battlements had lowered his spirits.

Isobel's hair was soft as silk, fragrant with her scent. He lay at her side, head pillowed on one hand and studied her. *Isobel.* Other than Isobel, Lucien had never lain long enough with a woman to watch her lying in a doze. Something in his chest twisted.

Mine.

* * *

Feeling a tug on her hair, Isobel opened her eyes.

'Will you sleep till dawn?' Lucien's broad shoulders were silhouetted by candlelight as he looked down at her. 'We've not eaten. I'm hungry.'

'We could ring for Girande. She can bring us a tray.'

'No, there's something you must see. After that we can eat in the hall.' Leaning forwards, he pressed a kiss to her forehead.

As they dressed, the imprint of his kiss lingered on Isobel's brow. There had been nothing sexual about it—it had felt like a kiss of affection. Of tenderness. Glancing sidelong at him, Isobel found herself smiling. Lucien was sparing with gestures of affection. He usually only gave them when he was intent on seduction. Was her cynical, martial husband learning to love her?

'What must I see?' she asked.

In the act of buckling on his belt, he looked across, eyes shadowed. 'It concerns Morwenna.'

Isobel felt her face fall. 'Oh?'

'I thought I saw…never mind, I will sound like a madman. There's a chest of Morwenna's clothes somewhere. I must find it.'

'What colour is it?'

'It is plain oak. Unpainted, but carved.'

'The design of the carving?'

'Roundels, I think.'

Isobel had a vague memory of Elise sorting through a coffer with roundels on the sides. She had assumed it was full of bedlinen awaiting repair. 'I think it is in the storage chamber below the chapel.'

The coffer was in the lower chamber. Isobel watched, tense with worry, as Lucien knelt in front of it and threw back the lid. Gowns and veils were dragged out and thrown to one side. A pair of shoes followed, then another pair. Some boots. A couple of girdles. A sturdy black cloak. As though in a dream, Isobel snatched them up again, shaking them out, folding them. *What does Lucien want with Morwenna's clothes?*

'It's not here,' he said, leaning back on his heels.

'What? What is not here?'

'Her scarlet cloak. It's gone.'

'Elise was tidying these things,' Isobel told him, holding Morwenna's gowns to her chest. Until she knew what this was about, she was reluctant to confess that Elise had been doing more than that, that she had turned out the entire chest. 'I shall ask her if she has seen a red cloak.'

'Elise? Yes, if you wouldn't mind.' Scowling, Lucien shoved his hand through his hair and came to his feet. He noticed her holding the clothes. 'Lord, Isobel, there's no need to do that,' he said. He took them and dropped them carelessly into the coffer.

'Lucien, whatever is the matter?'

'Nothing. I…' Heaving a great sigh, he jerked his head at the coffer. 'I want these burned.'

'Burned?' Isobel was shocked. 'I can understand you might not like reminders of Morwenna lying about, but to burn them—it is pure waste. There's good cloth there. Her things should go to charity; someone in the village will be glad of them.'

His eyes glittered, hard as glass. 'Very well, do what you will…as long as I don't have to see them again.'

She looked thoughtfully at him. 'Lucien, please tell me what is troubling you.'

He gave a short laugh, though he looked anything but amused. 'She's haunting me.'

'Morwenna?'

'Who else? There was a woman on the battlements when I rode in. Singing. Whoever she was, her voice was the echo of Morwenna's. It drew me like a siren's.'

'And…?'

He gave a bitter laugh. 'I would swear she heard me hail her, but the blasted woman vanished. I tried to find her, but—well, you'll have seen the mist to-night—it swallowed her. I didn't see her face, just the red cloak.'

Isobel stared at him. 'Lucien, Elise was definitely sorting through this chest. I think we should go and speak to her.'

Chapter Eighteen

They had missed supper. Servants were clearing away cups and serving platters when they reached the hall. Elise was not there. Isobel and Lucien took their places at a deserted table and wine was placed before them. A lad darted off to fetch food.

Lucien was heaping braised rabbit on to their trencher, when Isobel saw Solène at the other end of the hall. She waved her over. 'Solène, where is Elise?'

Solène's gaze fixed with apparent fascination at a neat darn in the tablecloth. 'Oh, my lady, please don't ask. I'm not supposed to say anything until morning.'

Lucien's head shot up. Isobel laid a hand on his thigh. 'Allow me, my lord.' She smiled at Solène. 'Solène? We are waiting...'

Solène shifted, she was looking anywhere but at Lucien. 'My lady, I swore not to say anything tonight, but...but...Elise has gone.'

'Gone? Where? What do you mean, she has gone?'

Solène clasped her hands. They were honest hands, gardener's hands worn down by toiling in the castle garden.

'Elise has left Ravenshold. My lady, I would have told you tomorrow, she was most anxious that I should convey her thanks to you. She told me you have helped her beyond measure. She is most grateful and said to wish you well.'

'Elise has gone away?'

'Yes, my lady.'

'But why? I thought she was happy here. I thought you and she shared an interest and—'

Solène shook her head. 'Elise did not come to Ravenshold by chance, my lady. She came to find out about her sister.'

Lucien put down his knife. 'Her *sister*?'

Finally, Solène looked at him, she was quivering from head to toe.

'Yes, my lord, her sister.' Solène lifted her chin. 'Elise came to Ravenshold to learn whether her sister—your first Countess—had been murdered.'

Isobel gasped. White about the mouth, Lucien came slowly to his feet.

'I told her how it was, my lord,' Solène said, speaking in a rush. 'I told her how...troubled Countess Morwenna had been. At first she refused to believe me.'

After a moment's silence, Lucien glanced shrewdly at Isobel. 'Do you recall? Elise wriggled out of telling us her full name. I realise why. It is Elise Chantier.'

'Yes, my lord, that is so.' Solène plucked at her skirts. 'My lord, I swear I never said anything amiss. All I did was try to lead her to the truth.'

'Before I married her, Morwenna was known as Morwenna Chantier,' Lucien said. 'Think, Isobel, how Elise took pains to avoid me. Whenever I saw her, she was skulking in the shadows. That shyness is affected. She didn't want to be noticed, she must have been afraid I would see a family resemblance.'

Elise is Morwenna's sister. Isobel's mind raced. *That is why she attached herself to me at the Abbey—it was a ploy to gain access to Ravenshold!* She rubbed the bridge of her nose. 'Elise found the east tower so terrifying she took to her heels rather than stay in it. I couldn't understand why, but this explains it. She was overwhelmed by evidence of her sister's fragility.'

'Yes, my lady,' Solène said. 'Elise was hit hard by what she saw in the east tower. Although initially she refused to accept that Countess Morwenna had become so very ill.'

'Elise told you she is Morwenna's sister.' Lucien gave Solène a penetrating look. 'What else did she say?'

'Not much, my lord. We discussed Countess Morwenna's interest in herbs; she revealed nothing of herself. Her main concern was that I should convey her thanks to Countess Isobel. Oh—she did mention a cloak, a red one. She has taken it as a remembrance of her sister. She asked me to make it plain she has taken nothing else.' Solène gave a small bob of a curtsy. 'Will that be all, my lord? I hope I set her straight. I did not think it was my place to prevent her from leaving.'

'I understand. And you are right—you could not have prevented her leaving.' Lucien's mouth twisted. 'Thank you, Solène.'

'You are welcome, my lord.' Solène moved away.

Lucien exchanged glances with Isobel, and heaved a great sigh. 'It was Elise singing on the battlements.'

'It would seem so.'

He leaned back in his chair. 'I cannot tell you how much that relieves my mind.'

'You did not truly think that Morwenna had come back to life?'

'No, but it gave me pause.' Reaching for her hand, he kissed it. 'You are infinitely precious to me, Isobel. I would not want to lose you.'

Wild joy rushed through her. *Lucien loves me. I am infinitely precious to him.*

'It made me realise what would happen if our marriage had to be annulled,' he added.

'Oh?'

'Think.' His voice became confidential. 'Isobel, if our marriage was declared unlawful, any child I may have given you would be illegitimate. You could stay with me, of course, but you would be my mistress, not my wife.'

Joy left her. Of course. The legality of their marriage was not his main concern. Lucien must have been wondering if he had got her with child. His priority was that his child should be legitimate. Something of her inner turmoil must have shown on her face, for his gaze sharpened.

'Isobel? Are you unwell?'

He does not love me. She pinned on a bright smile. 'I am well, my lord,' she said, searching for words to hide her distress. 'My lord, in light of what Solène has told us, perhaps we should not give Morwenna's belongings away. Elise might come back. She might want them.'

He picked up his knife with a frown. 'Very well. They may stay in storage. As long as I don't have to look at them.'

Isobel had lost her appetite. All through Christmas guilt had been a lead weight inside her. The holly clusters were losing their freshness—Twelfth Night would be upon them before they could blink. Soon, the festive greenery would be burned. January was here.

It seemed to have rushed at her. *Angelina may have had her child. I should have told Lucien.* Sick with dread, sick with waiting to hear from Turenne, Isobel picked at the rabbit. For the sake of appearances, she forced down a sliver or two. She knew the news would come soon, she just knew it. *I shall tell him tonight.*

Lucien was working his way through a spiced cream pie when Sir Gawain entered. He came directly to the table. 'A messenger has arrived, from Turenne, Lady Isobel. I have taken the liberty of asking him to come in.'

'Thank you, Sir Gawain,' Isobel heard herself saying. Miracle of miracles, her voice was steady.

A messenger from Turenne. Angelina has had her baby. If it is a girl, everything will go on as before. But if it is a boy, Turenne is no longer mine. I will have brought Lucien nothing but a chest of silver pennies.

She looked at Lucien. 'I should like to greet my stepmother's envoy in private, my lord.' If she was about to be humiliated, she did not want the entire castle to witness it.

Lucien pushed the cream pie aside. 'We'll greet him together. In the solar.'

Eager for his supper, Angelina's envoy said little. Before you could blink, he had handed Isobel a scroll and bowed himself out.

Isobel moved under the light of a cresset, and snapped the seal. Brown letters swam before her...

My dear daughter in marriage,
God send that this missive finds you and Lord d'Aveyron in good health. It is my pleasure to inform you that yesterday I was brought to bed of a son. He is thriving and, God willing, will continue to do so. He is named Gautier, in honour of your dear father. He...

The letter ran on, most of it in praise of the new heir to Turenne. Isobel let it curl back on itself, she would finish it later. She was pleased to have a brother, she had always wanted one but—

Lucien tossed a log into the fire, poking it with his boot. 'Isobel?'

Isobel's throat closed up, she could not speak. Avoiding his eyes, she handed him the letter.

He stared down at it, following the lines of ink with his finger as he read. 'A son? Angelina has a son?'

Lucien's voice sounded perfectly normal, one might imagine that he was no more than mildly surprised. One might think from his tone that it was nothing to him that his wife—the heiress of Turenne—had brought him not even an acre.

Angelina's triumph—a male heir for Turenne— is my downfall. I am not an heiress, Lucien will no longer want me. Sick to her bones, she glanced up at him and caught the tail end of a smile.

'Well? Who would have thought it? Gautier finally produced a son. You have been displaced, Isobel. Displaced.'

Lucien's smile was a puzzle. He did not seem remotely upset. Beyond speech, Isobel could only stare. Which was why she saw the moment he realised. Those blue eyes searched hers. Curiosity was followed by realisation, and it was as though shutters had slammed down between them.

'You knew,' he said. His voice was flat. Dead. 'You knew Angelina was with child and you did not tell me.'

'Lucien, I—'

'You knew and you said nothing.'

His eyes were so bleak, she couldn't meet his gaze. 'Lucien, I'm sorry. I should have told you.'

'You should. *Mon Dieu*, what were you thinking? I am your husband and this—' he waved the scroll in front of her '—this concerns me as much as you.'

'Forgive me, Lucien, I was wrong. I bitterly regret not telling you. I hoped Angelina would have a girl. I wanted to bring you lands. I wanted to be the heiress you hoped for.'

He thrust the scroll at her, his face set in stone. 'Say no more, my lady. You damn me with your every word. I trust you will have the sense to bed down with your ladies tonight.' With a bow, he stalked from the solar.

'Lucien, wait…' But Isobel spoke to the air, Lucien had gone.

Lucien stormed into the bedchamber. The bitter taste in his mouth was as nothing compared to the bitterness of his feelings. *She deceived me. She thinks all I care for is her father's land. Lord, she must loathe me.*

He paced the chamber, and the candlelight shook in the draught. On the wall, his shadow did an ugly, wavering dance. Isobel's belief that he cared only for land was like a blow to the heart. She thought him mercenary. She didn't trust him.

Despite my first marriage, I was prepared to trust her. Yet she does not accord me the same honour.

Absently, he rubbed his chest with the heel of his hand. His chest hurt; Lord, he could feel real physical pain. It was probably indigestion. He sank on to the bed with a sigh. Reaching for her pillow, he brought it to his nose and inhaled. Roses. Honeysuckle. *Isobel.* The pain intensified. God help him, it was not indigestion. He hurt because of Isobel. *I love her.*

Throwing the pillow aside, disgusted with himself, he put his head in his hands. For the second time in his life he had fallen in love with a deceitful woman. *She should have told me about Angelina. She should think better of me than to judge me purely mercenary.*

On the floor, something caught the light. It was the brooch, the diamond moon that he had given her. Going over, he picked it up and went to put it in her jewel box. Searching the jewel box for the rose silk pouch, he pushed a sackcloth sachet aside. Some dried leaves spilled out and his stomach fell away.

Herbs? Why the devil does Isobel keep herbs in her jewel box?

Lucien ripped open the sachet, rubbing the herbs between his fingers. It was a blend, he could smell rosemary and sage, but there were other ingredients he could not identify. A russet-coloured residue clung to his fingers. *Mon Dieu*, what witch's concoction was this?

Was his second marriage turning into the mirror of his first? Was she dosing herself? If so, she must stop. A few days since, Lucien had wondered whether Morwenna's habit of testing various remedies on herself might have been the cause of her worsening malaise. Had Morwenna brought her illness upon herself by trying out so many pills and potions? It was too late to know the truth of what had happened to Morwenna, but he wasn't prepared to take the risk with Isobel. Not with Isobel.

Someone tapped lightly on the door.

He wrenched it open. Isobel. The candle in her hand made her eyes glow like green fire. They were huge. Anxious.

'May I come in?'

'Please do. I wish to speak to you.'

She put the candle on a coffer. 'I came to apologise. I—'

'Never mind that.' He held up the sachet. 'What the devil is this?'

She flinched. 'Oh dear.'

'Isobel?'

Her eyelashes fell. She stared at the sachet, chewing her lip. 'I am sorry, Lucien. I can see that tonight is going to be a night of apologies.'

'You've been dosing yourself with this stuff?'

'Yes, but I stopped, when—'

'Lord, Isobel. What's in it? What's it for?'

'Lucien, please forgive me. It…it is a blend of herbs to prevent conception.'

Isobel braced herself for an explosion of fury.

Lucien twisted away and stared into the fire, shoulders lifting and falling with each breath. Several moments slipped by. But for the faint popping of the fire, all was quiet. Tonight, the wind had died and all of Champagne was muffled in mist.

He turned. His brow was creased, his mouth tight. He dangled the pouch in front of her, and she caught a whiff of rosemary.

'Isobel, it grieves me to hear you do not want my child—'

'Lucien…that's not true—'

'Let us set that aside for now.' The muscle beneath his scar flickered. 'Are you taking these herbs? I want this quite plain—I do not wish you to take them.'

'They are everyday herbs, and I no longer take them,' she said, watching him warily. Hopefully. Lucien seemed more concerned about the herbs than about her lack of trust in him. Keeping news of Angelina's baby from him had been a grave error, but he was definitely more concerned about the herbs.

'Thank God.' He tossed the pouch onto the fire. 'You are not to take them again.'

'I won't.'

'Good.'

Isobel's pulse thudded, crazy with hope. He really did not want her to take them—anger at her attempts to prevent conception was not uppermost in his mind. *Lucien cares about me. He doesn't want to admit it, but I am more to him than the means of acquiring lands. He cares for me, I know he does.* 'The same herbs are used in the kitchens.'

'You are not to get more.'

'Lucien, I won't.' Reaching for his hand, she was heartened when his fingers slowly closed on hers. 'I'm sorry I didn't tell you I was taking them.'

'Why did you? You know I wanted an heir.'

'I was afraid. I told myself that I was afraid because...'

'Because of your mother?'

'Yes. Being forced to witness... Mama was brought to bed in childbirth so many times, and in the end it *killed* her.' She took a deep breath. 'But that was not the whole of it. I was unsure of you. Of what our marriage would be.'

His hand slid up her arm. His blue eyes were thoughtful. 'Discovering about Morwenna can't have helped.'

'You were not the man I had expected.'

He grimaced. 'You are disappointed.'

'Far from it,' she said warmly, squeezing his hand. 'I expected a careless tourney champion, a knight who lived for tourneys and trophies. What I saw when I arrived at Ravenshold led me to believe that you had been neglecting your responsibilities.'

'The dilapidation. The east tower...'

'Exactly.' Isobel smiled, and lifted his hand to her cheek. 'Lucien, it has taken a while but I have learned your true worth.'

'Ravenshold was neglected because Morwenna had charge of it. Visiting her was a penance to be avoided whenever possible.'

'I understand. You took to tourneying to forget her. Lucien, I am so sorry I deceived you over the herbs. And I truly regret not telling you my step-mother was carrying a child.' She searched his face, looking deep into those blue eyes. 'Will you forgive me?'

He tipped his head to one side, and slowly his lips turned up at the corners. Taking her firmly by the waist, he tugged her to him. 'I shall think about it, little dove. Go on. I rather like this apologising.'

Isobel narrowed her eyes at him. 'You are not playing fair.'

'Go on.'

She attempted to wriggle free and his hold tightened. 'I am banned from the bedchamber, my lord. Don't you remember?'

'Oh, that. I was angry. Disappointed.'

Isobel felt her face fall. Even though he had not admitted it, she knew he cared for her. But she must be a disappointment to him. 'Lucien, I am not the heiress you were promised. I bring nothing to this marriage but a box of silver. If you…' her voice cracked '…if you wish for an annulment, I shall not fight it.'

Scar livid in the firelight, he studied her. 'An annulment? You wish for an annulment?'

'Saints, no. But, Lucien, you wanted a dynastic marriage. You thought to annexe the lands of Turenne to your own. I was meant to bring revenues and I bring nothing. I have no lands, no revenues.'

He tipped up her chin. Blue eyes were smiling into hers. 'You bring me yourself, Isobel. That is more than enough. I am well pleased with my bargain. In any case, our marriage is young, there is plenty of time for children.'

Isobel couldn't miss his less-than-subtle glance towards the bed. Her heart soared. 'I am no longer banished to sleep elsewhere?'

'Lord, no.'

She couldn't help herself, she hugged him. 'Oh, Lucien, I love you so much. I am sorry I took those herbs. And I wish I had told you about Angelina's baby.'

'Apology accepted.' His head lowered and their lips met. With a murmur of approval, he shifted, looping his hands round her waist. The fire was warm at her back and Lucien's strong body stood before her. *This is happiness.*

'Isobel?'

'Mmm?'

His expression was sober. 'You have taught me much. The balance must be even—it is my turn to apologise.' Tenderly, he brushed his fingertips down her cheek. 'When we met in the Abbey lodge I confess duty was uppermost in my mind. I was determined to fulfil my father's wishes.'

'You were set on honouring our betrothal agreement.'

'Yes. I thought of your lands too, I will confess it.' He flashed her a smile, and pressed suggestively against her. 'And your beauty, of course. I was much moved by your beauty.'

Her cheeks warmed. She looked at his mouth. 'Mmm, I see what you mean about this apologising. It's…interesting. Quite stimulating, in fact.'

His eyes glinted. He dropped a swift kiss on her lips. When Isobel tried to prolong it, he eluded her.

'A moment, little dove, if you please. I haven't finished. When we married I believed love was about possession.'

'I remember someone telling me that love was a decision.'

'I did, didn't I?' He shook his head. 'If only it were that simple. In the solar this evening, you opened my eyes and I saw myself in a new light, as a man who thinks only of lands or possessions. I had never looked at myself from a woman's standpoint before, and it was something of a shock. I didn't much like what I saw. Isobel, I will never be the courtly knight you yearned for. Bernez and his songs will never move me, but believe me when I say I love you. You may be my second lady, but you are first in my heart. It is not enough for me to possess your body. I need your love.'

'You have it, Lucien. I love you.'

'And I love you, little dove. And that is no decision—it seems I cannot help myself.' He gave her a crooked smile, and lifted his shoulders. 'I love you.'

Leaning in for a kiss, Lucien began walking her towards the bed. This time he didn't pull back when she wound her arms round his neck and sought to prolong the kiss. Long fingers reached for the pins on her veil. It drifted away, and he lowered her on to the blue coverlet, kissing her, caressing her face, her neck, her breasts. As he reached for the hem of her gown, Isobel's mind went hazy with desire.

Her last coherent thought was that if this was how Lucien apologised, she was going to have to think of other ways they could cross each other. She wasn't looking for quarrels, but she did so love his way of apologising…

* * * * *